If you're going to try and
steal the Holy Grail,
watch out for
*THE MAN FROM GREEK AND ROMAN*
JAMES GOLDMAN'S
"swift and nifty"* new thriller
based on the most sensational
archaeological discovery
of the century!

"A HIGHLY ENJOYABLE THRILLER . . . GREAT FUN!"

—*Library Journal*

---

"No quick summary can do justice to the subtlety and the excitement of the plot . . . Always swift and sometimes blinding . . . An intelligent and meticulously executed work that is also thoroughly entertaining!"

—*Best Sellers*

---

"A MARVELOUS READ FROM ITS INTRIGUING BEGINNING TO ITS INGENIOUS END!"

—Peter Maas, author of *Serpico*

**Publishers Weekly*

# The Man from GREEK AND ROMAN

A Novel by

James Goldman

For My Bobby

*This low-priced Bantam Book has been completely reset in a type face designed for easy reading, and was printed from new plates. It contains the complete text of the original hard-cover edition.*
NOT ONE WORD HAS BEEN OMITTED.

THE MAN FROM GREEK AND ROMAN
*A Bantam Book*

*PRINTING HISTORY*
*Random House edition published October 1974*
*Literary Guild edition published February 1975*
*Bantam edition / October 1975*



*Published simultaneously in the United States and Canada*

---

*Bantam Books are published by Bantam Books, Inc. Its trademark, consisting of the words "Bantam Books" and the portrayal of a bantam, is registered in the United States Patent Office and in other countries. Marca Registrada. Bantam Books, Inc., 666 Fifth Avenue, New York, New York 10019.*

---

PRINTED IN THE UNITED STATES OF AMERICA

# The Man from GREEK AND ROMAN

# Preamble

The chalice sat between them, gleaming on the table. Neither man was looking at it.

Mannheim sat there rather like a wealthy turtle, little arms and legs but round and massive in the middle. Turtle's eyes, as well, with heavy lids hung low; so low that even when he looked at you directly, it was hard to tell.

VanStraaten sat across the table from him, casual and calm, unmarked by all the travel and the stress. The sleepless night before, the dark trip out to Kennedy at seven for the early flight, then straight to the chalet and, through it all, the knowledge of how delicate and pivotal this scene would be.

The general nature of the deal was clear, they'd come that far. The vital questions, provenance and price, had yet to be discussed but they were skilled negotiators, both of them, and there was very little tension in the room that showed. Outside, beyond the picture windows, moonlight rippled on the lake and faintly touched the mountains in the distance. The lake, an almost perfect crescent, gently curved away and, at its very tip, Geneva glimmered in the night.

No sound at all. Then Mannheim rumbled, cleared his throat. "My dear VanStraaten." Mannheim spoke six languages, each with an accent; he was a man without a native tongue. "My dear boy, at some point, we must speak of numbers."

"At some point." VanStraaten had a charming smile: he used it. "But before we talk about the money, we must talk about the provenance."

"The history of the chalice." Mannheim nodded. "Yes, of course."

VanStraaten crossed his legs, leaned back, away from the issue.

"I've acquired many rare things in my time but this," his hand flicked toward the chalice, "is beyond rare and it has to have a history beyond dispute."

"Of course, dear boy. Would I be sitting here if—"

"Let me finish. I must know who owned it; when and where and how. Those are the questions everyone is going to ask. Not just the scholars but the press and people on the street. I need to know the answers."

There was silence.

"May I know them?"

Mannheim shook his head.

VanStraaten's voice was calm. "Why not?"

"What use would I be then, dear boy?" The old man heaved up from his chair, all five feet six of him, and headed for the brandy. "I have done this kind of thing before, you know. For friends. They have some treasures which they want to sell, I help them and, without exception, they insist I take a small commission." He was pouring; steady hands. "If you knew what I know"—his smile was angelic—"you could make the deal without me."

"If you think—" VanStraaten stopped himself. "The fact remains, I need to know. I can't just pop up with a treasure of this magnitude unless it has a history."

"I give you my assurance—"

"Your assurance. I want papers from you, Mannheim; affidavits, documents, sworn testimony."

"You must trust me."

"That's my bottom line. No provenance, no deal."

"You'll have your answers when the time comes."

"Now." VanStraaten on his feet.

"My dear boy." Mannheim, oddly graceful, moving

toward him, brandy in his hand. "I am a wealthy man, well-known and much respected. If I promise papers, they will come to you."

He held the brandy out. VanStraaten made no move.

"Drink." Mannheim smiled, his old eyes sparkling, and his cheeks looked fresh and rosy, as they always did when girls or money circled near him. "Think of what I have at stake and drink your brandy."

Nothing happened for a moment. Then VanStraaten took the glass.

The talk was stilted for a while but they seemed quite friendly later as they spoke of numbers, settling on three-six: three million for the owner of the chalice and a small commission of six hundred thousand for the middleman. More brandies followed and a late good night.

Which, more or less, is how it all began.

# I

She spoke. "It's not the dullness of your work I mind so much, it's the sterility."

He didn't register a thing. It was his custom not to let his feelings show. Besides, he had a hunch it made her furious.

"Are you alive or dead? Say something so I'll know."

Apparently, it did. He thought of things that might be said. Things like "My darling, what's becoming of us," or "I can't bear it any more," or "Aw, go fuck yourself." That last was tempting. He imagined saying it. It made him smile.

"If I knew what made you tick, I wonder if I'd ever wind you up again."

His smile grew.

"It's late," he said. "You want a drink?" God knew he did.

They were in Dido's studio. She was sitting on a Hudson fender drinking tiger's milk. She drank the stuff religiously. It seemed to work; she looked delectable.

She shook her head. "You booze too much." He didn't, he was sure of it, but every time she told him so, it frightened him a little.

"How'd it go today?" he asked.

She cast a knowing eye across the mass of automotive parts surrounding her. "Terrific."

For all he knew, she meant it. Dido was an artist in search of a style. She'd tried all the fashionable styles on for size and, like nightgowns on a mannequin, they all looked reasonably good on her and reasonably lifeless. Recently, she'd gone back for a second time to *objets trouvés* and she spent all these days with welding torch and hammer, pounding, putting pieces of Detroit together. It was *passé* and she knew it. Surely.

In other years, they would have talked about it. Long and serious and heartfelt talks. Good times. But his Art had a big A and hers didn't: she could make with both hands all the things that he could only write about, and more and more the talk would end with Dido saying, "What the hell do you know anyway? You've got no talent."

It was true enough. He didn't and she did. How much? Well, once there was a time but he was not about to think about it so he stood and stretched and said, "I'm going up. You coming?"

"In a little."

Melvil nodded, "See you later," started up the stairs.

Her studio took up the ground floor of the carriage house; they ate and drank and entertained in three large rooms upstairs. He'd bought the house in '61, back in the days when 82nd between York and First was not a place where anyone who made a living lived. He'd liked the neighborhood, all neat cold-water walk-ups and old brownstones cut up into little pieces. On the sidewalks you heard German or Hungarian or English with a brogue, and there were quiet bars where people with blue collars went and he and Dido sat beside them, getting buzzed on beer.

He poured some J&B, a civilized amount, not one drop more, and turned. His living room. He raked it with a savage eye. Its charm was lost on him. "Your charm is lost on me," he said and headed for the kitchen and some ice. The irritating thing, of course, was that the room was charming. They had taste and flair and humor, both of them, and in the days when love was in the air, they'd done the whole place lovingly.

He opened up the fridge. No human food. There never was. Just tiger's milk, organic honey, sea whelk or some goddam thing and a year's supply of crunchy Granola. He wasn't hungry anyway.

He yanked the freezer open. Naturally, no ice. He'd used it, naturally, the night before and it had slipped his mind or what was left of it and Dido, naturally, had other things to think about. He scratched up what shards he could and hurled them, melting, into his glass.

What did she have to think about? Tomorrow was important to him and he'd wanted her to share it, hadn't he, and did she have to shoot him down? She didn't really mean the things she said . . . so why, why did she have to say them.

His glass was empty. What to do? Refill it. Then what? Work? He checked his watch—ten-thirty, not too late—and started for his study.

Melvil loved his work. All aspects of it, even what he did at The Museum. The job involved some paper work, administrative nonsense, but most days were spent on writing and research and Melvil had no little reputation in his field, a fact which constantly surprised him. It wasn't that he felt ashamed of what he wrote. The articles, the pieces in the learned journals, they were cleanly done and well thought out but somehow small and not important. They were things that any man might do. It was his own work that he lived for.

He closed his study door, sat at his desk and waited for the calm to come. Great place, his study. Tiny. In the days when carriages were kept downstairs, it had been quarters for a groom. Now bookshelves covered all the wall space, top to bottom. Custom-built. He'd done the sawing and the heavy work and Dido did the pretty stuff along the edges, where it showed. They'd built the desk, too, more or less. The top had warped a little but he liked that and the drawers refused to open but he liked that, too.

He took a sip, felt better, pulled the notebook toward him, carefully surveyed his pencils, chose one—choosing pencils was important—squinted at the half-filled page. He always worked in pencil so he could erase and no one in the world would ever know the stupid things he thought from time to time. He frowned—his eyes weren't going, were they—took his glasses off and checked them. Clean enough. He jammed them on again, bent forward. There.

He read. ". . . if I take the chalice as the central symbol." Would it work? It might. He found it an exciting possibility, to use the chalice as the central symbol of his book. The idea had been growing on him slowly, ever since the day VanStraaten walked into his office—was it just three months ago?—and dropped the photos on his desk.

His mind began to move. No racing thoughts, no disconnected insights; none of that. But not pure logic, either. Never cold. Ideas, the good ones, came with feelings, both at once. And slowly, like a crystal growing, what he meant to say next formed itself. "The function of—" *Gah-droom!* The floor shook.

Dido. Back at work. Connecting bumpers to her fucking hub caps. *Vrrung!* She knew he might be writing, didn't she? "The function of—" *Gah-droom* again. She damn well knew. He drank a little, choked a little, filled his glass a little. That was better. *Vroinng!* "The function of—" *Kong-oong!*

He brought the bottle to his desk. Save time, economy of movement. *Rat-a-tat!* A riveting machine? Impossible. It must be in his mind. He wondered, now and then, about his mind. If one sat down and thought about it, which one wasn't much inclined to do, he had strange fantasies. Not sick, you understand; no fetishes, perversions. Just odd.

He didn't sleep with Dido much, not any more; and yet, he never dreamed of other girls. Well, hardly ever. There was Sally Ann who worked in Cataloguing and VanStraaten's secretary, the untouchable Serena Burton. He'd undress them now and then, imagining a little, never going very far. And sometimes, girls he'd pass by on the streets. He'd think of walking close beside them, holding hands. How warm and friendly and they'd take him home and talk, tell everything, and so would he, keep nothing back, and they would fold their arms around him, tender, soft, fade out, the end. No sex. God, he was forty-one and didn't even make it in his dreams.

He smiled. Funny. Paradoxes always were. The paradox was he was horny all the time. He remembered being horny in his teens: pure torture. Ugly, which he wasn't; tall and skinny, which he was. What kind of girl could possibly be interested? Many kinds, he saw now, thinking back, but he was sixteen and he never knew. Things were no better at Wisconsin: two affairs and three degrees, so much for seven years in Madison. But then he got the teaching post at Harvard, grew the beard and Dido came along. He liked the beard, she didn't, and one night—she'd let him feel her up but that was all—he offered to remove the beard if she'd remove her panties and the rest was history. Ancient history and, besides, it didn't matter.

What he dreamed about was work. The book. To write one thing that had a life. One major, genuinely important work on the philosophy of art. Everything depended on it and on good days he was sure he had it in him. He could feel it like a lump inside. And centuries from now, when wise men talked about why things were beautiful, they'd put his name with Kant's and Aristotle's. "He belongs with the immortals, Melvil West. There is no truth, of course, but he came close."

The trouble with the dream, the only trouble with it was he hadn't started writing yet. Just notes and notes, for years and years. He looked up: binders, neatly filled in longhand, stretched for yards along the shelves. It bothered him from time to time and every now and then he'd start, just have a go, plunge in. The words would come so surely and he'd do a paragraph, a page, a chapter, and he'd read it over next day and it wasn't good enough. It had to be so good, each word, each thought. He needed to prepare more, that was all. He wasn't ready yet.

But it would happen, absolutely, and the book would live. He wouldn't, though; he'd die. Odd thing, but in the dream he worked himself to death. He'd always worked long hours but recently it seemed he never left his desk. He kept some notebooks at the office and he'd stay at The Museum till eight or nine and then, home to the study. Weekends, too, and in the dream he'd have the book oh nearly done but he was tired, oh so tired and he'd let his head rest for a moment on the page and bingo: dead as dust. And in the morning, Dido–it was always Dido–she'd come in and think he was asleep and shake him and he'd topple to the floor and God the grief and guilt she'd feel. Poor Dido.

Melvil raised his head up sharply. Everything was still: no *vrrung*, no *rat-a-tat*. He checked his watch: twelve-thirty. Any luck she'd be asleep now, safe to go to bed. He closed the notebook, put the pencil in the pencil cup, stood up, recapped the bottle, took it to the little bar. How did that poem go? "And let there be no moaning of the bar when I pull out to sea." Cheap sentiment.

He stood there in the bedroom doorway. He could make her out, just barely, curled up on the far edge of the king-size bed. They still slept in the same bed.

Why? Why not? The salesman had told them it would last for twenty years and they had eight to go. She looked so tiny, all curled up, and vulnerable. He felt a little bit like crying but instead he dragged his trousers off.

He fumbled in the closet, soft, no noise, got his pajamas off the hook—they never saw each other naked any more—eased into them and very carefully slipped into bed. She stirred. His heart stopped: what if she came over, what if, God forbid, she wanted to? How could he and how could he not? She sighed and went on sleeping.

He tugged the pillow tight around his ears and, with an effort, didn't think about his life. No images at all. He tried to feel his toes, and for a moment, wasn't sure he could. He felt a little tightness in his stomach, like a ball. The thing began to rise. He wondered for a moment what it was and then he knew. He thought perhaps he just might let the scream be heard, then thought the better of it, closed his eyes and let the lights go out.

# II

He was moving at a good clip, west on 82nd Street. The sun was shining. Warm for April, gorgeous, and he felt like singing. Big day.

He'd been up since seven. Too excited, couldn't sleep. He tiptoed from the room, no sense in waking Dido, shaving with extra care and showered, took a long time with his hair. He had good hair, liked it, parted it on the left like Cary Grant. He knew what he was wearing, had it all picked out: the new gray pin stripe—bought at Brooks and never worn, he'd saved it for today—white shirt, the Cardin tie that Dido gave him. Dido had great taste in ties.

He got dressed in the living room, made orange juice, toast and coffee, left a note downstairs. "Dear Dido, See you five. Love, M." He signed it love. Well, what the hell.

He marched along, gut flat and shoulders back, past Second Avenue, then Third, old walk-ups, tenements with tacky new brick faces. Lex, then Park. Apartment buildings now, rich people, limousines. Then, up ahead, its marble glinting in the brilliant sun, the massive, bastard-Greco-Roman face of The Museum.

The steps weren't steep at all today. He started trotting up. "*Gut morgen*, Vest." Old Graz of Arms and Armor. Melvil waved. "Bik tay ahet." "Big day," Melvil agreed and went on trotting to the top.

"Good morning, Dr. West." Old Bindle, gray and

friendly at the door, on guard since 1930. Melvil grinned, "The same to you," and strode into the hall.

It almost always picked his spirits up, that hall. The place was like a railroad station, needlessly enormous. Late Victorian extravagance, it rose up, he supposed, a hundred feet and stretched out, end to end, like football fields.

He turned left, passed the empty Information Desk and moved, his footsteps echoing, through the deserted marble space and into Greek and Roman Art: his territory, home sweet home. Past eyeless busts on pedestals, by the crowded reliefs on the Badminton Sarcophagus and into Gallery 6, a sort of corridor, Mycenaean things, all early stuff, Egyptian influence. He smiled at them, liking what he saw.

Then, at the Sardis column, with the restaurant in front of him, sharp left and up the stairs. He never used the elevators; stairs, the walk to work, that's all the exercise he got these days. Up past VanStraaten's office on the landing. Second floor: more Greek and Roman. His was the only collection housed on two floors, a small distinction but on good days like today he felt absurdly proud of it.

Big strides now, moving faster, straight ahead past Greek pots and some more Greek pots, then left a few more steps and presto, on his right, the unmarked door.

There should have been lettering on it saying CURATORIAL OFFICES, GREEK AND ROMAN ART but there wasn't. All the other office doors had lettering: ISLAMIC ART or NEAR EASTERN ART or WESTERN EUROPEAN ARTS which had an s, no one knew why. No more than anyone knew why his door was blank. He'd asked once, out of curiosity, and Maintenance had told him to expect a memo but it never came.

There was a buzzer for announcing visitors. The door was kept locked. Each department had a different lock that opened to a different key. Staff members had their own and Melvil took his out and entered. Only to be greeted by another flight of stairs.

He bounded up, just felt like bounding. Miss McCann was at her desk. They had arrived at The Museum together, more or less, in August 1961. She'd been a pale and sweet-faced miss of twenty-five then. She was still a miss and still pale but a little sadder now. He liked her.

"You know what day it is today, Kate?" Breathing deep, not really winded.

"Bet I do." She found a lovely smile for him. "Here's the schedule for it." And she handed him a paper.

"Thanks." It wasn't every day that had a schedule, not in Greek and Roman. In fact, of all the stagnant backwaters in The Museum, none compared to Melvil's. As a rule, it was a paralyzed department. Literally; nothing ever moved. No new displays, no special shows or exhibitions. Now and then, there'd been an acquisition and he'd have to shift a vase or something, but the statues in the lower halls had been there since the roof went up. Which had a lot to do with Melvil's fondness for his job: free time. He sometimes had whole weeks to spend on nothing but his own research.

He headed down the corridor. Books left and right, long rows. All scholarly, old friends: bound volumes of the *Zeitschrift* going back to God knows when, *Denkmälers, Monumenti, Lexikons.* Tools of the trade. Then past rooms housing the Assistant Curator, the Associate Curator, the Curatorial Assistants, none of whom he cared for very much. And, finally, his own sweet door.

It was a really pleasant room: good size, walls lined with shelves all crammed with books and papers, roll-top desk, an easy chair and footstool, leather worn and cracked. The windows, two of them, looked west, across the Museum parking lot and onto the spring green of Central Park.

He sat down, kept his desk top closed—the mess inside was terrible—and looked out at the park. Not much was new. The garbage by the oak was fresh and he was sure he hadn't seen that inner tube before. He shook his head and turned and slid his eye across the schedule Kate had given him.

Reminders, mostly. Call Photography about the blowups, see if Printing had the handouts ready, check with Catering, a meeting with Security, another with Display, VanStraaten at 1:30, on and on, and at the bottom: 5:00—Reception.

Canapés and cocktails for the patrons and the press. Collectors, scholars, critics, all the art world of New York, jammed in and buzzing with excitement. Wondering what was it The Museum had bought, what treasure were they going to see. And then a sudden hush and heads would turn. His moment. Well, VanStraaten's, too, but Melvil rather liked it, sharing things with Pieter. In they'd come and then a few well-chosen words but he'd been having trouble choosing, making little speeches up for days, all awful but he'd think of something. Then VanStraaten would unveil it, pull the velvet off the pedestal and by tomorrow morning all the world would know he had a treasure just as great as London's Elgin Marbles or the Louvre's Winged Victory.

He had no business feeling proud—he hadn't made the chalice, he was just the keeper of it—but he did. The kind of pride he'd felt, back when he was a kid, just knowing Einstein was alive; that he existed. It was how he'd felt that day in February when VanStraaten walked into his office unannounced and handed him the envelope. Postmarked Geneva. Thick. The photos of the chalice spilled out on his desk. Heart-stopping. Grainy black and white and poorly lit and still the beauty of the piece leaped off the paper at him and he sat there numbed.

"You think it's genuine?" VanStraaten had to ask him twice.

It couldn't be. The piece could not exist. Ask any scholar and he'd tell you no, it wasn't possible. But there it was, beyond the reach of any other artist of its time. Of course, they'd have it tested, run it through the mill, but there was genius in it. Unmistakable. Nobody could have done it but Pasiteles.

"I think—" he'd had to clear his throat, "I think it's real."

VanStraatten knew the period, knew how impossible it was. "I think so, too," he said, "and where's the brandy?"

There had been a lot of brandy and the next day he had gone with Pieter to the Board, been eloquent which wasn't like him, and at sunup Pieter took off for Geneva to inspect the chalice, have it tested, make the deal. Then three long weeks of waiting and in early March he'd sat downstairs with Pieter in his office looking at the packing crate. They opened it together.

It was then he knew the chalice was the keystone of his book. He touched it, held it in his hands. The piece was more exquisite, full of life, than anything he'd ever seen. He'd felt connected to it, as if it had been created just for him and in the hours he'd studied it since then, he found it inexhaustible, so full it was of line that spoke, of golden shapes and figures molded into meaning. There were times when, late at night, he'd take it from his office safe and almost—just in his imgaination, nothing real and not in words—when he could almost hear it speaking.

To this day, the chalice was a secret. No announcement, not a syllable, no dribs and drabs of story, dreary press releases through the weeks of prepara tion. Just one big announcement: *blam.*

He jumped: the phone was ringing. Who? It might be Pieter's office, the unattainable Miss Burton on the line. Pale, delicate, and he began unzippering her, his porcelian Serena. White, so white of skin and small of breast, so soft. The longing welled up like a pain and yes, by God, he'd ask her out.

"Hello?" His voice was hoarse.

"I read I'm seeing you at five."

His Dido: suddenly, he wanted her. "That's right."

"Is five a where or is it a when?"

"It's here at five o'clock." She couldn't have forgotten.

"What is?"

She knew it was important; she remembered. It was just her way of teasing him.

"You don't mind if I don't make it, do you?"

"Why? What's more important?"

She laughed. "You want a list?"

He wasn't angry, just the old knots in his stomach. "Dido, it's the biggest evening of my life."

"Some life." The line went dead.

Why did she do this to him? On this day of all days. If she cared for him at all—but did she? Did he care for her? What did he feel? He turned, looked out the window at the park. Kids playing. Had he ever wanted kids? He had, at least he thought so, but she'd always told him soon, not yet but next year, maybe next year. Little Melvils, what a ludicrous idea. He blinked and shrugged, no matter, and his phone began to ring.

# III

Photography had screwed up with the blowups and Publicity checked in to say the handouts came out smudged and Catering was in hysterics and Security was nervous so he went and held their hands awhile and it was twenty after one, no time for lunch or he'd be late to Pieter's office.

It was just to check and double-check details. The timing and the placement, who did what and when. So much to think about; no time to think. He hadn't thought at all since Dido's call. Well, maybe just a little. Thoughts like what if Dido didn't come and would Miss Burton smile upon him. On the whole, though, he had kept himself tuned out. He was a master at it, he could tune out street noise, radios, the voices in his head. He felt good as he trotted up the stairs.

Brass letters on the door: EXECUTIVE OFFICES. He buzzed and got an answer. In he went and there she was. Exquisite, limpid, Dresden doll Miss Burton, sitting in her little office just outside of Pieter's. Ah, but what was in her eyes? Was it a greeting? It was hard to tell, her eyes kept moving and she stood so quickly, smiled so quickly, showed him in.

First thing he saw, there on the great oak table, was his chalice. He knew everything about it—height in centimeters: 30.48; weight in grams: 451.59—yet every time he saw it, there was fresh surprise.

"Come on," said Pieter, "come and say hello to Waldo."

Waldo Sitwell, first-string critic for the *Times*, was sitting at the table staring stupidly, it seemed to Melvil, at the chalice. Sitwell was a power, and a big one, in the little world of art, no more insensitive or dense than other leading critics, and Melvil, if you pressed him, couldn't tell you why he thought the man was such a loathesome creep. He did have birdlike bones, wee hands, a massive buttocks, out of all proportion, and a flaky drift of dandruff on his shoulders. Maybe that was why.

"Hello," said Melvil, moved into the room.

VanStraaten's office was a large and graceful place, great windows on Fifth Avenue, a scattering of armchairs (Chippendale), a breakfront (Adams), and a massive round oak table (Tudor) in the center which VanStraaten used as a desk. By the windows, on display, were models of projected wings, some of which The Museum was actually building.

Sitwell mumbled something, went on staring. VanStraaten, standing just behind him, made a pistol out of thumb and forefinger, shot him cleanly through the head and said, "We had a one-fifteen appointment, other matters to discuss, and I'm afraid he caught us with our chalice out." A likely story. It was Pieter playing politics. The *Times*, for turgid reasons of its own, was after Pieter's head and he was making nice and handing them a scoop. Why not?

"Extraordinary," Sitwell murmured. "Such economy, such elegance of line."

Why did he find that irritating? It was true enough.

VanStraaten pulled a chair up, sat. "If you have any questions, Waldo, West can fill you in."

"Good." Sitwell took his notebook out. "It's not my field at all, you know. I haven't studied Roman plate since college."

Melvil smiled his oily smile. "What can I tell you?"

Sitwell's pen was ready. "Basic data first. Who made it, when and where?"

Melvil kept it brief. "The chalice was made by Pasiteles in the middle of the first century B.C., most probably at his workshop in Rome."

"Pasiteles? Should I have heard of him?"

"No reason why." The man knew nothing.

"Any other basic data?"

"Only that the chalice was created for somebody named Josephus A."

"Josephus A? Who was he?" Sitwell frowned.

"We can't be sure. Our best guess is Josephus Ariticus, the Roman proconsul in Antioch."

"Josephus." Sitwell wrote it down. "How do you know all this?"

"It's printed on the bottom." Which it was. On the underside of the base in letters beautifully engraved in clear and careful pointillé: PASITELES and, after it, JOSEPHUS A.

"Extraordinary," Sitwell said.

He didn't know the half of it. "We have very little Greek or Roman plate," said Melvil, getting interested in spite of himself, "and any piece of gold or silver is a rarity. Great quantities were made, of course, for royalty and temple decoration, but it's lost forever. Almost nothing has come down to us."

"Why lost forever? How can you be sure?"

"Because most plate, you see, got melted down. Invading troops would sack a temple or a palace and they'd take the gold and silver, all of it, and melt it into ingots. Made it easier to carry off. On top of which, you have the Greek and Roman burial customs. When they died, they took no treasure with them, didn't need it for their afterlife, like the Egyptians. Open an Egyptian tomb, it's filled with precious things. Greek and Roman graves have bits of armor now and then, and bones. That's all. What little plate we have survived because, quite literally, it was buried treasure."

"Buried treasure." Sitwell chuckled. "Sounds like pirates."

"Not at all. Imagine you're a wealthy man. The enemy is at the gates. You take your gold and silver and you dig a hole and bury it, and then you go to battle. If you live, you come back home and dig it up again. Whoever buried this," he nodded toward the chalice, "didn't make it."

"Fascinating." Sitwell sat back, capped his pen.

"There's more. What makes the chalice even rarer is the fact it's signed. Most pieces have no signature. The ordinary craftsman never signed his name. It was a privilege given only to the greatest masters. And Pasiteles was taken, in his time, to be the greatest master of them all."

"Pasiteles, of course," and Sitwell snapped his fingers. "Knew I knew the name."

"The Elder Pliny, in his *Natural History*, Volume Thirty-six, describes him as the finest artist of the century and possibly the greatest goldsmith of all time. Till now, of course, we've had to take his word for it."

"You don't mean ..." Sitwell sat up very straight. "You mean to say . . ." His voice trailed off.

"Exactly." Melvil nodded. "All his work is lost. We haven't any. Not one piece survives. Except, of course, that object on the table. You are looking at the only known example of the greatest goldsmith of all time."

Melvil paused. He'd put that rather well, he thought; and he'd been civil, not insulting. He had more to say, about the beauty of the piece, its meaning, the perfection of its form. But that was personal and not for Sitwell.

"That's incredible. Fantastic." Sitwell paused and

looked at the chalice. "This is more than just another acquisition. This is an event."

"We think so," Pieter said. "A lot of books are going to have to be rewritten."

"More than that." Sitwell uncapped his pen, eyes bright. "There hasn't been a story like this, not for years. Where did you get it from, whose was it, and how much did it cost?"

VanStraaten smiled. "One thing at a time."

They started with the money question. That was Pieter's ball and Melvil let him carry it. All the press release would have to say was "for an undisclosed amount." Pieter felt quite strongly on this subject: that museums were private institutions and that prices paid for acquisitions were a private matter. Melvil thought so, too. On top of which, he hadn't wanted anyone to know the price. Not that three six was high; the chalice had a worth beyond all dollars. But he'd wanted people just to see the chalice for itself, for what it was; back in the 60's, when all those crowds had come to look at Rembrandt's *Aristotle*, all they had was money in their eyes.

"Where did you find it, Pieter? Where'd it come from?" They were on to that now. "From a highly reputable European dealer." Press release again. Not very informative but it was all they knew. Pieter, when he came back from Geneva, told him how he'd pressed to get the provenance. "I almost blew the deal," he'd said, "and all I got was that it belonged to an important collector whose family owned it for generations. When I asked for more, the answer I got was taxes." Melvil had nodded. Happened all the time. A fact of life for all museums. It went like this: Suppose you're an Italian and you want to sell this Leonardo that's been in your family since forever. You face two big problems: (1) it's a national treasure and you can't sell it out of the country which is where the big money is; (2) whatever you sell it for, you pay income taxes. The result was deals like this one—middlemen, no names, no facts—and public statements like today.

Still Melvil longed to know the provenance. The chalice was authentic, he had no concerns of that kind, and the provenance would be a good one; Mannheim was a famous figure, reputations were at stake. But where, he longed to know, where was it found? What else was with it in the excavation? Pots, utensils, weaponry, more gold or silver, evidence to add to knowledge of the time. It was a time of ferment, after all, an era that produced a Jesus. Burning questions of research and scholarship.

"That's nonsense, Waldo." Pieter's voice was sharp. "The Boston made a deal like this two months ago. No questions asked."

"The Boston isn't my museum." Then Sitwell's voice went confidential. "Was it smuggled? You can tell me, Pieter. Was it stolen? Is it hot?"

"I'm not a fence, if that's your question." Pieter's face went white.

"You're covering, this story is a cover-up."

"You call it anything you like and if you call yourself a critic, criticize the chalice. It's not an article of commerce, it's a work of art."

VanStraaten was terrific. Lots of people didn't like him. Rich, attractive, social, family stretching back to Pieter Stuyvesant. On top of which, he was a scholar and a skillful bureaucrat, a natural at raising money, hard as nails when necessary and he had a nose for art and damn good taste. He was a lot to take and Melvil took him undiluted.

"Tell him, Pieter." Good God, had he said that?

Sitwell spun on him. "I took your little lecture, West. I knew it all but—"

"Knew it all?" The rage felt wonderful. "Sitwell, you don't know shit from Shinola."

Sitwell shot up to his feet. "I know a story when I

hear one. All this song and dance about Pasiteles, you boys can stuff it in your Bulletin. This thing is rarer than the Golden Fleece. I want my story. You know what my story is? My story is how much? My story is whose was it, where'd it come from? That's my story and I'll sink the two of you to get it."

More was said, a lot of it not very sensible. The door slammed and the room became extremely quiet.

"Jesus, Pieter . . ." Melvil sat. "I don't know what came over me."

VanStraaten stood there, looked at him and slowly shook his head. "Shinola." And he started laughing. "It was worth it."

There were sherries, several of them. Pieter poured.

It was the last nice thing that happened.

# IV

Dido's voice was in his head. He didn't want to hear what it was saying. Tune it out. He was a master, wasn't he? Just push the switch, go blank. He looked down, tried to see himself in his martini. No one there. He wondered where he was.

In point of fact, he knew perfectly well. He was sitting all alone in Beggi's, 84th and Second, and his steak was getting cold. The place was quiet, empty. Almost two, he'd have to go home soon. Home. Did he have one? Interesting question. It had been a long, long day; a long, long trail a-winding.

He had stayed too long with Pieter and the afternoon had been a race, a million things to do. One final sherry, out the door, no unapproachable Miss Burton at her desk—no talk, no date, no luck, no time to think about it. Down the stairs and through the halls and into the Blumenthal Patio.

Remarkable room. Two stories high and big enough for basketball, the patio had been hauled off intact from Velez Blanco, an early Renaissance castle in southeastern Spain. Beautifully proportioned marble columns, carvings of exquisite quality, a lacy loggia running round it fit for Juliet. The Museum used the place for important receptions and at the moment all was chaos.

Everyone was shouting, arguing, milling aimlessly. The people from Photography had managed to come up with blowups of the chalice and were snarling at the people from Display about where the hell to put them. The people from Catering were busy setting tables up and dropping glasses and the people from Security were milling ominously around the empty velvet-covered pedestal that stood before the dais. Everyone was temperamental, everyone had feelings to be soothed, and Catering had lost its keys and couldn't open up its bins to get its liquor out and some fool had misplaced the easels for the blowups and the handouts came from Printing with VanStraaten's name misspelled and it was almost five when Pieter came and put the chalice on its pedestal. The curtains closed around it and Security took up their posts and Melvil tore up to his office, washed and changed his shirt and thought about the gracious little speech he had to make and what in God's name would it be.

When he got back to the Patio, the clans were gathering. Old Graz of Arms and Armor had "gut vishes" for him and he said hello to Snead, the mousy Curator of the much-despised American Wing, and Gribble of Near Eastern Art, who thought the chalice should have gone to his department and he had a point, was sulking in a corner and the universally detested Racine-Brissac of European Paintings was holding court as usual.

Guests started coming in. No sign of Dido, so he angled for the bar and belted down a quick martini, looked around. He saw Kropotkin of the *Post* and Sybil Schwartz who wrote for *Time* and Simon Prinz of *Newsweek*. Every critic in New York would be there. Still no Dido. Why, for God's sake, should it matter if she came or not. He had another quick one. Potter Grant, the Chairman of the Board, came striding in, surrounded by a cluster of lesser Trustees. The Patio was filling up.

Melvil took a fresh martini, wandered through the crowd, shook hands, big smile. People seemed to seek him out, so many people. Scraps of bright Museum chatter floated past him: "... wonder what it cost ... a thousand shares at fifty-two ... the food is terrible ... another meeting of the living dead ..." That must be Dido. Melvil turned. It was. She came, she came.

She looked sensational in something orange and silky. Dido always wore bright colors to Museum affairs, the few she came to, "*pour épater les zombies,*" as she liked to put it. And he meant to say how nice she looked but "Hi" was all he said.

She bared her teeth, took his martini in her hand.

"You came," he said.

"I came, I saw, let's go."

Just teasing him. "We can't. I have to make a speech."

"In English?"

He let it pass. "Besides, you haven't seen the chalice yet."

She shrugged.

He smiled. "Thanks for coming."

"No," she said, voice low, eyes looking straight at his, "No, you're not glad I'm here at all."

It wasn't true and he was going to deny it, tell her how he cared, but Grant was standing on the dais tapping at the microphones. The noise died down and Grant—a decent fellow, always gave a case of Scotch at Christmas—started phumperhing along. No need to listen, so he didn't. Didn't register a thing till someone said his name and Dido nudged him in the ribs.

"You're on," she whispered.

"Doctor West?" His name again. Who said it? Grant. Christ, he was next. His speech.

He made it to the dais, seeing nothing, mind a blank. What was he going to say? He'd had it all worked out. "Ladies and gentlemen." That's how it started; he was right so far. What next, what did he tell them next?

Suppose he told them what he felt. Sensational idea. What did he feel, exactly? Nothing much except—his eyes went to the curtains covering the chalice—he could tell them what the chalice made him feel if only there were words for it. No words: some aesthetician he was, a philosopher who had no words. He blinked, then smiled at all the pepople, turned and held his hand out to VanStraaten.

Everyone applauded. He had done a gracious thing; imagine that. A wordless introduction. And VanStraaten took his hand and did the rest. He spoke with wit and ease, with charming seriousness, about Pasiteles in general and the chalice in particular and with a simple gesture, no dramatics, reached out with his hand and pulled the cord.

The curtains parted. Quiet in the room. All eyes were on the chalice. Even Dido's. Large and clear and gray, such lovely eyes, but what was in them? It seemed desperately important that she love his chalice, find it good. She stood so far away.

Then Pieter asked if there were any questions. "None? In that event . . ."

A voice rose. "Just a little query, if I may."

VanStraaten looked delighted. "Waldo Sitwell of the *Times*."

Sitwell edged forward through the crowd. "You haven't told us what it cost."

"You'll find that in the press release."

"It says 'an undisclosed amount.' "

"That's right."

"Why not disclose it?"

"Because of circumstances surrounding the acquisition."

"What circumstances?"

"In view of them," VanStraaten went on smoothly, "The Museum has undertaken not to make the figures public."

"You're evading my question."

"Surely not. As you know, in the art world, even in the world in general for that matter, valuable things are bought and sold without announcing what the price was. May I ask you what you paid for your apartment?"

"That's my business."

"But of course."

Some laughter rippled. Sitwell, to his credit, grinned. "Touché," he said, "but there are issues here which, as a scholar, you should be the first to recognize. That's not a piece of real estate," he nodded toward the chalice, "and it's not your property. It is a masterpiece and it belongs to all mankind. I have a need to know about it; everything about it. Don't you?" This last was to Kropotkin of the *Post* who thought a moment, nodded, took his pad and pencil out.

"It's not a story that we're looking for; it's knowledge." Sitwell's voice rang with conviction, pencils everywhere were coming out. "When was the piece discovered? Where? Whose was it? You can't stand there and produce it like a rabhit from a hat and fob us off with undisclosed amounts and nameless European dealers. If you know the answers and won't speak, that's inexcusable; and if you bought it without knowing, that is irresponsible or worse."

From that point on, things got a little sticky. Voices rose, a glass broke, pens and pencils scribbled busily and Dido said, "I loved your speech." VanStraaten dealt with all the more coherent questions, firm but gracious, holding to the press release.

It ended, finally, and there was general movement to the bar. He grabbed a drink and Dido kept on saying things like "Not since Daniel Webster" and he had to smile a lot, he knew so many smiling people and when Potter Grant came up and shook his hand, congratulating him on his performance, Dido broke out with the giggles. Melvil had another quick martini, just to pick the spirits up. It didn't help.

He was feeling no better at all as they moved down

the sweeping marble steps and into the April evening. Silence. Dido broke it with another burst of giggles and he nearly hit her. Gales of effortless invective whistled through his mind. All the rotten things he longed to say and never did; just once, to let it all fly loose.

Instead, he walked along, not talking, on the curb side like a good boy. Pointless custom, man along the outside by the curb. A lot of what he did was pointless. They were walking east on 82nd Street. Another silent night.

"What do you always mock me for?" It wasn't much to say but it was something.

"Do I?" Dido seemed surprised. He nodded. "I don't know." She shrugged, then hunched her shoulders.

"Think we ought to talk about it?"

"I don't know," again.

"I mean, you liked the chalice, didn't you?"

"Yes. Yes, I really did. It's beautiful."

"What was so funny?"

"Nothing much."

"I mean, just tell me what the joke was. Was it me?" She shook her head.

The street was dark, not many people out. A car went by. She looked so pretty; really nice. He touched her.

"Don't do that." Not sharp; just mostly bored, as if he'd brought up birth control, some issue settled years ago.

He shriveled up inside but all he said was "Sure, okay." They made it through another block and Melvil wondered, for the first time, if she was as miserable as he was. What a thought. Did Dido suffer, too? Did she have moments, all alone among her automotive parts, times when she wept? Was her life slipping past her, did she grieve? It must be so. He wondered if she'd tell him but he couldn't ask her: it was much too hard and did he care and did it matter and what difference would it make?

"Let's go to bed."

She stopped and looked at him. "You mean to sleep?"

"No, not exactly."

"Oh." She started walking briskly.

"Hey." He caught up. "All I did was ask. I mean, is that so terrible? We used to, every now and then, like once a day back when we met or don't you for the love of God remember?"

She stopped abruptly. "Do you love me, Melvil?"

They were on a corner, Lexington he thought, and she was looking at him straight and hard. Of course he did. A lot. He tried to feel it: nothing came. He used to love her; bet your ass he did. The first time she'd come into class, he'd stumbled through his lecture absolutely numb. She wore a white angora sweater. He saw her in it now. His eyes filled up. "I love you."

"No, you don't." She said it dully, like an old familiar fact.

"I do."

She shook her head.

He nodded.

Clearly, this was going nowhere. What next? What do you say next? Or do? Do was better than say. He'd so something. Something brilliant. What was brilliant? He was sweating. Hold her close. Right. That's a brilliant thing to do. He reached out.

"Touch me, Melvil, and I'll kick you in the balls. If I can find them."

It stopped him. "Jesus, Dido, that's a hell of a remark."

" 'Let's go to bed,' he says." The words came out like bits of ice: "You haven't wanted me for years." He started to deny it but she went on talking and he missed it so he asked her to repeat it and she said it, firm and clear. "Let's call it quits," she said.

He froze. That's how it felt, as if he actually were numbed by ice. He couldn't feel his lips or fingers and his ears rang and the night looked white. "You mean not be together any more?"

"It's no good, Melvil. I suppose it never really was but that's beside the point. It doesn't matter who did what or where it all went wrong . . ."

Her lips were moving, she was talking, but he couldn't hear. He had a vision of himself, a fantasy, a flash. Snow: everywhere, as far as you could see, just snow and ice and he was all alone, a tiny figure in the middle distance, freezing to death. That's what life without her would be like. He'd die.

". . . the point is, what we're doing to each other, well, it's murder."

"No!" It sounded far off but his throat hurt so he must have screamed it. Then the words came tumbling out; he was amazed how fast they came. He loved her, it was all his fault, they'd try again, she'd see how good he was, how different he could be, he'd change, be anything she wanted but she couldn't leave him.

"Not so loud."

He wasn't shouting.

"It's embarrassing, for God's sake."

"You can't leave me."

"Take it easy."

"I won't let you."

"We'll discuss it."

"No."

Somebody definitely was shouting now; somebody else. He looked around, he found it. Brownstone, second floor. "You woke my kids up, Jesus Christ, go fight it out at home."

Dido made a kind of strangled cry and turned and ran. He didn't feel like running so he leaned against the building. "I'm sorry," Melvil said, "about your kids." The window slammed.

"I'm sorry, really sorry."

"Me too, mister, but we're closing and you gotta go."

Lights were going out in Beggi's. Melvil nodded, gave the waiter twenty, told him to keep the change, went out the door and set his course for home. The street was empty now, except for papers, cartons, broken bottles, scraps of garbage, candy wrappers and a pair of shoes. Who'd leave his shoes? Why do a thing like that? The night was full of mysteries.

All the lights were off. You'd think she might have left the hall light burning. Melvil shrugged and, first try, got the key in the lock.

He closed the door behind him, double-locked it, hooked the chain. No sound at all. He started up the stairs. They seemed peculiarly steep. He thought he'd rest a minute. Things were swirling in a kind of gentle, pleasant way, like palm trees. Lots of things: a chalice, Sitwell's butt, Miss Burton's boobs, a white angora sweater. *Halfway up the stairs* . . . How did it go? *And all kinds of funny thoughts run round my head: "It isn't really anywhere! It's somewhere else instead!"* He had no memory of it but he cried himself to sleep.

# V

*Gah-droom.* The house shook. Melvil blinked awake and bolted upright into pain. His back felt broken, must have had an accident. Where was he? *Dronng.* Where Dido was, was home and that was Dido. Yes, but where exactly was he? On the stairs. What was he doing on the stairs? Passed out, he'd passed out, that was it and bit by bit the night came back. He saw it all.

Eventually, he'd have to stand up. Slow and careful—there: a little bent but he was standing. There was daylight outside. Morning. What time in the morning? Almost ten. Staff meeting. He groaned. Staff meetings were important. Had to be there. Left foot, right foot, up the stairs. Cold shower, shave, the teeth, the hair, fresh clothes, wrong tie, to hell with it. He hurried down the stairs, no breakfast, hailed a cab.

Staff meetings were held once a month in the Staff Dining Room, a moderately elegant establishment just off the public restaurant. The meetings, presided over by the President and the Director, were attended by Department Heads and their Associate Curators. The Museum, in practice, operated rather like a large university: each department was essentially autonomous, free to handle its own affairs in its own way. Minor acquisitions, questions of display or discipline, matters of tenure and promotion, and the general play of politics, these were departmental matters. In the main, only questions of overall policy came down from the Board of Trustees. And, of course, the overriding, all consuming, ever-present issue of money.

Take his chalice, for instance. It had to be paid for. The Museum had funds for minor purchases but major ones were made with money borrowed from the bank. The Museum was into Chase Manhattan for three million six. The way out was simple enough: you deaccessioned, you took something off your shelves and sold it.

Simple, but for Melvil it was murder. Each department had to give up something—that was what the meeting was about—but Greek and Roman had the chalice, had to come up with the greatest share. Three quarters of a million: seven-fifty. Finding objects of such value, things no one would miss, and ripping them from his collection, losing them forever. He had put it off, of course, and his report was due, what could he say? The taxi bounced. He sat there, eyes shut tight.

VanStraaten, looking vigorous and keen, was talking when he got there. Slinking noiselessly to the empty chair next to Waterford, his Assistant Curator, Melvil sat and listened in. ". . . but if they do attack us, gentlemen, if that should happen, we must fight."

Fighting? Was there fighting? Was the country in another war? He looked around the table. Tension; something going on. In front of everyone, the usual blank pad, fresh pencils and the front page of the morning's *Times*. There must be something in the paper. He looked down and found it: a three-column picture of his chalice and a headline—METROPOLITAN ACQUIRES GREATEST CHALICE IN THE WORLD.

The subhead was more difficult to see. He frowned and brought it into focus: "Source and Purchase Price Kept Secret." Then Sitwell's by-line and the article.

New York City, Thursday, 18 April. A magnificent gold chalice, officially described as "the greatest in the world," was unveiled at private ceremonies yesterday at the Metropolitan Museum. A masterwork "of such extraordinary merit that the history of Western Art may need revision," the chalice bears the signature of its creator, the immortal gold-and-silversmith Pasiteles.

Described by Museum Director Pieter VanStraaten as "utterly unique, the only genuine example of Pasiteles known to exist," the chalice was acquired for "an undisclosed amount" from "a highly reputable European dealer." It will be placed on public display later this month."

Melvil drifted down the page. Some stuff about Pasiteles, some drivel from the press release he'd helped to write, some quotes from scholars here and there. All harmless, nothing bad. And then he found it.

Museum authorities, when pressed, firmly declined to disclose any data concerning the price or source of the chalice. When asked the reasons for this lack of candor, there was no response.

Both the public and the academic community have a legitimate interest in the answers to these questions. On their behalf, The New York Times is instituting an investigation to determine the source of the chalice and by what means it came to the Museum.

There was a good bit more but Melvil's eyes were tearing and besides VanStraaten seemed to be talking to him.

"Sorry, Pieter. Beg your pardon?" Melvil cleared his throat and sat up straight; it hurt.

"I wondered if the *Times* had called you yet."

"Not yet." God knew what calls were waiting for him in the office.

"Gentlemen, we must expect a lot of pressure." Pieter's eyes were bright: he liked tight corners, taking chances, he had taken on the *Times* before. "Potter and I are both of the opinion that there is an issue here well worth defending. Namely, our independence as an institution. If you're questioned by the press, just send them on to me. That's all, except for deaccessioning reports—and Melvil, would you stay a minute."

"Yes, of course." Around him, people rose and went. He stood. He walked. He talked. He listened, paying close attention to each word that Pieter said. He was to call the other papers and the magazines, to feel them out, were any of them taking up the story.

Right. He went out briskly, made it to the Sardis column, stood there looking up the stairs. The office, get Kropotkin on the phone and Sybil Schwartz. He couldn't do it, not just yet. What could he do? Go home to Dido, take her in his arms? Go see Serena, take her in his arms? He did the next best thing.

His Aphrodite's breasts were firm and full. Her legs were straight and strong, her belly soft yet muscular, her heart-shaped face was pure and sensual, all innocence and lust. Her nose was smashed off and her arms were lost but Melvil didn't mind. She was a Roman copy of a Greek original and on his bad days he would spend an hour or more in Gallery 4 just looking at her. Sometimes he'd let her come to life and glide down from her pedestal. Or else he'd conjure up the girl herself, the one who posed two thousand years before. He'd see her standing in the dappled shade beneath a cypress, smiling at him with her eyes because she mustn't let her lips move.

Could he deaccession her, he wondered. Academic question: she was an important piece, no pun intended, and the Board would never put her up for sale. But if he had to? Could he lose her if he had to? Never; no. Or Dido? Could he deaccession Dido, leave her, give her up to someone else, imagine life without her?

He shivered, left his Aphrodite, wandered on. What could he live without? What did he really need? His books, his notes, a quiet place. A little peace. He leaned against a wall and closed his eyes. Knots in the stomach. Eat. He had to eat and talk to Sybil Schwartz and deaccession something.

He could do that, yes. Go to the Departmental Storage Room and look for something there to deaccession. Wouldn't have to find it, all he had to do was look. Besides, he felt so peaceful there. He liked his Storage Room. Each Curatorial Department had one. It was where the things that weren't on view were stored. And Melvil's was enormous, like a mini-warehouse, holding three or four times the amount of art and artifacts that were on exhibition.

He did the stairs and found the door, got out his key and opened up. The shelves stretched on and on, all crammed with pots and jars and busts and carvings, every last one tagged and catalogued. There was a monster metal card file with a card for every object. Naked bulbs hung down from the high ceiling.

Surely there were things here The Museum could live without. Particularly because most of it was never put on view. Nobody ever saw the stuff. He started down the aisle, slowly. It was dizzying. His eyes burned and this thing inside his head was throbbing. What he needed was a drink or two—he started singing—"or three or four or more. In loveland, with me and my gal." There was a lot of echo and he thought he sounded pretty good.

He sat down by a row of old oil jars and closed his eyes. "Play 'Melancholy Baby.'" Well, why not; it's what he was. "'Cuddle up and don't feel blue.'" He was sounding like Crosby. "'All your tears are foolish fancies—'."

"Jeez, Dr. West, you scared me shitless."

Melvil looked up. It was Criswell, one of the Departmental Technicians. Another euphemism. They were porters, really, and they fetched and hauled and cleaned and dusted.

"How's it going, Criswell?"

"It's a hard life." Melvil nodded. "You're not sick or anything?"

"I felt like singing. Do you ever feel like singing, Criswell?"

"No, sir."

"Never?" Melvil stood. "We have to deaccession something, Criswell. Seven-fifty worth of something. Anything in here you wouldn't miss?"

"Well, Dr. West, the way I feel is you could sell it all off. By the time I finish dusting Roman down at that end, shit, the Greek stuff's all fucked up again."

Melvil had a quick flash of what Criswell's life was like. A task without an end, like Sisyphus. Every day, the poor son of a bitch, dustcloth in hand, caught in an epic of Grecian proportions—it didn't bear thinking about. He checked his watch. 11:30. Would the bar at the Stanhope be open?

A moderately elegant hotel much favored by prosperous and curiously furtive-looking Europeans, the Stanhope stood across from the Museum, at 81st and Fifth. Melvil moved through The Museum's delivery entrance just across the street and paused. A pleasant day it was: light breeze, sun shining, warm. Fashionable people strolling on the avenue; the fountain, just beside him, splashing. Voices floated softly; children playing, mothers calling. Pretty girl across the street, there, down the block. He squinted through the hazy sun.

His spirits lifted: pretty girls affected him that way. This one was walking close, hips touching, hand in hand with an attractive young man. Melvil smiled: love was nice and gee, the girl was really pretty. Lovely legs, slim hips, flat tummy—looked a lot like Dido—head erect, fine glossy hair.

The couple stopped and kissed and Melvil felt his heart stop. Was it? No, it couldn't be. He just had Dido on his mind, that's all. Like back in high school when he had this crush on Imogene Fiocchi and he saw her everyplace; her face was everywhere, like Dido's now.

He nodded briskly, with decision, started toward the Stanhope. The couple, he couldn't help noticing, was moving again. The man was blond and big, thick arms and shoulders, powerful. They turned down 82nd Sreet.

He lived on 82nd Street. With Dido. Maybe it was Dido after all. Who could the guy be? Cousin? Everyone had cousins; but their hips were touching and the way they kissed. He closed his eyes tight. Whoever the guy was and whatever was going on, he didn't want to know. He turned and started following.

It wouldn't do to get too close. He'd never shadowed anyone before. How did you do it? Crouch behind things, dart through doorways? In broad daylight? No, you looked like you were doing something else, like window-shopping but there were no shops on 82nd Street or else you put on some disguise or bought a paper, they were always buying papers, in the movies anyway, but if you stuck your head behind a paper how, for God's sake, could you see where you were going and if Dido turned around, he'd die.

But Dido didn't and he stayed a half a block behind the whole way home. He pulled up, leaned against a building as they stopped. She got her key out. They'd shake hands and say goodbye. Old flame, that's what he was. Some fellow Dido knew from college, maybe; only the guy looked twenty-five which didn't put him on the campus, not in Dido's time. And anyway, she touched his cheek and led the way inside.

What now? He was as modern as the next man. What the hell. He never played around but that was his decision. There was nothing, absolutely nothing wrong or bad or anything about a little action on the side. It was the normal thing, O.K. by him and if you wanted to be really fair about it, Dido hadn't had much screwing lately. Girls get horny, it's allowed.

There were a lot of things he just might do. Storm in and tear the house apart or pick a fight with someone on the street or find a bar and go get blind. A lot of possibilities and for a moment he imagined beating the guy to a bloody pulp, blow after blow, and Dido watching, eyes big, too afraid to scream. He'd like the feel of that: nice picture, but he'd never hit another person. Even in the army. Two years in Korea, playing safe and smart behind the lines except for when the lines had moved too fast and there he'd been, live ammo and a bayonet and even then he hadn't struck. No hits, no errors.

No, the thing to do was not to think about it. He turned and started back toward The Museum. It was nothing, everybody did it, no harm done. He didn't care, not even if she'd played around before. A little slap and tickle? Let it go. Forget it.

"Hello, Dido?" He was calling from the Stanhope bar. "It's me."

"Oh. Hi." She sounded normal. That was good. Or bad; depending how you analyzed it.

"How are things?" He kept it bland, no shades of meaning. It was one o'clock or so now. He was hardly buzzed at all.

"Okay." That could mean anything.

He'd worked hard on his next line. "Thought I might come home a little early."

"Any time. I won't be here." God, she was leaving him; and she could say it, just like that.

Say something. "Oh," he said. Then, thinking fast, "Where are you going?"

"There's an opening at the Whitney and you hate the Whitney." That was true enough. "And there's a party after. I'll be late, so come home any time."

He wasn't getting through to her. "I meant like kind of coming now."

There was a pause. Or was there? "Sure," she said. "You sick or anything?"

"Not me, I'm fine. It's just . . ." What was it just, he should have had a reason ready and was that a whisper in the background? The rustle of jockey shorts? "I overslept and didn't take a shower and I feel like, you know, cleaning up."

"You feel like cleaning up?" Did she believe it. Was she stalling?

"Be there in a minute."

He was there in five. She stood above him, looking down the stairs, her knowing smile on. The one that knew him inside out. "You don't look any tackier than usual," she said.

He shrugged and started up. How did she look, that was the question. Any signs of haste, a button buttoned wrong, hair out of place? He couldn't tell.

"I'll go and shower." He headed for the bedroom. Evidence, that's what he'd come for; evidence of any kind. Like what? He'd know it when he saw it. She was saying something.

". . . what we talked about last night." The bed looked neat. Too neat? She wasn't much at making beds and usually there were wrinkles. His hands were trembling just enough to give him trouble with his buttons so he pulled the shirt off over his head and mumbled, "What about it?"

"You were pretty smashed and sometimes when you're smashed, you don't remember."

*. . . in the balls. If I can find them.* "I remember."

"What's so funny?"

"Nothing's funny." He sat down on the bed to take his trousers off.

"Then what are you grinning about?"

"Was I grinning? I'm sorry." The bed was full of wrinkles now. He'd made them, sitting on it and he'd never know. He shifted, taking off his shoes. The wrinkles shifted, too, new shapes they made and interesting lines and she was saying what?

". . . his name is Drake and you'll be hearing from him."

Drake? Whose name was Drake? He pulled his socks off.

"He's my lawyer. Aren't you listening?"

Lawyer? What did Dido need a lawyer for? His legs looked long; amazing, what long legs he had.

"I need him for the simple reason that you can't get a divorce without one."

Melvil felt cold again, just like last night, same ice and snow and he was freezing. And this stuff about divorce; what was it? She was there last night. She'd heard him. It was settled. No. He'd told her no. Is that so hard to understand, for Christ's sake? No means no, she wasn't leaving him, not now or any other goddam time.

He heard a voice. The voice was saying things like "No means no, God damn you." All his thoughts but not his voice, a thick voice, loud. He looked down. Dido. Dido lying on the bed. Someone had thrown her there and he was standing over her and she was smiling at him like a mantis. Was it mantises that ate their mates? Was mantises the plural? Sounded odd and he was feeling dizzy, ringing in his ears.

He stepped back. "I'm sorry." He was naked—what had happened to his underwear? "I'm sorry, Dido." It was wrong, not having clothes on, Dido wouldn't like it so he turned away.

He started for the bathroom. He was near the doorway when she spoke. "You've got an ugly body, you know that?" He knew. "It's ugly and your dick is small."

He found the shower somehow and he washed.

# VI

They were sitting in VanStraaten's office. Just himself and Pieter and the unreachable Miss Burton. It was after two and he was feeling fine. Just fine. His mind was cool and clear and he could prove it: he could think back and remember anything he wanted. He remembered drying off and dressing, being in a taxicab and sitting at his desk. That's where he'd been when Kate had told him Pieter wanted him and that was why he was in Pieter's office.

Pieter wanted him because the *Times* had found the Customs declaration. Pieter told him so, that's how he knew. Just now. "The *Times* has found the Customs declaration," Pieter said.

He nodded. Art works have to be declared and once the *Times* decided to go after them it had been bound to happen. The Museum had held its line, stuck to its principles, no real harm done. Just that tomorrow everyone would know that three six was the price and that the chalice had been carried to the States by Adolf Mannheim.

Melvil hadn't met him but he'd really wanted to. A legendary figure, millionaire, self-made, and with a really decent art collection of his own. Which meant he had a lot of friends with art collections and he'd done this kind of thing before. The Cleveland got its Goya through him just a year ago and there were other deals, a Greco for the National or someplace. Melvil wasn't sure. The thing about him, though, the big thing was he'd made his fortune making movies. In the 40's back when Melvil was a kid. Terrific movies like the one where Cooper was a soldier and that Gable epic and the chase with Cary Grant and Melvil's favorite pirate picture starring—come on, who? You know his name.

"Damn Sitwell, anyway." VanStraaten frowned, then grinned. "I wonder what he paid for his apartment."

Melvil grinned back, chanced a quick look at Miss Burton, looked away. Oh sweet, never-to-be-touched Serena, how about a date tonight? He uncrossed his legs and tried to pay attention.

"My guess . . ." Pieter paused. "My guess is they'll go after Mannheim and he'll tell them what he told me—taxes, privacy—and that'll be the end of it. We'll have some pressure for a day or two, so when the calls come in . . . are you all right?"

"I'm fine."

"Just stick to our position. We're a private institution, it's a private matter, they can like it, lump it, go to court or go to hell. Okay?"

"Okay."

"That's all—except, Miss Burton, see if you can find where Mannheim is in case I need to talk to him."

He stood up, meeting over, time to go. Miss Burton stood up, too. Quick flash of thigh. White, perfect, smooth, like scissor blades.

She showed him out. They stood there in her little office, just the two of them. So close. Say something. It was now or absolutely never.

"Miss Burton?"

"Doctor West?" She sat, looked up at him.

"Serena . . ." He was fiddling with his glasses, forty-one and fiddling. "Are you free for dinner?"

There. He'd said it. Desperate men do desperate things. He watched her face for signs. Keenly: he was a keen observer of her face. He saw her lips move.

"Dinner when?"

He'd left it out, the vital part. "Tonight."

She frowned. "I don't know . . . I have work to do . . ." and then her head moved. Up and down it went; that's nodding, she was nodding. "Yes, if dinner's early, yes I will."

He felt like bounding up the stairs. Two-thirty, Eastern Standard Time. He was to meet her in her office, five o'clock. Two hours and a half. The afternoon would never end. Each minute took so long, the way the minutes did when it was Sunday morning and his dad was going to take him to a Tarzan movie and it didn't start till after dinner: agony.

He sat down at his desk. 2:32. The phone buzzed. It was Kate. Would he speak to Kropotkin? Hell yes, put him on. Good old Kropotkin. "Absolutely, anything you want to know, what can I tell you? Sure, we paid three-six. To whom? To Mannheim, Adolf Mannheim, you know, the producer of . . . Was he the owner? No. As to who owned it, The Museum's position . . . What?"

"I just had Mannheim on the phone."

Sneaky bastard; knew the answers when he asked the questions. "What did he have to say?"

"Not a hell of a lot. Some garbage about the tax problems and rights of privacy."

"I guess that's that."

"The hell that's that. Come on, West. Give. Whose was it? Is it hot? Who got the money? Was it smuggled? Did you—"

Kate walked in looking harried, steno pad in hand. He covered up the mouthpiece. "Trouble?"

"I've got Sybil Schwartz on one line and some guy from AP on another and the *Daily News* just—"

"Have them call VanStraaten."

"They want you."

His head began to ache. He nodded it. "Okay,

okay." Then, into the mouthpiece, "Look, Kropotkin—"

"No. You look. You look in your files and come up with some facts."

"What facts? You want to know about Pasiteles, I'll tell you—"

"Screw Pasiteles."

"You call yourself a critic? Shame on you, Kropotkin."

"West, I'm giving you a final chance."

"I'm taking it." He hung up and the phone buzzed.

"Schwartz here," Sybil said, sounding like the man she might have been.

"Hi, Sybil, what's the good word?" No good words at all. Just questions. Which he couldn't answer.

"You know as much as we do. Mannheim offered it for sale. VanStraaten snapped it up. He'd have been crazy not to. Why come down on us? It's standard practice."

"Doesn't it bother you?"

"Why should it?" But it did. A little.

"Well, it bothers us a lot."

"Us?"

"*Time.*" Voice deep, she tolled it like a bell. "And don't you give me standard practice. Lawlessness runs rampant in America's museums today. You know what happened at the Bliss Collection. They . . ."

He knew. He put the phone down on his memo pad. 2:40. Five o'clock would never come. He looked out at the park. A lot of new debris around. He didn't care, he wasn't in the mood. What was he in the mood for? Feeling good, that's what he wanted, just to go on feeling good and thoughts of home were pressing in. He picked the phone up.

"Sybil?"

"I'm still talking."

"Call me when you're finished."

Click, he clicked her off. The damn thing buzzed at once. Associated Press. Yes, Adolf Mannheim; yes, three million six; yes, that was all he had to say. Another buzz. The *Daily News.* He told them something. Buzzing, there was altogether too much buzzing going on.

He spent the next two hours in the tunnel. Favorite place of his. His visits there were fairly secret. Kate knew, naturally, she had to cover for him when he went; and Pieter, over drinks sometimes, they'd talk about the place and Bindle had a running joke, had he been tunneling today? It had some long official name, like "Intra-Departmental Storeroom, Supplementary," but Melvil called it the tunnel because that's what it was. For reasons he'd forgotten if he ever knew them, the thing was dug out, deep down, underneath the ground and paved and walled with brick when The Museum went up. And then abandoned. A good forty feet wide and arching twenty feet or so in height, the tunnel stretched from one end of the building to the other, from 80th to 83rd Street.

It had stretched there, dark and empty for a long time. Then, as The Museum acquired more than it could hold, the tunnel had been fenced off into areas and each department had a huge cage crammed with uncatalogued junk. Over the decades, expeditions went out and bequests came in and the cream was skimmed off, all the good stuff catalogued and put away upstairs. The rest went to the tunnel to be stored and sorted out someday. Every major museum in the world had a place like the tunnel.

Melvil opened up the Greek and Roman cage, switched on the light and blinked around. Dust, cobwebs, sagging shelves, half-opened crates: a mess. He'd found some great things here from time to time: some jewelry from a Persian expedition that was absolutely Mexican, a marble bust of Nero with MADE IN ITALY stamped on the bottom, modern kitchen pots mixed in with ancient pottery, someone's burnoose, a box of tent pegs, nineteenth-century Mason jars.

What was his mood today? Which crate to open? Something from the Lowenthal Bequest. There, faded letters: GIFT OF ALMA B. AND SIMON LOWENTHAL. He'd wonder sometimes who they'd been, old Simon and his Alma. Half the crates were theirs. He picked one labeled Antioch: why not, it's where his chalice came from. Once great city on the left bank of the Orontes, home of the mighty Selucid kings, center of letters and the arts, evangelized by Simon and Barnabas and, just perhaps, by Peter himself.

He lifted up the lid. Good God, what junk. A sea of pots and pot shards, broken perfume phials, oil jars. It wasn't junk, not really; it was simply not museum quality. There was no use for it at all. The whole place should be deaccessioned. Only someone had to catalogue it first and that would cost more than the stuff was worth.

He rummaged through the bits and pieces, shrugged, picked up a tiny clay amphora, handles long since lost. Whose was it once? That was the game he really liked to play, the thing that drew him down here. He'd imagine everything. The phial, he decided, came from Pergamon, that miracle of Greek achievement on the Asia Minor coast. Blue water bright, sun splashing down on marble temples.

Usually the thing, whatever it was, belonged to some beautiful woman. Today was no exception and Diana, he decided, was her name. She was of noble birth. She lived in a villa on the sea near the agora. She was tall and pale and, in general, looked remarkable like Serena Burton. The amphora held some rare perfume and every morning she'd arise, like Botticelli's Venus only more so, pick up her beloved amphora and glide down the polished corridor to her bath.

As a rule, these baths took a long time to imagine. There were so many decisions: the precise size and shape of her breasts, the diameter and color of her nipples. Were they hard, erect? Was she easy to arouse? Or was she sensual but somnolent, a drowsing tigress? And the difficult question of moles and birthmarks, those little touches that could take a fantasy and make it real.

Once he had Diana just the way he wanted her, he let her ease into the bath. She drifted, floating, smiling secretly. They always smiled secretly, his girls, because they all had secret lovers. Mighty men, these lovers were: great muscles, brave and strong, around forty years old, sort of intellectual-looking and with really big dicks.

Diana was out of the tub. Amphora in hand, she was anointing herself with myrrh in very private places when she turned and gasped. Footsteps. Her lover's footsteps. Arms outstretched, she raced into the corridor and there he was. Magnificent. He saw her, cried her name, opened his arms and checked his watch. Ten after five. Son of a bitch.

Melvil jumped up, pivoted, tore out of the cage, slammed the door, thundered down the tunnel floor and up the stairs. He was wheezing when he made it to the mezzanine. She'd wait, she'd be there, had to be. She'd never think he'd stood her up.

EXECUTIVE OFFICES: there on the door. He reached out for the buzzer, hesitated, ran a hand covered with dust through his hair, smudged his necktie as he straightened it, tugged his cuffs, buttoned his jacket, thought of crossing his fingers but rejected the impulse as childish and buzzed. He started counting, got to three. It buzzed back. He went in. She looked up from her desk and smiled. At him.

So many smiles; at almost everything he said. And now—he leaned across the table toward her; not too close, just closer—he had made her laugh.

"He said that? Pieter really said that?"

Melvil nodded and the waiter put down fresh martinis.

"What did you say?"

They were sitting in the Stanhope bar and she had asked about the scene with Sitwell, she'd heard shouting through the walls. He longed to tell her his Shinola line but it would shock her and he couldn't think of how to clean it up.

The bar was full of people. Didn't matter, it was safe. O.K. to be there with her and he nodded to old Graz across the room. But dinner was another matter. Where to take her? Dinner was a date and married men did not . . . He grinned. He had a secret. It was thrilling: secret talks in secret places. Secret things.

He ordered a Sancerre for dinner. Inexpensive wine but very nice. He watched her as she looked around the room. She liked it, he could tell.

Pieter had taken him to lunch at Le Canard a number of times. Nice atmosphere, nice food and prices out of sight. Safe places for Curators with secrets.

"Melvil?" No more Doctor West. "It's funny being here." Her face was flushed. All those martinis—was she tight? He hadn't meant to get her tight. Or had he?

"Funny? Why?"

"It's just . . . I've made so many reservations here for Pieter and I never thought—" She looked away and smiled. "Thanks."

Her hand was on the table and he let his brush against it as he reached out for his glass to test the wine. He couldn't taste it but he said he found it good. The waiter poured and went away.

A seafood something came and then some lamb

and she was interested in him, she really was. So full of questions, all about his work, the chalice, Pieter, where they went together, what they did. And he was being charming, clever; you could tell the way she smiled. Her eyes were shining and she touched his hand.

He looked away. His glass was empty. What had happened to the wine? All gone, the bottle empty and the coffee cold. All over, dinner over, time to go. He paid with his American Express card. Good he had one. The Museum had gotten them for all the Curators. His wallet was so thin; she hadn't noticed, had she? Taxi money, that was all.

He sat beside her in the cab. Not touching her, not quite. He had to make his move, do something; in a minute she'd be gone. He shifted, put his arm up on the seat behind her. Slowly, very slowly so she wouldn't notice it, he brought it down around her shoulders. There—he had her, he was holding her. She didn't pull away. His heart pounding and the cab drew up. A brownstone in the Sixties somewhere, east of Second. This was it.

"Okay if I come up with you a minute?" Said: he'd said it.

Back the answer came; no pause, no hesitation. "Please come up. I'd like you to."

He felt a little dizzy on the sidewalk. Not from alcohol, of course, but everything looked slightly white and far away. She took a key out, opened up a door. He followed her. There were a lot of stairs. To paradise. The song went through his head.

She opened up another door, turned on a light inside. He couldn't move. "Come on," she said, "and don't look till I fold my bed up, it's a mess."

Her bed. Were those the marks her breasts had made, were those her hips? He watched her smooth the sheets and tried to listen as she told him not to mind the books all piled in the corner or the clothing on the chair. Her clothes.

"Come sit," she said. She had the Castro folded, plumped a cushion down. He sat. A tiny place. One room. He had a sudden ache for tiny places, for the one he'd had at Harvard in the days when anything was possible.

"You want a Scotch? I've got some."

"Please." Through lips that felt like Silly Putty.

"There's no soda, it's expensive, do you mind?"

He didn't mind, not anything. He watched her move. Light, quick, a bird: like Dido only Dido was a pterodactyl and Serena was a dove. The drink was in his hand. She sat down close, within his reach. Her voice was sweet, a little slurred, and she was telling him how much she liked her job, how nice it was and Pieter was and he was.

He was nice. The girl thought he was nice. She meant it. From the heart. Her heart belonged to him; it might, it would, it did. He felt a sudden rush of something, God, if only he could open up his heart to her. Why not? He knew her inside out, he'd always known her, she'd been living in his dreams and he could tell her everything. Pour all his feelings into her. He looked down. Christ, his thing was sticking up, it hurt, what if she saw it, awful, how could it go sticking up like that when all his feelings were so pure? He looked into her eyes, saw longing. There was longing in her eyes. For him and suddenly he wanted her to see it.

"Oh, Serena."

In his arms, he had her in his arms. Her lips kept moving, she was talking. Soft, how soft her lips were. And her body, little breasts, so delicate.

"No, Melvil, please . . ."

He loved her, he was sure of it. He told her so but she was wriggling, rigid, pushing him away. He grabbed for her, she mustn't go, his fingers held her, then she wrenched and something tore, he heard a tearing sound.

"No. Stop it." She was standing.

"But you like me, don't you?"

"Yes, I do." Her lips were trembling. Were those tears? "I do but I'm in love with Pieter."

Ice. He felt encased in ice but "Oh" was all he said.

"I love him but he has a wife and I know it's hopeless and he doesn't know but I can't stop it." She was weeping and he'd torn her dress, he'd torn it down the front. "And you're his friend and you could tell me all about him, little things . . ."

"I don't know."

"He's all I've talked about all evening. I'm so sorry, Melvil."

Fool. To think a girl could love him. And the shame of it. Oh Jesus, he was so ashamed. His face was in his hands. He couldn't think, he couldn't hear, that roaring in his ears and he was sweating and the room was turning and he wasn't going to vomit, was he, oh my God.

He had to get out, run away. He stood. His fault, he was so sorry, please forgive him. Laughter, it was Dido laughing at him. Aw gee, Dido, have a heart. Was that the doorknob? Turn it, make it turn. He turned it, turned the corner, everything was turning, cars were turning, he was turning, too.

He didn't fall. His feet kept moving. He could see them, far off, down there on the sidewalk. Noises in his ears. What were they? Voices? Dido laughing and his mother whispered something. It was Mom, no doubt about it, and she said—what was it? Never mind; if it was anything important, she'd repeat it. She was always telling him how bad he was. She never used the word but he could tell she meant it. Like just yesterday. He'd come home late from school. He had his bag of marbles in his hand.

He looked down at his hand. It held a key. He

watched the key. It went into a lock. It fit. Another knob, another door; then stairs. He saw an empty bed. He couldn't: it was Dido's bed. When she came home, dear God, he couldn't, that was all but where to go? One final turn. He saw a sofa. Could he make it? Sure, he could. He hoped it was a friendly place.

# VII

The ringing was a telephone. Eyes closed, he reached out for it. Odd: no phone. No bedside table, either. Very odd. A little frightening, in fact. He bolted upright, eyes open.

Living room. That's where he was. The sofa, he was sitting on the sofa and the phone was on the coffee table and the room was dim. How early was it? 7:30. Ringing phones at 7:30—someone sick or dead?"

"Hello?" he said but very little sound came out.

"Hello, hello. I want to talk to Melvil West, please. This is Sitwell, Waldo Sitwell of the *Times*."

At 7:30? Thoughtless bastard, he could go to hell. He slammed the phone down, stretched, felt terrible. He had his clothes on; strange, he'd slept with all his clothes on. Two nights in a row. What had he done last night? Serena. Lovely girl. They'd had some drinks, some dinner. He was starting to remember when the phone went off again.

"Sitwell?" His voice was working now. "You take it, Sitwell, and you stick it—"

"West?" VanStraaten's voice. "Is that you, West? Are you all right?"

"I'm fine."

"I'm leaving for the office. Can you get there right away?"

"What's up?"

The line went dead. He stood and started for the bedroom. Empty bed. No Dido. She was out, still out. With whom and doing what? He hurled his clothes off, shaved too fast and nicked himself. The shower was a killer, icy cold.

The taxi let him out at The Museum. 8:30. It was Saturday, so things were quiet; no one on the street, no traffic. He was feeling better now; the shower hadn't hurt. Nor had the tiger's milk. He'd never touched the stuff before but there was nothing else. He hurried up the steps. First Sitwell, then Van-Straaten: there was trouble.

No two ways about it. "Jesus Christ, West, did you ever in your fucking life?" VanStraaten was standing by the big round table. Morning paper on the table. *Times.* VanStraaten shoved it toward him. "I mean, did you fucking ever?"

Melvil hurried to the table. Paper was inverted, upside down, but there it was, front page again, his chalice. Even bigger picture than the last time, took up half the page. Over it, the headline read: IS THIS THE HOLY GRAIL? He shook his head—not possible—and turned the paper right side up.

IS THIS THE HOLY GRAIL? the banner headline asked. Then, just beneath, in smaller type: "Famed English Scholar Identifies Pasiteles Chalice." And, under that: "Claims Chalice Stolen from Excavation Site."

"Is it a joke?" VanStraaten shook his head. "I mean, for God's sake, in this day and age, the Holy Grail?"

"You look like hell."

"Worked late, that's all. You mind if I sit down?"

He sat. It had to be a joke, a hoax, a put-on, something. "Who's the famous English scholar? Anyone I ever heard of?"

"What would you say to Sir Winston Hunter-Donne?"

"Sir Winston Hunter-Donne?" Fantastic man; like Arnold Toynbee: only more so. Melvil blinked. He'd started reading Hunter-Donne when he was ten or so and Hunter-Donne was sixty-something. That made the Great Man eight-five or more. He was a Nobel

Laureate, an aristocrat with close ties to the Royal Family, a master of prose, a penetrating and original historian and an absolutely world-class archeologist. "You've got to be kidding."

"Read it and weep."

"Then he's got to be senile. I mean, the chalice is authentic, it's a genuine Pasiteles."

"He doesn't deny that for a minute. What he claims is that he found the goddam thing four months ago in Somerset and—read it for yourself." He shoved the *Times* at Melvil, lit a cigarette.

Special to The New York Times. Glastonbury, Somerset, April 21—In a hastily summoned press conference at his expedition headquarters here, Sir Winston Hunter-Donne identified the so-called "world's greatest chalice" by Pasiteles unveiled in New York Thursday as "in all probability the Holy Grail."

Sir Winston, generally considered the greatest living authority in his field, went on to say that he had himself unearthed the chalice at his nearby excavations in South Cadbury. No announcement was made of the find, which occurred in January, and "before the chalice could be adequately studied and tested, it was stolen, along with a number of other Arthurian relics, from my laboratory."

Sir Winston's claim was substantiated by authorities at Scotland Yard. The theft, no report of which was made public, has been under investigation without success since January. According to Yard spokesmen, the chalice disappeared along with objects of lesser value and importance, all relating to King Arthur.

Serious excavations at South Cadbury have been going on, under Sir Winston's direction, since 1966. Scholarly opinion, doubtful at first, has been shifting through the years as more and more objects and artefacts have been unearthed indicating that the legendary English king may not have been so legendary after all.

"The appearance of my chalice in New York," Sir Winston stated, "has been brought to the attention of Her Majesty's Government and, pending authentication, appropriate measures will be taken to assure the return of this national treasure."

When asked for his reasons for believing that the chalice is, indeed, the Holy Grail, Sir Winston said, "It is my belief that the chalice was brought here to Glastonbury in the First Century A.D. by Joseph of Arimathea who was present at the crucifixion of Our Lord and who took possession of the chalice at that time."

Legends concerning Joseph and the Grail have been traced back as far as the Eleventh Century. When asked for reasons why he took these ancient legends to be fact, Sir Winston said, "A generation ago, King Arthur himself was taken to be legendary. Today we know the man existed: not a king, perhaps, but a national hero nevertheless. In 1966, when I began these excavations, Camelot was merely legend. Now, as we discover find after find, it begins to seem that Camelot was real as well."

Sir Winston declined to speculate as to how the chalice might have reached New York. When asked about (Continued on Page 28)

Melvil was turning to the page when VanStraaten said, "You've got the gist of it." Some gist. It wasn't possible. His chalice couldn't be Sir Winston's; it was his, it's place was here in his museum. He felt a little spurt of panic—but the whole thing was absurd.

"The old man must be crazy, Pieter."

"As a loon. It's not his chalice and there never was a Holy Grail." The phone rang. "Get it, will you? Christ, it's going to be like that all day. We've got to make a statement and we can't until I talk to Mannheim."

Melvil had the phone. "Hi, Waldo."

"What's the little bastard want?"

"He says to tell you he's been on the line to Cardinal Kellerman."

"So what? Why tell me?" Pieter took the phone. "Top of the morning, Waldo. Great to hear your voice." He listened, nodded. "Absolutely. Anytime." Another pause. "You'll have our statement later in the day." He put the phone down carefully. "Cardinal Kellerman would like to see the chalice but he wants to talk to Rome first."

"To the Vatican?"

"He wants to be sure of the Church's position: was

there a Holy Grail or wasn't there." His voice began to rise. "They've had two thousand years to make up their minds. Don't they know by now?" The phone went off again. "Look, call Miss Burton, get her over here and get some people in to answer calls and get me Mannheim on the phone."

"Right." He was not about to call Serena, couldn't face her, saw her for a moment, dress all torn, her eyes. "Where's Mannheim?"

"Jesus, Melvil, in the crapper, how do I know? Try the chalet in Geneva where I met him. If he's not there, track him down. We've got to have that provenance." He slammed a hand down on the table. "Weeks ago, he should have sent it weeks ago. I cable and I call. 'Don't worry, Pieter dear,' he tells me. Worry? Christ, we're out three million six, our neck is on the block, the Holy Grail, for God's sake. Get him for me."

Melvil tried. It wasn't easy. Outside in Serena's office, pulled a chair up to her desk—he couldn't sit in her place, couldn't do it—found her Wheeldex, opened it to M. The phone began to ring. It kept on ringing and he talked to *Newsweek* and Kropotkin and the AP, God knows what he told them, something, statement later in the day, and Sybil Schwartz hung up on him. He wasn't feeling very well. He found the number for Geneva, dialed it, no delay, it rang. A deep voice spoke to him in German but it wasn't German. Swiss? Was Swiss a language? Anyway. Herr Mannheim, it was clear, was *nicht zu Hause*. Where was he? *Wo Herr Mannheim?* Maybe London. Where in London? Maybe *zu Hause*. Where was his house? Savoy Hotel.

The lines to London were busy and his phones were ringing and someone from Reuthers swore at him or was it the other way around and finally he got through, had the Savoy on the line and Mannheim didn't answer. Wait, for God's sake, don't hang up. He had some questions. Could he have Reception? Yes, he could. Yes, Mr. Mannheim kept a suite at the hotel. Yes, he had been there earlier that week. Where was he now? Perhaps in France, perhaps America. Where in America? He had a town house in New York. And where in France? A villa on the Riviera. Cap d'Antibes.

Great: he was gaining on it. Phone book—K, L, M. No Adolf Mannheim. Try the Operator, that's-a-boy. The number was unlisted. Could he have it? No. Who could? Nobody could. He told them where to put their number. Now what? France, the Riviera, Cap d'Antibes. The digits on the dial were blurry and he didn't know the number; how, for God's sake, did you dial Information in Antibes? He dialed O and could the Operator help him? Yes she could, she was a darling. Melvil told her so and heard a lot of hissing and some crackles and a faint voice said, "*Renseignements.*" He had it: Information. Could she tell him—no, she couldn't, not in English and his French was fine for reading but he couldn't speak it very well, but, finally he got the number.

It rang. A lady answered.

"*Allô?*"

"*Monsieur Mannheim, s'il vous plaît.*"

"*Pas ici.*"

"*Où est-il?*"

"Sorry but my French is rotten."

"So is mine. I'm trying to reach Mr. Mannheim."

"Same here but the old fart stood me up. Invites me on the *Samovar* and then takes off without me."

"The *Samovar*?"

"His boat."

"He's on a boat?"

"You sound nice. What's your name?"

"What kind of a boat? Is it—"

"It's lonely here and I'm a little tight. Where are you calling from?"

"New York."

"That's how it goes."

"Is it a big boat? Would it have a telephone?"

"It's got a crew of thirty-three and lots of telephones. You didn't tell me what your name was. Mine is Nancy."

"Nancy, does it have a number?"

"Sure I do. It's—"

"I don't want your number."

"Why not? Don't you like me?"

"Nancy, please . . ."

"You're not so hot yourself, you know."

"For God's sake, Nancy, I have got to talk to Mr. Mannheim."

"When you get him, tell him he can fuck himself."

The line went dead.

"West?" Pieter, standing in the office doorway. "Have you found him?"

"More or less. He's on the *Samovar.*"

From there on, it was easy. "Mannheim?" Louder. "Mannheim?" Louder. "Mannheim, it's VanStraaten." The call had been routed from New York to Paris to Marseilles to Radio Grasse. The *Samovar* was in the Gulf of Lions and the reception, apparently, was terrible. Melvil sat near Pieter at the big oak table. It was two o'clock.

"VanStraaten. It's VanStraaten." Pause. "You're goddamn right, I read about the Grail. That's why I'm calling." Pause. "You've got the papers? No, I can't wait till they get here." Louder. "Give it to me on the phone. I need the facts. I've got to make a statement to the press—hello, hello, for Christ's sake."

Melvil straightened up and paid attention. This was terribly important. "Who? Who owned it?" Pieter's pencil moved. "He lives where? What's he doing in a place like that?" Gold pencil, up and down it went, so fast. He watched it go. "His father? When?"

Black marks and squiggles, all across the page; he wondered what they meant.

"Melvil?" The call was over. Pieter moved his chair around the table, close beside him. "Help me write this thing."

They worked it out together and it went like this:

> The Pasiteles chalice, recently acquired by The Metropolitan Museum of Art, was, until its purchase, part of a notable collection of Greek and Roman artefacts belonging to Dr. Stefan Kalman. Dr. Kalman, a well-known scholar and collector, makes his home in Calvi, the luxurious resort and seaport on the northern coast of Corsica.
>
> The chalice has been part of Dr. Kalman's collection since it was unearthed by his father, Dr. Bela Kalman, the distinguished archeologist. The elder Kalman, who devoted his life to the excavation and study of the extraordinary menhirs of Corsica, is the author of several monographs on the subject. He discovered the chalice, along with other artefacts of the period, in 1927 while working at an excavation near Corte in the Corsican interior.
>
> The Museum must, therefore, beg to differ with Sir Winston Hunter-Donne as to the circumstances surrounding the discovery of the chalice.
>
> The chalice came to the attention of Mr. Adolf Mannheim, the illustrious film producer, many years ago on the occasion of one of his frequent visits to Calvi aboard his yacht, the *Samovar*. Recognizing the rarity and importance of the chalice, Mr. Mannheim, after long and quiet persuasion, was finally able to bring Dr. Kalman to part with the treasure.
>
> The Museum is grateful to Mr. Mannheim for his efforts and to Dr. Kalman for his generosity and vision in relinquishing this masterpiece.

VanStraaten put his pencil down, sat back and stretched. "I don't know, Melvil, what do you think?"

"I think 'generosity and vision' is a little much." He stood up, rubbed his eyes and looked with longing toward the sherry.

"I could use one, too." VanStraaten went to the decanter, poured. "You ever hear of Stefan Kalman?"

"No." No reason why he should have.

"Check him out for me tomorrow, will you?"

"Sure." It meant some calls to fellow Curators and they'd have heard of him or not; it wouldn't mean much either way. Collectors were a funny bunch and some of them were secretive, anonymous . . .

"The father, too."

"What bothers you?"

"It's nothing." Pieter handed him a sherry. "Only, Melvil, could the chalice have been found in Corsica?"

"The Romans colonized the island, sure it could. They built whole cities there." He looked at Pieter. "You're not worried, are you?"

"No. It's just . . ."

"Look, Pieter, Hunter-Donne is eighty-something. Old men make mistakes."

"I know. It's just . . ." He smiled. "You've never had a cognac and cigars with Adolf Mannheim. What the hell." He started for the phone. "Let's hit it."

It was dark out by the time they finished calling in the statement to the more important magazines and papers. Time to go. They went. The day had been a long one but it wasn't over.

# VIII

"You know what I think, Pieter?"

"What about?"

"Oh, life in general."

"Tell me."

They were having brandies in VanStraaten's living room. Big room with lots of books and music in it, terraces and windows overlooking Central Park. A penthouse on Fifth Avenue. He didn't get there very often. Pieter's life and his, their private lives, just didn't cross. They worked together, drank together, had a late meal now and then together and then Pieter always left, so eagerly, for home and his Alicia. Pieter's second wife, Alicia. The first, a Whitney girl or something, disagreeable divorce, in all the papers, got a fortune for a settlement. Was it the women, Dido and Alicia, were they the reason why it didn't work? They'd gone to dinner once: disaster.

"What I think is . . ." What exactly did he think? *Life is real and life is earnest*—the grammar school he'd gone to had been big on nineteenth-century poetry. Life was like that for him—but not for Pieter. Pieter had a good time. How did Pieter do it? Why not ask—and he was going to when Alicia came in.

Alicia, Alicia, as lovely as her name. Slim, tall, so elegant and bright. Amusing, too; she said such funny things. Like Irene Dunne or Carole Lombard, someone like that: perfect and beyond his reach but there for him to look at. So he looked and laughed, they all did, had a few and he kept thinking he could have a good time, too, if this were his. This home, those city lights now swimming just a little, and a woman like Alicia.

He was exhausted which was why the brandy hit him when he hit the street; not hard, not really and he didn't feel like walking but there were no taxicabs. The house was dark and quiet; not a sound. No Dido. Up the stairs. He wondered where she was, then wondered why he wondered. Did he love her? Would he die if she divorced him, would he really freeze to death. Deep questions. Much too deep.

He made it through the dimness to the bar and poured himself a nightcap, started for the kitchen for some ice, remembered that there wasn't any, headed for the bathroom. God, the pleasures of the bath. To sink into the water, lie there drifting, half afloat.

He flipped the light on, squinted at the glare, reached for the spigots, watched the water pour. The bedroom was too far away. He pulled his clothes off, left them in a heap—he was a neat boy and he'd pick it all up later on—switched off the lights and sank into the tub.

He left the water running till his chest was covered. That was vital, water on the chest. It got cold when you breathed on it, your chest did, if it wasn't under water.

The faucet dripped a little, very slowly, but he liked that. It was comforting. Steady things were comforting, things like his job or taking notes forever on the book he'd never write. It would be nice to write it, though: the fame and the respect. The book would be a huge success. How many printings would it have? The water went on dripping, and just for the fun of it he started counting plops, one for each printing. He was somewhere over twenty when he fell asleep.

The dream was ugly. That was all he knew. A lot of pain and hurting and the memory of blood. He woke up shivering, skin puckered, water cold and listened to the voices in the bedroom. No. He shook his head. The sounds were from the dream.

They came again, all whispery and very real. He felt like screaming. Burglars. Jesus Christ. They'd find him. Helpless. In the tub. They'd kill him. They were crazy, burglars were. Not like the old days, when the guys who broke in were professionals and didn't hurt you. What to do?

He bit his lip, tried not to breathe. They'd never try the bathroom. Would they? Why, what for? What's in a bathroom? Drugs. That's what they came for, what they wanted. Jesus. He stood up. His knees were wobbly and he couldn't feel his feet. The room was dark. His clothes: he had to get his clothes on. It was horrible, the thought of being naked when the knife went in and somehow it would hurt less if he couldn't see his flesh.

The trouser legs were all scrunched up, all twisted. Get them straight, come on, no noise. He slipped, scraped himself against the sink, held on. He jammed his legs through, tugged them up and zipped the zipper—that was vital. Shirt next. He crouched down, felt around and found it. Inside out? He couldn't tell. It didn't matter.

Barefoot, he trembled to the door. His breathing was so loud. He listened. They were there, still there. If he could make it through the hall—there was a tiny hall outside the bathroom door—if he could do that, he could make it to the stairs and down and out.

He put his hand out, touched the knob, then turned it. Slowly, ease it around, then inch the door by tiny fractions, take your time. He had it wide enough and slipped into the hallway. Up ahead, the bedroom door stood open and the light was on. He'd have to be quiet, really quiet.

Right. He took a step. The fucking floorboards; Jesus. He stood absolutely still. They'd heard him, hadn't they? He waited. No one came. Another step. Another. He was close now, really close. It wouldn't matter if he made a noise now, he could beat them down the stairs, he knew the way, they didn't, that was an advantage, he could make it.

He was poised, all set to go, when Dido walked across his line of vision. In the bedroom, calm and smiling, naked as a tooth. It struck him funny. Boy, some hero; scared to death and it was only Dido. He felt like laughing, and apparently he did because this giant of a man came whipping through the bedroom door and down the hall and grabbed him.

Something hard smashed into his stomach and there was no air to breathe and he was face down on the bedroom carpet with his arms all bent behind him and the pain was blinding.

"Don't kill him." It was Dido screaming. "That's my fucking husband."

What ensued was never very clear to Melvil. His arms were set free and after a while he could move them, and when the pain was better he sat up and saw Dido with the same blond guy he'd seen her with the other day. Except the guy was naked now, with balls the size of cantaloupes, dick hanging down below his knees.

It seemed important to get to his feet, so he did. The room was very quiet; no one was saying anything. It was obvious to Melvil that something really ought to be said, so he cleared his throat and spoke. "How do you do?" was what he said. "I'm Melvil West. Has Dido offered you a drink?"

He of the long dick blinked and shook his head. "No thanks."

"Sure you won't join me?" Melvil smiled pleasantly. It wasn't hard. "The bar's through here." The words came tumbling out, no need to think. "I came home inadvertently to get some clothes. Just for a day or two. We've got a sort of mess at The Museum and I need to be there. Neat or soda?"

"Soda, please."

He filled his glass, chatting on and on. "We have this chalice, possibly you're read about it in the papers. Lovely thing. It goes on exhibition next week. You must come and see it. Ask for me, I'll see you're let right in."

There was a valise open on the bed now. He was packing it: two shirts, two socks, two suits of underwear; all twos, just like the ark. Dido sat at the end of the bed, eyes like slits, not saying anything, just watching him. "In any event, there seems to be some confusion as to where the chalice came from and until it's all cleared up," he closed the valise, "I'm afraid I have to man my desk." He smiled, kissed Dido lightly on the cheek. "My shoes are in the bathroom. I'll just get them and be off. Take care."

He nodded to them from the bedroom doorway, made it to the bathroom where he vomited, changed clothes and went out into the night. He found it hard to see where he was going; everything was clear enough but what he couldn't seem to do was pay attention. He began to count the sidewalk lines, to see how many squares there were between Third and Lex and how did that compare to Lex and Park. The results were interesting and he made a mental note to write them down.

Park Avenue was empty, not a car in sight. The pavement looked inviting in the streetlight, dark and soft, a licorice road. He wondered where it went. What if you followed it forever? Would you get to Candyland? He used to spend a lot of time in Candyland but that was very long ago indeed, way back when everybody was alive.

He crossed and moved on. Dido was a funny girl, she did such funny things. He laughed a little, softly, just to be polite. Big day ahead. He'd better hurry. Lots to do and he was late.

He half ran up the marble stairs. The door was locked. He looked inside. No Bindle, good and gray, to let him in, and everything inside was dark. How could that be? He started knocking on the door. The Museum was always open, seven days a week. Even Mondays, when the public couldn't come, a lot of work went on. He banged some more. He had so much to do.

He saw some lights inside. Two, three. Lights bobbing up and down. What could this be? Another robbery? He squinted. Lights were shining on him and the door was open.

"Okay, mister, what's the big idea?"

"I've got a lot of work to do." He started forward. Something stopped him. Hands. Some hands were holding him. "I work here."

"Sure you do."

"I'm—" Perfectly ridiculous: he knew his name as well as he knew anything. "I'm Melvil West."

"I don't care who you are. It's four o'clock."

He had his wallet out now. "Look. It says so. Melvil West. It's on my card. I'm Curator of Greek and Roman and I've got to go to work."

"I'm sorry, Mr. West. You can't come in."

"I can't?"

"It's four A.M., why don't you go home, get some rest."

"I can't do that."

"You can't stay here."

"What can I do, then? I don't know. What should I do?"

"You feel okay?"

"I'm fine."

"Come back at eight, I guess, that's all."

"At eight o'clock, I'll write that down."

He wrote it on his card.

# IX

Sunday was a blur. He had no memory of most of it. The day went past him like a movie out of focus, now and then an isolated section crystal clear.

The guards and flashlights he remembered. After that, a sticky counter top and cups of coffee and the seals in Central Park asleep in morning sunlight. Really clear these things were: he could see the cake crumbs on the counter and the whiskers on the seals. He'd even counted them; the numbers seemed important at the time but, in the long run, not worth remembering.

It was seven after eight, exactly seven, when he got to The Museum. It wasn't Bindle at the door, but someone nice. The halls were empty and he'd liked that and he'd spent some time with Aphrodite.

Later, he was at his desk. Big books were open on it. Volumes of the Encyclopaedia Britannica, Thirteenth Edition. He had Volume 15 open to page 514. Why 514? What was there on it? Then he saw:

> Joseph of Arimathea, in the New Testament, a worthy Jew who had been converted by Jesus Christ. He is mentioned by the Four Evangelists, who are in substantial agreement concerning him: after the Crucifixion, he went to Pilate and asked for the body of Jesus, subsequently prepared it for burial and laid it in a tomb.

He knew all that; well, more or less. Why was he reading it? Old Hunter-Donne. Of course. Old Hunter-Donne was claiming that this Joseph brought his chalice to England. Couldn't be. Or could it? How sure was he that his chalice came from Antioch? And there were Romans everywhere in England in those days. A lot of ways it could have gotten there. And what if Hunter-Donne had actually found his chalice? Eighty-five or not, he was a great man and he'd dug up something, hadn't he?

Hard questions. Much too hard. He let his eye slip down the page. "The striking character of this single appearance of Joseph of Arimathea led to the rise of numerous legends. Thus William of Malmesbury says he was sent to Britain by St. Phillip and, having received a small island in Somersetshire, there constructed 'with twisted twigs' the first Christian church in Britain—afterwards to become the Abbey of Glastonbury . . . Joseph also plays a large part in the various versions of The Legend of the Holy Grail. *See* GRAIL, THE HOLY."

Did he have to see it? Surely, as an educated man, he knew a lot about the Grail: the harvest legends and the *Nibelungenlied,* but still the book said see it so he did. Or started to but all the words he saw kept sounding meaningless. He'd pick a word at random—*grail,* for instance—and he'd say it ten or fifteen times out loud. It made no sense at all.

Anyway, his thoughts kept slipping, sliding off on things. Like all the names connected with his chalice. So many names. He made a list so he could keep them straight. Sir Winston Hunter-Donne, the British Government, the Queen and Scotland Yard, VanStraaten, Mannheim, Dr. Kalman, Cardinal Kellerman, the Pope in Rome. What did they want his chalice for? What did it mean to them?

He had the brandy out now and was feeling deeply philosophical. What was his chalice anyway? Once, long ago, an artist made it, shaped it to convey his thoughts and feelings, made it into something beautiful. What was it to Josephus, he whose name was on the base? A drinking vessel, an attractive container of liquids.

Really deep stuff, all of this. He stretched out on the floor to think more clearly. What did his chalice mean to Hunter-Donne? It was an object of archeological significance, historical evidence about King Arthur. To Scotland Yard it was a stolen article of great value, a mystery, a theft to be investigated. And for the British Government it would be a National Treasure, something all the people had a stake in.

The Vatican and Cardinal Kellerman were easy. What if the chalice really was the Holy Grail? If it was—it couldn't be, but if it was—that turned it into the holiest, most sacred relic in existence. VanStraaten, Melvil suspected, thought about the chalice in terms of publicity and attendance figures and how terrific it made him look compared to all the Museum Directors who didn't have the luck to buy it. And for Dr. Kalman it meant money, pure and simple, to the tune of three million and then some. And to Mannheim? Money, too; he did these things for his commission.

A knotty business, full of moral and aesthetic implications. And what about old Melvil, lying on the floor here. What was the chalice to him? He felt a sudden urge to see it, to be near it, touch it with his fingers. But he'd have to stand up, wouldn't he, and cross the room and down the hallway to the safe. So far.

He sank back, still thinking hard. What did it mean to him? Well, to begin with, it was his. He owned it in the sense that any man owns any thing: he keeps it for a while. When death came, or retirement . . . he sighed. But there was more to it than that. It went deep, very deep . . .

His sleep was terrible. No rest in it at all. He dreamt about his mom and dad and how he kept on failing them, year after year, no matter what he did.

And Dido had sharp teeth, like fangs, and she was looking at his thing and licking her lips and then some faceless man was chasing him with a phallic symbol bigger than a smokestack and he opened up the departmental safe to see his chalice and it wasn't there; just lots of notes from everybody saying why Her Majesty or whoever had to have it back.

He woke up feeling rotten. It was dark out, early evening, eight o'clock or so. He stretched. The floor was hard but better than the stairs; it was his way of sleeping around. Dido did a better way; he'd have to try it. Find a girl, a nice girl somewhere, ask her out, impress her with his wit and wisdom, fill her full of booze and bingo. Like Serena. None of that: think nice thoughts.

On his feet now, Melvil looked around the room. He'd have to spend the night; if he went out, he couldn't get back in and there was nowhere else where he could be. He thought of Hamlet. Could he live in his office and count himself a king of infinite space? He didn't have bad dreams, not really, not like Hamlet did.

He nodded: maybe he could make it here. Why not? What else did he need? He had a bathroom and a telephone and books and they could slip his food in through a slot in the door. He had a window, too, so he could watch the seasons change. The work he might get done, the things he could accomplish, all the books he'd write.

He took his notebooks from the shelf and put them on his desk. Not all of them but just his Plato notebook and his Aristotle and the one on Pericles himself and one on drama, one on architecture and a book on pots and vases, full of amphorae and kraters.

Once they were on his desk, they had to be arranged just so. It took a while to get them right, each in its proper place and opened to its proper page. He sat back then and looked. Impressive. Melvil nodded, Melvil smiled.

All these years of reading, thinking, organizing; the analysis, the graphs and charts, the insights and discoveries. When would he write his book? When would it start? Why not this minute, why not now? He knew enough, he was prepared, he had his thoughts in order, he had notes, notes up the asshole, notes that stretched for miles. He was ready, he could put the first word down, he knew how it began.

He pulled the typing table to his desk, took the cover off the Smith-Corona, threw it on the floor. He opened up his stationery drawer, pulled out a lovely sheet of clear white paper, stuck it in the machine. He was ready. No, not quite. The paper wasn't straight. That was important. There: he'd fixed it.

Hands above the keys, he paused, then stopped. No carbon. He wasn't going to fall in that trap, write a masterpiece and have no copy. Remember Carlyle. Leaving his only copy of the French Revolution in the carriage or wherever, losing it, starting again. It was enough to write a great book once: you couldn't ask a man to do it over.

He hunted for some carbon paper, found it, put it in, made sure it wasn't backwards, got the paper straight. Now. And with no hesitation whatever he centered the carriage at the top of the page and in capital letters wrote: PROPAEDEUTIC.

What a word. One of his favorites. He'd discovered it at sixteen reading Aristotle and he'd gone directly to the dictionary, just the way he always did, and looked it up. "The body of principles or rules introductory to any art, science or subject of special study." It was not an easy word to introduce in conversation. He had tried, on numerous occasions. The reaction generally was a look of irritation and an "Aw, for Chrissake, Melvil."

So he'd saved it. All these years. To put it there.

Page 1, top, center. PROPAEDEUTIC. He sat back, smiled, and looked at it awhile. Surely it was right. It meant exactly what it said. His readers would know. They'd be educated people, academics. What philosopher would hit you with an "Aw, for Chrissake, Melvil?" Never happen.

Even so. Still looking at it, frowning now. Was PROPAEDEUTIC absolutely right, was it the perfect word? Why was it preferable to INTRODUCTION or INTRODUCTORY REMARKS or BASIC PRINCIPLES or PREFACE? What was wrong with PREFACE? It was shorter, more familiar. Sure, but wasn't it pedestrian?

He got up, started walking back and forth. He'd been dead certain, all these years, just how to start and now the paper was in the machine, blank, waiting to be written on, to bear his thoughts. What thoughts? Did he have an original idea? He grabbed the paper, tore it out of the machine. Why had he done that? What a stupid thing to do.

Fool. Inspiration: that was what he needed. Get the chalice out for inspiration. Through the door and down the hallway, storeroom door, throw on the light. The Departmental safe. His fingers jiggled but he got it right the second time and there it was. He heard it speaking so he spoke back. "Here I am," he said.

He moved his notebooks, rearranged them, making room, there in the center. Just the place. He moved his desk light but it kept on throwing shadows on the figures, couldn't get it right. He brought a floor lamp over. Better. He could see it now. He sat back. Yes, the words would come, the page would fill with thoughts, the deepest things in life were in this piece, the reasons and the meanings. Something stirred inside him and he moved his hands out, struck a key.

From this point on, his memory of the night was spotty. A lot of paper went into the machine and out again; some of it blank and some with words. Like "Beauty is" and "Form" and "Oh, my God," and "Jesus, please." All crumpled into balls and thrown around. There was a lot of brandy, too, and lots of talk. Talk to the chalice, to the walls.

He was reasonably sure he hadn't cried. He wanted to. God knows. He had no home, no wife, his work was hopeless, empty, he was nothing: thoughts like that.

On impulse, he got pencil, paper, made a list of all the things he didn't have. "No friends, no sex, no book, no talent, no ability, no happy memories, no past, no future . . ."

For some nut reason, it began to cheer him up. "No fun, no girls, no appetite, no love, no hope . . ."

He was smiling when he fell asleep.

# X

He woke up feeling great. The eyes popped open, nice and clear. He knew exactly where he was, as if he slept there all the time. The floor was full of paper balls but what the hell: new day, new week, bright Monday morning.

He got up from the floor, stretched; nothing hurt. He looked out the window. Sunshine on the park, some interesting new garbage. He was humming, actually humming, as he washed up in the tiny bathroom. Razor: had he brought one: He opened the valise and there it was. He shaved and brushed the hair, put on fresh socks and underwear, new suit and tie, went to the mirror and checked himself. You had to overlook the eyes; or, more specifically, the purple blotches under them. A little sleep would fix that up and otherwise he looked terrific.

7:30. Lock the chalice up. Then jogging down the stairs, the Sardis column, right turn, down the hall. Nobody stirring, not this time of day. No trouble at the door, he fooled them: getting in was no-no but they had no regulations saying he couldn't get out.

More stairs, more jogging, down to Fifth and straight ahead to Madison. Some coffe shop or deli would be open. He was famished, ravenous; he'd order eggs and more eggs, bacon, ham, potatoes, muffins, Danish, toast and jam. What kind of jam? Strawberry. Definitely strawberry.

He found a place and darted in, sat down and saw the morning paper. On the counter. There it was. Big print. NEW CHALICE COMPLICATIONS. New? What now? The subhead gave the answer: "France Initiates Investigation." France, for Christ's sake? How was France involved? He started reading.

> Special to The New York Times. Paris—The Ministry of Culture, acting on reports that the "mystery chalice" recently acquired by the Metropolitan Museum was found in Corsica, has ordered an investigation of the matter.
>
> According to department spokesmen, should it be established that the chalice was indeed unearthed on French soil—Corsica being a Department of France—appropriate action would be taken through diplomatic channels for the return of the treasure.
>
> The chalice has, since its discovery in 1927, been part of the collection of Dr. Stefan Kalman, a resident of Calvi, Corsica and a citizen of France. According to high sources here, Dr. Kalman, as the legal owner of the chalice, has the right to dispose of it however he chooses so long as the chalice remains on French soil. No action is anticipated until or unless it can be definitely established that the chalice was spirited illegally across French borders.
>
> Attempts to reach Dr. Kalman at his residence in Calvi have proved unsuccessful. According to government records, Dr. Kalman's father, the archeologist Bela Kalman, established residence in Corsica in 1926. Copies of monographs reporting his research on the Corsican menhirs—large, upright monumental stones bearing mystico-religious carvings of enormous antiquity—are on file in the Bibliothèque Nationale.

There was more, a lot more, but Melvil didn't feel like reading it. He ought to eat, eat something, hadn't eaten since—when was it?—days ago. He couldn't. Anger: that's why he was shaking. Rage, it was an outrage. All the world was fighting for his chalice and no one was looking at it. It was made for looking, not for owning. Was he all alone in loving it? Did no one care? Outrageous and the guy behind the counter asked him what was wrong and Melvil would have told him if it hadn't been so complicated. Down his money went, he slammed it down and stormed off back to The Museum.

No one had gotten around to picking up his paper balls so he did it himself. There were an awful lot of them. He left a few, picked up his precious notebooks, fought an impulse down to heave them into Central Park with all the other garbage, jammed them on the shelves, threw out the brandy bottle—it was empty—and the phone rang.

It was Sitwell, for the love of God, and full of questions. What did he know about the Kalman Collection, would The Museum resist a French move to regain the chalice, what position did he take about the Grail and was there interest from the Vatican? He snapped some answers, anything, just get him off the phone. And then Photography called in and could they have the chalice for an hour or so. He sent Waterford up with it and Simon Prinz was on the line, downright abusive so he got abusive back and suddenly he'd had enough, no more, the phone could go to hell. He told it so, went steaming out, no notion where to go, just going. He was down the stairs when Kate called after him: VanStraaten on the phone and he was wanted.

"Can't it wait?"

"I'll ask." He waited. "No, he needs you right away."

What now? What new catastrophe? He leaned against the wall. The anger went away, all gone, and it had felt so good. He rubbed his forehead, then his eyes, went out his door, the Greek and Roman door, the door with nothing on it.

Miss Burton wasn't at her desk, and just as well. There was a stranger in VanStraaten's office: nice man, clear gray eyes, good handshake. Said his name was Sandborn.

"Mr. Sandborn's with the State Department." VanStraaten, sounding very earnest. Something very earnest must be going on; he wondered what it was.

VanStraaten told him. "He has come to ask for cooperation."

Melvil nodded briskly. "Yes, of course." He had a lot of respect for the State Department and they could have his cooperation anytime. A picture of Cordell Hull came into his mind; you had to respect a face like that and any man who worked for Mr. Hull—Sandborn seemed to be talking to him. It was only courteous to listen.

". . . close allies whom we cannot afford to offend. Should either London or Paris approach us officially, we shall want to extend to them our full and friendly cooperation." Melvil nodded; he had friendly feelings for London and Paris himself. But not for Sandborn. Sandborn wasn't friendly, not a friend. "If either government, or both, approach us, our response must be a fair one. We must know the facts and we have, therefore, submitted a request to the CIA to investigate the matter."

The CIA? Melvil didn't like the CIA. Why didn't he? What had it ever done to him? And was it an "it" or was it a "they"? He had the answer someplace, knew he knew but Sandborn kept on talking, sounding like a news release and Melvil wondered if he had a button, turn him off.

Eventually, he went away and Pieter stormed about. The fucking government, the chalice was the property of The Museum and if the fucking government came after it, he'd fight them for it. Melvil nodded. Pieter would, he'd do it, yes, and he could count on Melvil and could Melvil go now?

"One more thing. You ready for it?" Melvil shrugged. "I heard from Cardinal Kellerman this morning. Wants to see the chalice and would three tomorrow be convenient."

Melvil nodded. He would have to get it from Photography and bring it down. It might be nice to do that now.

"No, wait," VanStraaten said. "He's going to have some expert with him that they're flying in from Rome."

From Rome? The Vatican was coming for his chalice. Jesus Christ. "What are we going to do?"

"We let them look. There is no Holy Grail; there never was. They might as well lay claim to Noah's Ark."

Good point. They might as well. Except that Hunter-Donne believed there was a Holy Grail and Hunter-Donne was very great and Melvil West was very small. He stood there on the landing, just outside the door to Pieter's office. Stairs. Stairs going up, stairs going down. Which way to go? Down. Down is easier than up.

He wandered, looked at all the people. Mostly kids. Schoolkids looking bored to death, shuffling along in clumps, their teachers droning on about how great the art was. Weekdays, for the most part no one came to The Museum except these kids. Some lofty purpose his Museum was serving: boring kids to death.

He thought of seeing Aphrodite. Not today, he wasn't in the mood. He moved along, his eyes perversely looking at everything that wasn't Art. Things like the fire extinguishers and water fountains, switch plates, doorframes, electrical outlets. He wondered if the people who came to The Museum thought they were art objects. Why not? A switch plate by Cellini; not impossible. They looked at all the paintings with such dull eyes, seeing nothing. Maybe he could lead a tour, just herd a bunch of them together, show them the Leonardo elevator.

What good did The Museum do? Yes, what was it for? That was deep, a question worth considering but there was something that he had to do. He had to pee but there was something else. The chalice. That was it; he had to get the chalice from Photography. He turned and wandered toward the stairs.

The Photography Department occupied tremendous quarters on the top floor of the Museum. Nearly the entire floor except for the Poison Room. Melvil liked the idea that there was a Poison Room: it sounded dangerous. It was. All things of cloth—the tapestries and costumes and the ancient fabrics—all these things were treated there, preserved or fumigated or coated with something and a person could get killed inside.

He climbed and climbed, climbed all the stairs. He found the buzzer and he buzzed it. Someone came and let him in. Yes, they were finished with the chalice, he could have it, sign the forms and take it away.

He saw it where they'd been photographing it, against a backdrop of black velvet. He went to it, picked it up, held it carefully in both hands, thanked everybody for taking such good care of it, went out the door and started down the stairs.

The chalice felt warm in his hands, as if it had a life. He stopped, looked at it closely. Were the figures moving? It was hard to tell. The stairs were moving, though; no doubt of that. He sat down. Everyone was going to come and get his chalice. All the world was gasping for it. Queens and Popes and diplomats and secret agents. Everywhere you looked, someone was after it. They didn't love it, no, or find it beautiful. They wanted it, that's all.

He wiped his forehead. There were hands now everywhere his eyes went, hands all tugging at his chalice. It was terrible. They'd hurt it. Someone had to stop them but there wasn't anybody anywhere. Just Melvil.

It was then it came to him. He stood. The stairs were steady and the hands were gone. Except for his hands. Only his hands were on the chalice.

# XI

It was like walking through a beaded curtain into daylight. Everything was clear. No detail was too small. He knew exactly what to do.

He had some string in his office and he had some brown wrapping paper. He would wrap the chalice in the wrapping paper and tie it with the string. He made his way at a steady and reasonable pace down the stairs, then to the Greek and Roman Department, then up to his office. Kate was at her desk out front. He stopped. He showed her the chalice. She said it was lovely. He told her he was going to put it in the Departmental safe for the Cardinal to see tomorrow and she smiled and nodded.

He went into his office. He found the paper and the string. Exactly where he knew they'd be. He spread the paper flat out, smoothed it, put the chalice on the paper, wrapped it very, very carefully. He put the string around it and he tied it with a bow. The package looked very neat.

He then got his valise, closed it, put it next to the package on his desk. The next thing was to sign the forms. You couldn't take packages or valises out of the building without a form to give the guard authorizing you to take them out and Curators had the authority to sign the form and he was a Curator so he authorized himself.

He picked up the phone, dialed Kate, asked her to get him some supplies from Stationery so she wouldn't be at her desk when he went away. Then he picked up the package in one hand and the valise in the other and he went out of his office, down the corridor, through the outer office, down the stairs, through the long, long Mycenaean gallery and into the great entrance hall. Here and there, he saw a colleague scuttling crabwise across the floor: poor Snead of the American Wing, Gribble of Ancient Near Eastern. He nodded to them, cordially enough but just the least bit formal, moved on to the entranceway.

Bindle was there. He nodded graciously to Bindle. Bindle nodded in reply. He held the signed form out to Bindle. Bindle shrugged it off. He shrugged back, returned the form to his pocket and, movements firm and steady, went on down the stairs.

He saw an empty cab. He hailed it, waited till it stopped completely, got in, settled back and gave his home address. Would Dido be there? If she was there, would he see her? If he saw her, would he talk to her? If he talked, what would he say? Goodbye? I'm sorry? Have a good life. Thanks for everything? I hate you? Lots of luck?

The cab stopped. He paid the driver, tipped him fairly, got out, crossed the sidewalk, put his key in the lock and opened the door. *Droong!* Dido was home. *Braanng, bronnng!* Working hard, she was. That was a mercy. Meant he could see her or not see her: up to him. Taking the valise and package with him, he went firmly up the stairs and straight to the bedroom. He put his valise on the bed, opened it, took out what was soiled, jammed it as full as he could with underthings and shirts. The valise didn't want to close but he bent it to his will.

That done, he opened the top drawer of his bureau, removed his bankbook and his passport. Hadn't used the passport since that conference in Buenos Aires three, four years ago. He checked it: good till next year. That was more than long enough. He put the bankbook and the passport carefully in his inside jacket pocket, picked up his valise and his package, left the room and went downstairs.

He paused a long time at the front door. Should he see her one last time? It was the only thing he wasn't sure about. She made him angry and she'd made him dream of dying and a lot of other things and even so, he wouldn't hurt her for the world.

She was hammering away when he came in. She looked adorable, frowning in concentration, an enchanting clown in baggy overalls. He stood there watching till she noticed him.

"You're home."

He nodded.

"Going someplace?"

He nodded again.

"I guess my lawyer got you."

"No." He frowned. "What lawyer?"

"The lawyer handling my divorce."

"That lawyer."

"Yes, that lawyer."

"No, he didn't get me." Why was it so hard talking to this woman? Was he scared of her? What power did she have? Just look at her, poor little thing. So much hard work, so much ambition but the talent wasn't there. That's heartbreak. And so pretty. Why not tell her so?"

"You're pretty."

"Thanks a lot and call my lawyer, will you."

Melvil shook his head. "I've gotta go."

"Go where?"

"Away."

'Where's that?"

"It's just away. Goodbye." He turned to go. He meant to tell her more. What kind of farewell speech was that, for God's sake?

"Call my lawyer, dammit."

Melvil turned back. "Why, what for?"

"I want you out of here, out of my house."

"As you can see, I'm going."

"I mean permanently."

"So do I. I'm leaving you."

"This minute? Now? *You're* leaving *me*?"

He nodded. "I feel very sorry, Dido, sorry for both of us and all the time we've wasted. Have a good life."

"Just a goddam minute." She looked ashen and her eyes filled up with tears. "You can't leave *me*. You can't do that." The tears were down her cheeks now.

"I feel very sorry—" No, he'd said that. It was time to go.

"Come back. You bastard. You come back. We'll try again. It hasn't been so bad. Come back here."

She was standing by her hopeless sculptures, white with rage and choking on her tears. He couldn't understand the things she was saying now. He'd loved her once, but where and when? He started playing "Where and When?" inside his head and turned the volume high to cover up the sounds she was making.

Disturbing business, seeing Dido, telling her goodbye. He'd lost that terrific feeling of calm and clarity and it took a while to get it back. It seemed a while; actually, all he did was walk a block or two. It was his neighborhood, eleven years or more he'd lived on 82nd and did anybody know him? Any friends behind the counter, hands to shake, one person he could say good morning to? Was it his fault? Had he missed a chance or was it all New York and what it did to people?

Anyway, he didn't live there any more. He had important things to do and time was of the essence; or it would be soon. He crossed the street and into the Chemical Bank. He'd started banking there when it was called the Chemical Corn because he thought the name was hilarious. It was a sad thing, all the old names ironed out, all flattened: no more Sohio, Union Carbide, New York Central. Terrible.

"Yes, sir? Can I help you?"

Melvil looked across the counter. Pretty girl, nice face. Should he ask her for a date? Was that why he was there? Nonsense: his mind was cool and crystal clear and he had come for money. He got his bankbook out, handed it across the counter.

"What would you like, sir?"

Pretty face but no intelligence at all. "I'd like some money, please."

"How much?" Fair question. How much was there? How much would he need? Was it all his to take or was some portion of it Dido's? Knotty questions. Could he see the book? He held it in his hands, commanded the numbers to hold still. $9,846.35. Almost ten thousand. The savings of his lifetime. Not a lot to show. A decision was called for; it was time to be decisive.

"Five," he said.

"Five what?" The pretty girl seemed puzzled. Surely, he'd been clear. "Five hundred?"

Was that what he'd meant? The five was right. The pretty girl was wearing the prettiest pin, a little gold butterfly. Just over her breast. Left or right? The five was right. "Five thousand, please."

The girl nodded. "Yes, sir. How would you like it?"

"Fives and tens," he answered automatically. He always asked for fives and tens.

She smiled. "Have you got a suitcase?"

Yes he did, as a matter of fact, but it was jammed with clothes and he was being stupid. He must pay attention, concentrate. He told her hundreds, please, and waited while she went away and did some things and in a little while there she was, back at the counter, smiling. She held a thick bundle of fresh, clean bills. She counted them very carefully. She asked him to count them, too, but he trusted her and didn't want to hurt her feelings.

He put the fresh clean money in his jacket pocket,

too thick for his billfold, never fit, thanked the pretty girl politely, went out to the street, found a taxi right away and asked the driver for the airport.

Which airport? It was a day full of decisions. Where was he going, exactly? He had been quite clear about it earlier. He'd known. The moment he resolved to take the chalice, he had known it all. Abroad. That's right, he was going abroad. He nodded, asked for Kennedy and got it.

It was 4:13 precisely. He was standing at the Pan Am ticket counter. He had decided on Pan Am because Pan Am flew everyplace and it would make things easier in case he changed his mind.

"Yes, sir? Can I help you?"

Another pretty girl and everyone was being so nice today, so helpful.

"I think," he said. "I think I've got to go to London."

She smiled. "When do you think you'd like to go?"

He was ahead of her this time, he knew the answer. "Right away."

"We have a flight at seven-thirty." Not till then? Three hours and a quarter. God, that was a hundred and ninety-five minutes. How many seconds? Six times five—too hard. He shrugged and nodded and she made a ticket out in his name, Melvil West, and asked to see his passport, smiled at the picture of him in it, gave it back and asked him how he'd like to pay.

He almost made his first mistake. He nearly gave her money. He had his hand inside his pocket, on the bills, before he realized how precious the money was to him. It was all he had, he'd need it where he was going and if it ran out, what would he do? So he gave her his American Express Card and she gave him his ticket, checked his valise for him and asked him, please, to be at Gate 15 no later than 6:30.

Time to kill. He looked around the terminal. Busy;

full of people going places. Yes, and he was one of them. He hadn't flown since—was it Buenos Aires?—not since then. He'd been to Europe several times; he'd seen the Prado and the Louvre and the Reichmuseum and the Tate and the Wallace Collection and the Jacquemart-Andre and it was 4:53 and nothing to do. He looked at magazines, discovered he was hungry, bought a Milky Way, devoured it, had instant indigestion and wandered into the bar.

Just one martini. Had to keep the head clear, that was vital. He sat down on a stool, carefully placed his brown paper package in his lap and asked for Plymouth gin with a twist on the rocks. It had no effect, none whatsoever, so he had a second one and by that time it was exactly 6:09.

He paid, got up, moved out, looked for the signs and found them: there it was—GATES 15–30 and a big long arrow pointing that way. So he went: up ramps, along broad corridors, past lots of gates and lots of people, on and on. His gate was always at the end; he wondered why.

There was a crowd at Gate 15. Two hundred people, maybe more. Just standing, waiting, every kind of people you could think of: mothers, babies, kids and old folks, pretty girls and plain ones. Surely one of them would say yes if he asked her out. Which one, he wondered? What would she be like? Good-looking, naturally. What kind of good looks? Did he have a dream girl? No, not really. Tall? Yes, she'd be tall. Well-rounded? Certainly. Intelligent, high forehead, dark—no blondes, please, thank you very much. Large eyes, good posture—posture was important. Yes—like that girl over there.

He couldn't take his eyes away. It was the oddest thing. The girl was very beautiful: refined, extraordinary bones, if only he could paint, and she reminded him of someone. But it wasn't just her face that caught him, or her figure. She was standing twenty feet or so away, with people all around her, crowded in, and he felt absolutely certain she was all alone, deserted, living in some desolated place. Her face was clear, no feeling showed, no reason in the world to think of her like that except she looked like—who? Someone magnificent and doomed and then he had it. In some book he'd read about the last Czar. There were pictures of his daughters, yes, and one of them, a princess named Tatiana; that was it, he knew because he'd had these fantasies about her at the time. For weeks. This girl looked like a Russian princess and a tinny voice was welcoming them all to Flight 11, nonstop to London's Heathrow Airport, would all Tourist passengers please get in line.

The crowd moved, shifting, shoving, forming itself. He let himself be moved around, he didn't mind. The girl had disappeared; no matter: he was with Tatiana at a ball in Petersburg. The Winter Palace, that was where they were, and everyone was there. Magnificent women, incredible jewels, an orchestra was playing, dancers whirling past and he was making small talk with this princess. Who was he, how'd he get invited? He was somebody important, naturally; a famous artist. He had been commissioned, that was it, to do a portrait of the princess. Every day he saw her. He set up his easel in some grand salon and in she'd come and pose and people were starting to grumble because the line was hardly moving.

They had a point. What was taking so long? He stood on tiptoe. Up ahead, way way ahead, there were trestle tables with purses, parcels, cases on them. And a funny kind of metal archway like a doorframe. "What's all that?" he asked aloud.

"Inspection." The answer came from this big lady next to him in line.

"Inspection?"

"On account of all the hijackers."

"The hijackers?" That rang a bell. What was it?

"We have to put up with it, I guess. They open absolutely everything. Why, just last week . . ."

They'd open up his package, find the chalice, call the cops. Christ, he was caught before he'd started. How could he explain, what could he say to anybody and the shame of it.

He found a chair. He sat. He felt like he was in a photograph. He couldn't hear a sound, no sound at all, and everything was black and white and crystal-clear and frozen. Nothing moved. He saw the veins on people's hands, the details of their luggage, he'd remember it forever.

But the picture had to break, it couldn't last, they'd start to move, his turn would come. Oh Jesus, what to do. Think. But he couldn't. Nothing worked inside his head; his mind was just as frozen as the photograph. He clenched his fists and drove his nails into his palms.

It got things moving, back to life. He saw his life, the years ahead, ignominy and ridicule, all scorn and laughter and the line was getting shorter. He'd be all alone soon and they'd see him, come to him and say, "I'll help you if you'll let me." What was that? His heart stopped. That was real. Someone had said it. Someone just behind him. Woman's voice. It spoke again. "You'll never get it through."

His stomach heaved. He fought it down. He turned and looked. His Russian princess. No expression on her face. "Is there a bomb inside?" Her eyes were very large and dark. He shook his head. "What's in it?" He was done for. Caught.

"What's in the package?"

# XII

What in hell, she wondered, could he have in there? She watched him as he tilted down the corridor toward Gate 15, her attention caught even before he was completely in focus. Nothing more than thirty feet away was ever quite in focus but she looked ridiculous in glasses and the thought of contact lenses made her queasy.

The way he held that package, like it was the world's last lunch. Demented: tie askew, hair wild, glasses crooked on his nose. But nice demented. There was something sort of dear about him and she wondered for a moment if he'd do. He was not at all the kind of man she usually considered. He was leaning now against a pillar, package cradled in one arm, attempting to clean his glasses with the end of his necktie. She had an impulse to take a Kleenex out and do it for him but instead she turned away and looked for someone else.

She always picked up someone when she traveled. She didn't mind being alone in private; sometimes days and days would go by and she wouldn't surface from her little place, shades drawn, just Carrie curled up by herself and that was fine. But out in public—all the planes and restaurants and shops and doing things—when she was moving in her brisk way through the world, then it was terrible to be alone. She didn't find it paradoxical at all, not even when she thought about it.

Usually, she took the morning flight. 10 A.M.

BOAC. It got you to the Dorchester a little short of midnight and a drink or two, a pill or two and sleep would come, in one form or another. She enjoyed herself in London, or she thought she did, and she'd see Doug tomorrow, lunch at Burke's, and Simon in the evening which was nice, or was it, but she wasn't coping with the problem: namely, she'd be boarding soon and not a proper man in sight.

She was sensational at coping, had that kind of mind, devoured problems with a brain like a computer; which meant it was queer of her to keep on looking at that odd man with the package. He was tall, nice body, good lines on his face. He led a sheltered life; that's why he was so nervous, planes and airports, taking off. Age: 40. Occupation: something scholarly and square. He ran a bookshop. Secondhand? No, there was something too alive in him for that. Old books, fine bindings, first editions. Antiquarian: he liked things past. He'd know everything there was to know about the sixteenth century but you'd have to help him cross the street.

He was sitting, slightly pigeon-toed, precious package on his lap. Rare books, illuminated manuscript? A Book of Hours or a Bible sold to some English collector and he couldn't trust the mails so he delivered it by hand. His hands were really shaking. He was reaching for his jacket pocket, check his passport or his ticket. Funny, when we're nervous, how we know we have things with us but we look and look again and—

Carrie blinked and looked again. That stuff was money. Wads of money. He had money in his hand and he was blinking at it, too, and looking as surprised as she was. Weird. And then he dropped it in his lap, as if his hand were numb, and went on looking at it and a few bills fluttered to the floor. She ought to help him: pick the money up and put it in his pocket, help him on the plane. He wasn't going to make it on his own.

She even took a step before she stopped herself. Life was hard enough. You don't go picking up demented antiquarians who don't know they've got money in their pockets. She'd had quite enough experience with weird ones, though you couldn't ever tell how weird they were until they got you to the bedroom. Usually she fought her way out. She was good at fighting, really dirty when she had to be, and afterwards she'd try to analyze it: Signs and Symptoms of Male Weirdness. As a rule, the quieter they were, the kinkier; repression breeds strange bedfellows. But she had a thing for quiet men, she liked them and a lot of them were really nice. How did you tell the nice ones from the uglies? Take this one, for instance. He was picking up his money now and looking kind of frantic. Nice or ugly: which?

And what about his bookshop? Something odd about it; had to be. Behind the curtains, dimly lit, the smell of dust and ancient leather, tins of polish, something very strange was going on. A smuggling ring? Who'd smuggle ancient books? Insane. She couldn't take her eyes off him. Was he insane? Like Doctors Frankenstein or Jekyll, someone wise and serious and kind and bent? He didn't look bent but they never did and anyway, the voice was telling Tourist passengers to get in line. He'd have to manage by himself.

The crowd was pretty dense and people pressed against her. People always did. She gave off something, she supposed; a scent of some kind. Even dogs would sniff around. There was a time, back when the ice was melting or whenever, when we really had a sense of smell and one Neanderthal would know another by his scent and Carrie was convinced it still went on. An aura was made up of lots of things. You'd meet a person, man or woman, didn't matter, and you'd sense them. It was more than what your eyes saw; there was something literally in the air and someone just behind her had his hand on her bottom.

Carrie liked her bottom. It was absolutely first-class, one of the few things about herself that she approved of. And she liked to have it played with; patted, slapped or kissed or pinched. Nice feelings; warm and safe and cared for. And exciting, too. A hard one at the right time, sharp and stinging and she'd sail right off, she loved it. But not at 5 P.M. at Kennedy, stuck in a goddam line. Some creep or two-bit pervert, cop a feel; they'd think twice next time.

Carrie spun around, her right hand flat and rigid, ready for the abdomen that had to be there. He was big. To hell with that, she'd let him have it anyway and she was going to, she'd have done it, left him doubled up and gasping on the floor, but someone made a panic sound. She stood there, tight, eyes darting, looking for the man who made it.

Panic had a sound, a noise its very own. She'd heard it in the past, at times and places that she didn't like to think about. She raked the crowd behind her, looking for it. There it was. Ten feet or so away. Her antiquarian. His face was chalky and his eyes were blank. It looked like sudden sickness, like a heart attack, but Carrie knew it wasn't. Nothing physical. He had a case of terror.

She watched him as he teetered, half-turned, groping, moving on stiff legs, package clutched to his chest, hands white and rigid. They wouldn't move, not those hands, not if two men tugged at them. She'd seen it and she knew. He dropped down on a bench. His knees were trembling. It was awful and she had to help him.

She was thinking now; the old computer clicked the possibilities. First, could he see her? Panic really made you blind, it worked that way. Then, it was dangerous to startle panic; any jolt and it exploded into violence. She veered off, moving in a circle, coming up behind him. Could he have a bomb in there? She didn't think so. Not the type. But what type was he?

She was getting closer. Just behind him. Nothing moved. His hair curled in the nicest way above his collar and his neck looked like a boy's, so young and innocent. Her hand reached out; she stopped it. Would he hear her when she spoke? You couldn't tell. What would she say? Calm, something calm and quiet; nothing startling. Voice low, soft and friendly.

"I'll help you if you'll let me," Carrie said. No movement. Nothing. Had he heard? She'd have to try again. "You'll never get it through."

It registered. He shifted. He was going to turn. She braced herself. He might strike out, he might do anything. His hands, still white, still clutched the package. There was cold sweat on his face; the forelock of his hair was damp with it. She had to ask. "Is there a bomb inside?"

He shook his head and she believed him. He was innocent, a good man, someone pure in dreadful trouble. Could he see her? Carrie wasn't sure. She bent down, closer, very close. Brown was the color of his eyes and there was moisture in them. Was it tears?

Her lips moved. "What's in it?" She was whispering. "What's in the package?" was what she said.

# XIII

He felt her hand. It lightly touched his shoulder when she whispered, "Don't be frightened. You can tell me." It was like a shock, her touch was, and his mind began to race in absolutely all directions. Could he tell her? Should he try another plane? Or take a boat? Was she a cop? What color were her eyes? Where could he run and hide? What if he checked the chalice, simply left it at the airport? What would happen if he asked her for a date?

No answers to the questions but he felt a little better. He was thinking. He was at his best when he was thinking. Never mind how mad the thoughts were; he was back in operation.

"Hi," he said. And then, because he wasn't sounding very clear, "Hello."

"Hello," she said. She straightened up, eyes never leaving his. Her face was grave. He couldn't tell what she was thinking. Would she pull her whistle out and blow it? Would she turn away and leave his life forever? Would she touch his shoulder one more time?

"May I sit down?" she said.

"Of course." He stood up, like the gentleman he was, and watched her move around the bench. She moved all over when she moved, as if her body were a single thing. When Dido moved, her back looked stiff and nothing went from side to side below her waist. He waited till she sat, then picked a spot out on the bench, not close but not too far.

"Well," he said. Not much of a beginning, didn't move things very much. He cleared his throat and tried a smile. His face felt stiff. "Nice weather for this time of year." She nodded thoughtfully, as if what he'd just said were interesting. It wasn't, was it? Why was she just sitting there, not saying anything? He'd have to sound her out.

"You going far?"

"To London."

Idiot; that's where the plane was going. "Yes, of course. A fascinating city, London. Very civilized. I like it there." She nodded. Not much of an interrogation, not so far. What did she want? Why had she asked about the package? If she were a cop, then wouldn't he be nabbed by now? She would have put a heavy hand upon his shoulder, not a light one. Ask her something clever, take her by surprise, throw a curve.

"You go to London often?" Stupid question but she seemed to be debating it. She frowned—two tiny lines between those eyes—she took a deep breath, bit her lip, leaned toward him.

"Listen." It was coming now; he'd find out what her game was. "We don't have a lot of time." He looked. The line was short now; twenty, thirty people. Christ. "I have to know what's in the package." He shook his head. "You have to tell me what it is." He shook again. She reached out, put her hand on his. A strong hand; firm, yet tapered like a girl's. Imagine that: both strong and delicate at once.

"What is it?" God, how could he dream of trusting her? "Is it a book?"

"A book?" He shook his head.

"Tell me."

"I can't."

"Okay, you win, I give up."

She was rising. She was standing. She was going.

"It's a chalice."

"In the package? There's a chalice in the package?" She sat down again. He nodded. "Is it worth a lot?"

He felt an urge to tell her everything. "It's very valuable."

"Right; a valuable chalice. Is it yours?"

That was a hard one. In a way, he felt it was; and so he told her. "In a way."

"Be straight with me, okay?"

He nodded.

"Did you steal it?"

"Not exactly."

"Is it stolen, yes or no?"

"I signed it out."

"You signed it out? Just what in hell does that mean?"

"Well, it means I've kind of borrowed it."

"You've borrowed it."

He hadn't tried to find a word for what he'd done but, on reflection, borrowed seemed to fit. He nodded firmly and risked a smile.

"Look," she said, "I'll find out later who you stole it from and why. Just tell me what it looks like."

"It's extremely beautiful."

"Describe it."

"Not in words, I can't; it's indescribable." She looked like she was going to hit him. "Anyway, you've seen it's picture in the papers."

"In the papers?"

"Sure; the chalice from the Metropolitan."

"The Metropolitan Museum?" Her face was blank, her mouth just slightly open. Silence. Then she spoke. "No shit," she said. "You mean to say you've got that thing in there? The one and only what's his name?"

"Pasiteles."

"You borrowed it?"

She doubted him. "You want to see it?"

"Christ no; not out here." Her head was shaking, there was wonder in her voice. "You took it, wrapped it up with string and walked it out and you are sitting here this minute with three million in your lap?"

"Three six."

"Fantastic." She was smiling. What was funny? Was she laughing at him? All the girls from long ago, he always thought they laughed at him and even though he'd never caught them at it he could hear them all the same. But not this girl. She wouldn't.

The speakers spoke. Some tinny voice was saying something indecipherable. He concentrated. "Final call," that's what it sounded like and she was talking to him, had her hand outstretched, not smiling any more.

"Give it to me."

"What?"

"You've got to give it to me."

She was reaching for his chalice. She was going to take it. She had used him all along, that's all it was, she wanted something and he had it.

"No." He shrank back on the bench, away from her.

"I'll take it through for you."

Why would she? Why would someone do a thing like that for someone else?

Her lips moved. She was whispering again. "I trust you."

What a crazy thing to say. It was the other way around: he had the chalice, it was up to him to do the trusting. She was sitting there, not moving; firm and strong, like Aphrodite only finer. She had come down from her pedestal. To find him. She knew everything, she knew it all, she had his whole life in her hands. He liked her hands. He took his chalice and he put it in them.

"Right," she said and cleared her throat. Then nodded. "Right," she said again. Her eyes looked misty and she hadn't even had the manners to say thank you. Young people. Melvil didn't know any young people but he knew they were different: had no manners, slept with anyone. Well he was anyone, as much as anybody, wasn't he? But at a time like this, how could he think of that? He almost said I'm sorry, came within an ace of it but her eyes looked funny, going through him in some funny way, not seeing him at all. Then tears. No doubt about it, those were tears. Big tears, yes, soft and round and running down her cheeks. He'd made her cry. What had he done?

"Don't do that." But it did no good. "Look, please don't cry."

"It's okay," she said, her voice all choked. "Just get in line."

The tears rolled on. Her eyes were red now, slightly swollen. She looked dreadful. It was hard for her to speak. "Go get in line. Don't know me. Don't look back. I'll meet you on the plane."

He stood. Her shoulders sloped, grief-stricken. Was she crazy? Not impossible. And what was all this "Don't look back" stuff? She could disappear, just take off with his chalice, he'd be on the plane and she'd be hell and gone. His Russian princess. Would she do that to him?

He bent down. He didn't know what he was going to say until he said it. "Here's the thing," he said. "I trust you, too."

She didn't seem to hear him. It was time to move. He turned and started out across the floor. It took a long time. There was almost no one left in line: a nervous mother with a little girl, a fat man with an attaché case. The mother had a shopping bag, a plastic carryall, a purse, an overnight case and what was it Robert Benchley said? "Traveling with children is like traveling third-class in Bulgaria."

He had a point and Melvil watched, half-mesmerized, as object after object came out on the table: dolls and crayons, picture books, a box of Oreos, a bright red rubber ball, assorted bath toys and a ragged blanket and a little pillow, it was absolutely endless. And when everything was out at last, then everything went in again.

Not once did Melvil turn around. He wanted to, God knows. The little girl was whining, tugging at her toys; she'd seen them and she wanted them and Melvil could have strangled her because by now his princess could be in a taxi, halfway to Manhattan. But he trusted her and trust was trust, whatever the hell trust was. He wouldn't look. He should have heard her sobbing but he didn't. She should be in line behind him with his chalice and her plan. But was she, was she?

Suddenly, the woman and the little girl were gone. The fat man opened up his case, then closed it, then went through the metal archway. It was Melvil's turn. He took it.

Nothing beeped, no lights flashed; he was clean. The security guard said thank you. Melvil told him he was welcome, moved the few steps to the gangway entrance where a hostess stood. She smiled at him and held her hand out. Did she want a tip? He didn't think so.

That was it: his boarding pass. He started fishing for it. In a moment, he'd be down the gangway, on the plane. Would she come after him? Would she get through? Or would she even try? He had to know. He turned.

She stood there by the long examination table. She looked bereft and brave, both things at once, as if she had lost everything in life except her courage. Slowly, it was playing in slow motion, Melvil saw the guard hold out his hands to take the package. For a moment, no response; then, firm and slow, she shook her head. She wasn't going to give it to him.

Melvil saw the guard frown. He was frowning, he was talking; then his hand went out again. Through it all, she stood there, huddled up, the package held against her breasts as if it were a baby and her head shook dumbly, side to side. Another guard came over, there were two guards now and Melvil couldn't stand it any more, he had to hear. He sidled closer.

"It's a federal regulation, miss," the guard was saying, "and you can't get on this plane except I see that package."

"No." Her voice was clear.

"For all I know, you've got a bomb in there."

"I don't." Her head still shook, her hands were white, like claws around his chalice.

"Look, you want to take this plane, I gotta see what's in there. You can stay here if you want to, miss the plane, that's fine with me—"

"I can't." A new sound in her voice. Hysteria? "I can't stay here."

"Okay, let's have it." Out again the hand came and she cringed as if the man had struck her. Then he shrugged and took his hand back. "Have it your way, I give up." "We're all done, Debbie." He was talking to the stewardess. "That's all; this one's not coming."

"Yes I am." She moved up to the table and she stood there looking tall and proud. Fresh tears were falling from her eyes; she didn't seem to know it. She looked different. No more grief. What was it on her face now? Melvil looked and had an absolute conviction this was real, the rage he saw and scorn, that it had happened to her, something terrible that she had lived through.

She was talking and her voice was flat and calm. Everything was in her hands; they seemed no part of her. Her hands were working on the package, tugging knots and tearing paper, ripping it apart. "You want to see my mother's ashes? Would you care to run your fingers through them? Shall I pour them on the table? Tell me."

"Take it easy." From the guard.

"I am a follower of regulations and a great believer in the law. I'm sorry if it makes a mess. I'll clean up after, if you like." She had the package halfway open.

"It's all right, miss. You don't have to."

"Yes I do. Here, look." She thrust the package toward him. "Can you see? I'm having trouble with the string. I'll get it."

"Come on, it's okay." The guard was moving now, around the table. "Sorry, miss, we didn't know, come on, you'll miss the plane." He touched her, took her arm. She made a little sound and stood there rigid. Couldn't move.

But Melvil could. "I'm with her, I'll take care of her," he said. He put his arm around her. She felt cold. He tugged. She didn't budge. "It's me," he said. "Come on, it's over, everything's all right." He tried again. She leaned against him, feeling heavy.

Melvil smiled at the stewardess. "She's fine," he said and moved on, holding her. He felt important. They were moving down the gangway, he could see the door ahead.

"I told you I was good at stories." Voice from far away.

He looked at her and nodded and she made a kind of grin.

"I'm fine," she said. "Let go." He did. She stood there. "See? I'm really fine." She handed him his chalice. "I'm a big girl and I'm very strong. Come on; let's have a drink or two."

Or three or four or more; he'd sung that sometime, someplace, long ago but she was striding, strong steps, through the doorway and he didn't want to lose her.

He felt tall, like marching, and he let his feet strike loud and hard against the floor. He'd made it, he was off and running and his heart soared, truly that was what it felt like, high and wide inside him. He was Galahad, or was it Lancelot; he had his chalice and his princess. Melvil West: would you believe it? He was airborne long before he left the ground.

# XIV

What was she going to do with him? Her shoulder ached. His head felt hard and heavy and she longed to wriggle out from under but she didn't. He was going to need his sleep. The plane was dark and quiet and her glass was empty for the fifth or sixth time. Numbers, she was good at numbers. Four o'clock: four in the morning, London time. They'd land at seven and what was she going to do?

She closed her eyes and let some numbers float. Eleven: that was Gardener's house in Boston; shutters white, bricks red and black for Carrie's room, the place where she had been a little girl. And 27: that was Carrie's age. And 28: that was the year that Carrie died. She'd known that ever since she'd been the number 13. It had come to her one day, no reason why, and she had always felt quite good about it. She was safe till then.

She looked at Melvil. Glasses all askew. She gently took them off and slipped them in a pocket. He had nice ears and the best eyelashes, long and thick. He would be good in bed, she knew it, and it would be good to be there with him. Bed was good.

Melvil was a funny name, she'd never met one, all the men she knew and not one Melvil and she'd asked him if it had a double *l* and *e*. It didn't, he was named for Melvil Dewey. Not the admiral or philosopher: the Dewey decimal one. His father had been a librarian. She never thought of librarians as going home or having families. They lived behind their desks, that's all, and scolded you when books were overdue. She liked books; or she used to, back when she was young and being smart had been the best defense.

The ache was in her arm now and her hand was getting numb. She shifted, needles tingling, and he groaned; exhausted, more unconscious than asleep, arms wound around the chalice, holding to the package like a man overboard.

He had shown the chalice to her shortly after takeoff. They were sitting more or less alone, back in the tail, nobody in the seats around them and the stewardess had brought their Scotch and soda, gone away when, wordlessly, he turned and put the chalice in her lap.

She looked at him. He smiled quickly, like a boy who'd pocketed the only Yo-Yo from the only five-and-dime, and then he nodded; quickly, too. She started fiddling with the string. The knots were tight, the package was a mess, her fingers felt like sausages.

At last, by accident, the string gave way and she began unwrapping it. She tried to do it quietly lest someone hear and turn and see it but the bloody wrapping crashed and thundered like a Liszt concerto. And, of course, he'd wrapped it stupidly, enough brown paper for a side of beef.

It was sudden when she saw it, like a magic trick. The endless paper sort of fell away and there it was. A strange piece, all its own, mysterious; and yet she felt she knew it. Like a perfect melody you've never heard before, each note both fresh and necessary, falling where you know it has to fall. She almost dropped it.

He was talking and his eyes looked glittery and full. "It's really something, isn't it?" She nodded. "Look," he said and turned it slightly in her hands. New shapes. "And here." Another turn. "You see?" Of course she saw. She wasn't stupid. It was beautiful and why, for God's sake, was she so upset?

Because he'd stolen it; that must be why. Because he shouldn't have and she had helped him get away with it without a thought. On impulse. He'd looked lost and dear and she'd been feeling—what in hell had she been feeling? It didn't matter, and besides she knew a lot of thieves, the rich kind mostly: film producers, oilmen, promoters. Rats, of course; but charming for the most part, interesting company and all they stole was money. This was different. It was wrong of him to steal this thing. What reason could he have that made it right? She hoped there was one.

"Why'd you steal it, Melvil?"

"But I didn't steal it."

"Right." She started wrapping it. "You signed it out."

He nodded. "That's exactly what I did. You see, I saw these hands."

She kept it calm. "What hands?"

He told her all about it. All about how he'd been sitting on the stairs and all these hands had come to take his chalice: Cardinal Kellerman, Sir Winston Hunter-Donne, the Queen, the Pope, the Government of France, the CIA, the State Department.

What he said was garbled. What he'd felt, the things that drove him, these were curiously clear. He loved this chalice, knew it was in danger and he had to save it. Sentimental thinking, if it qualified as thought at all.

"You think we've got the Grail here, Melvil?"

"I don't know. I doubt it but it's not impossible."

"I used to wish there were a Holy Grail." And Arthur, the once and future king, she'd wished him, too. Knights on white horses and one day when she was five or six, small numbers, she was out on Boston Common, lots of snow, and she was there with Nanny and she heard the hoofbeats close behind and she had braced herself to be scooped up and taken far away from Gardener's house but it was just a drunk who wanted money.

Carrie blinked. She had a lot of questions. She'd been clicking as she listened to his story, putting thoughts in order. There was much she had to ask but was he capable of answering?

"Look, Melvil, when you get to London, what's your first move?"

"Rent a car."

The answer came back fast, as if he knew what he was doing. She would have to wait, no point in pressing him for answers. Maybe in the morning.

Dinner came and went. They couldn't touch it, either of them. But the drinks kept coming. She had thought the drinking wouldn't hurt. He needed to let go: a little sweet oblivion.

It loosened him, he went on talking, all about the good things and the bad. His office and the way he watched the garbage out the window and his Aphrodite and the tunnel and his notebooks and the night he'd written "Propaedeutic" and the Stanhope bar and Pieter's penthouse and how much he liked him and Alicia, how beautiful she was and Waldo Sitwell and Serena Burton. Jesus, what a life.

And Dido. Bitch: and he kept saying decent things about her; Dido's mind and Dido's looks and Dido's talent. Auto parts, for Christ's sake, and the wheat germ in the fridge and he was getting slurry, going down and down. The drinks were a mistake, she should have seen this coming and she wished she had an up to give him—or a down; it didn't really matter which—but she was off ups and downs, no more of that.

He kept on talking, on and on, refusing to let go. Then suddenly—he had been laughing, something this Pieter had said that wasn't all that funny—suddenly his face was in his hands.

"I'm crying. Oh my God," he said and turned his face away from her.

She took his hand and patted it. He was no good at crying, didn't have the hang of it at all. Tight little sounds. She never cried. She held his hand against her cheek. Smooth skin he had.

"Melvil?"

"Sorry."

"Where'd you grow up?"

"Me? Milwaukee. It's a big town." He was breathing easier. "I hated it." He took a deep breath, leaned back, closed his eyes.

She had let him go to sleep.

Her arm was stiff, her head ached and her mouth felt like the green you see in fish tanks. She looked out the window. Orange and red. They would be over Ireland soon. He stirred and sighed: some dream or other. She would have to wake him soon. There were a lot of questions, things she had to know. Her fingers drummed, the way they always did when she was flipping through solutions. Flipping was the way it felt, as if her thoughts were down on punch cards.

It was time. She shook him gently. Nothing happened. "Melvil?" No response. She didn't want to wake the plane up; they had quiet things to say. She shook him harder and he sat bolt upright.

"Dido?"

"Shh."

He looked at her as if he didn't know her.

"Am I late?" he said. "What time is it?"

"You're on your way to London and it's six o'clock." She watched his face as everything came back to him. It was like watching a bereavement. Then he smiled.

"Oh, hi. It's you."

They both got up and went to wash. She looked as if she'd slept in last week's make-up, which was odd because she used no make-up if you didn't count some color around the eyes. She rather liked the lines to show. She scrubbed until it hurt. It didn't do much good.

She found him in the aisle, leaning, looking worse. He'd washed, she saw the soap that proved it, and he put some water on his hair and combed it. More or less.

She put him in his seat and hunted down a stewardess. The drinks were under lock and key but there was coffee. Hot, no flavor, but the burning felt good.

"Look," she said, "I've got some questions."

"Questions?"

He was blinking and his voice was rough. She'd have to take him through it slowly. "Do they know you've gone to England?"

"Does who know?"

"Does anybody, anyone at all?"

He frowned and shook his head. "No, I don't think so."

"Are you sure?"

"What difference does it make?"

"Go through the day. Who did you talk to?"

"Kate McCann and Dido and the teller at the bank, the taxi driver . . ." He was thinking hard. "That's all."

"And they don't know, you didn't say where you were going?"

"Not a word."

"Not bad. They'll find you on the Pan Am roster when they get around to it but that'll take a while. They'll interview your wife first and your friends and Pieter What's-his-name. That all takes time. There's just a chance they won't be waiting for you at the airport. Now—"

"Who won't be waiting?"

"Scotland Yard or Interpol, I don't know who."

"But no one knows I took the chalice."

"Are you kidding?" Was he smarter than he looked?

"Nobody knows it's gone."

She shook her head in disbelief. "You mean to say you walked out with the Holy Grail for all we know, for Jesus's sake, and no one knows it's missing?"

"They don't know it yet."

"Fantastic. Where do they think it is?"

"They think it's in my safe."

"That's some security you boys have got."

He nodded. "Someone ought to talk to them about it."

Time. It meant he had a little time to work in, room to move. How much time? Melvil told her: three o'clock. That's when the Cardinal was coming with his expert from the Vatican and Kate would cover for him—Dr. West was sick or something—Pieter would be there and he'd have someone open up the safe and that was when the shit would hit the fan.

Three. That was eight at night in London. He'd be safe all day today and with the panic and confusion and the interviews, he might, he just might make it through the night as well before all England started looking for him.

The stewardess came by with buns and coffee, everyone was up now. She was hungry and she wolfed her roll, inhaled it, grabbed a handful from the wagon, grinning at the dirty look she got. She had a running war with stewardesses; there was always something in the air between them instantly, like certain cats with certain dogs.

Her mouth was full and she was feeling marginally better when he put the question to her.

"Carrie, I've got no one else to ask and I've been thinking, look, if you were in my place, what would you do?"

What was she going to do with him? She heard the answer. Nothing. Loud and clear. Not anything at all. Hands off. It was his life, his future, his decision and she wasn't going near it.

"See, the thing is, I could get the chalice back in time. Just turn around and take the next flight, I could make it back by three o'clock."

She nodded. "Yes. You could." Detached and noncommittal.

"What do you think my chances are?"

"Of what?"

"Of finding out the truth. You see, if I could get to Hunter-Donne and if the chalice isn't his, if I could get to Corsica and talk to Stefan Kalman—"

"Have an if or two, why don't you?" Corsica, for God's sake? He'd be lucky if he got to Belgrave Square.

"I know." He nodded. "Yeah, and I should talk to Adolf Mannheim, too, I guess." His shoulders slumped a little. "Do you think I have a chance?"

"I'm not the oracle at Delphi."

"All I'm asking is—" He bit his lip. "You think it's crazy?"

"Melvil West, I wouldn't tell you if I knew."

"I ought to go back home, that's what you think."

"I don't think anything." Her eyes felt hot.

"That's all you've got to say?"

She nodded sharply once and turned away. She felt a little sick; the buns, that's all that was. A sinking feeling, too, but that was just because the plane was starting down. The seat-belt sign went on. She'd taxi to the Dorchester and God how good the bath would feel and she'd put on a new dress, maybe the Cardin or else the little Valentino with the vest. She looked sensational in slightly dyky clothes and that was how she'd feel: sensational.

She heard the paper rustling and she turned. He sat there frowning, struggling with his package, looking lost. The paper was in shreds, the string all knotted. Customs wouldn't look at Heathrow, never did; but even so, why take the risk. She'd brought him this far, what the hell. She grabbed her Vuitton shoulder bag, tugged at the zipper angrily. Of course it stuck. She hated Vuitton but she used it when she traveled; people recognized it and a girl alone got better treatment. One more tug. She had it open. Full of junk. She shoved and pushed, made room, then held her hand out.

"Give it here," she said. He paused a moment, then he gave it to her.

Down they went. A perfect landing, hardly any line at Immigration and the baggage came so fast. One ratty-looking case for him, three Gucci bags for her. Then straight through Customs, no one interested in anything, and there they were, uneasy in the airport lobby. What to say? She opened up her purse and handed him the package.

"Here," she said.

He took it. "Thanks."

She had a thing for exit lines; collected them. "Put out the light and then put out the light." "The rest is silence." No, all wrong, not exits, those were death scenes and she couldn't think but there was something, surely there was something that she had to tell him.

"Melvil with one *l*," she said.

"That's me." She wasn't certain: was he smiling?

"Take good care."

He nodded, bent down—was he going to kiss her?—straightened sharply, turned and went away.

She watched him go. She didn't feel a thing, no feelings whatsoever. Nothing stirred. He'd go up to the Pan Am counter, take the next plane home. She knew it, that's what he'd decided. Had to be. He'd make it back in time and make it up with Dido, make some kind of life.

She nodded to her porter, started for the taxi rank. Across the floor she went. She had a rule she never broke: Don't look back. Never look. Last looks don't pay, you see things you weren't meant to.

So she turned. She didn't see him. He was big and tall, he couldn't disappear but there was no one like that at the Pan Am counter, no one like that at BOAC. Then she saw him. He was in a line. Hertz Rent-A-Car. Four ugly sounding words: but there was singing in her ears; or was it ringing. Something rose inside her, round and warm. She ran. She must have done so, though she had no memory of it. All she could remember was his face and she was laughing, tugging at his arm.

# XV

The scenery blurred, the motor whined, the needle kept on pointing at 120 something. They were whistling west toward Bristol on the M-4 and he felt sensational. He'd burned his bridges, turned the corner, done it. He was off.

And she was with him. Wasn't life fantastic? Actually there. Behind the wheel, relaxed and sure, her left hand on the gear stick, shifting constantly. She'd asked if she could drive, she loved it, used to race in competition, nothing much, no prizes but she'd done it. Was there anything she couldn't do? He had a lot of questions. Like, for instance, first and foremost, what had made her come along?

The odd thing was, it seemed completely natural at the time. He'd gotten into line at Hertz and that seemed natural, too. No sense of a decision, nothing. Were the big decisions always like that? Choosing his career or Dido or the post at The Museum—they happened, that was all. And Carrie happened. Happened to be tugging at his arm and he had smiled and put the arm around her.

Just like that. But there was more to it, there had to be. He wondered if she liked him. Sure she did; a little. How much was a little? Stimulating question and her legs flashed as she shifted gears again. Long, white and more than lovely: legs that did things. Running, spinning, leaping, spreading and he winced and looked away.

They had been on the road an hour with another

two to go. The paper rustled on his lap. The London *Times* and Hunter-Donne was on the front page. He was news in England and the article had said he was—where was it? Melvil held the paper close and squinted. There: "Sir Winston, currently encamped at the site of his excavations at Cadbury Castle, South Cadbury, Somerset where the stolen chalice was discovered in mid-January. . . ."

A castle. Melvil put the paper down. Too much: they were going to a castle.

"Carrie?" Lots of questions. Which to ask? The wind was whistling so he said it louder. "Carrie? What's your last name?"

"Gardener."

Lovely name. He rolled it over in his mind, like a possession. Carrie Gardener.

"Carrie?"

"I'm from Boston and I'm twenty-seven and—" She shifted, slowed; an exit, Exit 17, and they were taking it. "And if you're wondering why I came along—" She pulled up at the crossroad, looked at him, then gunned the motor, spun the wheels, a lot of noise. "I'm wondering, too," she said.

Country road now; narrow, winding, low stone walls and hedges hemming in the sides. No room for cars to pass and she was driving down the middle—madness—and he held on, knuckles white. What was he doing here? He turned and faced the window so she wouldn't know his eyes were closed. The gears howled and the tires squealed like pigs in mortal combat. Endless, it would never end, not—she was throwing on the brakes. His eyes flew open.

"Jesus Christ, what is it?"

She looked wonderful, eyes bright, exhilarated. "Lunch," she said.

He turned and saw a country inn. He felt like hitting her.

The place was charming and the food, dear God,

he hadn't eaten, literally, since the week before. He had to watch it, not too much, but she was chewing up enough for both of them. In fact, he'd never seen such eating. Salmon and a slab of ham pie, half a chicken and assorted sandwiches and Cornish pasties. With dessert to come.

"You always eat like this?" he asked.

She nodded, grinned. Incredible. He started asking questions and the answers came between the bites, offhandedly, as if they didn't matter. Hadn't liked it much in Boston. Got out early. Went to school in lots of places. Traveled some. He asked her what she did.

"I write." Her mouth was full.

"What kind of writing?"

"Junk." She swallowed, took another bite.

"What kind of junk?"

She shrugged. "For magazines."

He pressed her but she didn't want to talk about it. It was garbage: fashion, interviews. He tried her family. She had two sisters: older. Father was a teacher, wrote some kind of books. He tried again.

"What kind of books?"

She mumbled it. "Philosophy."

He liked that. "Would I know his work?"

She said it in the oddest way: "He's Gardener."

Melvil stared at her. *The* Gardener? Johnathan Gardener of *Philosophy and Form* and *New Aesthetics for Old*? And more. He'd read them all. First-class. And famous—not like Hunter-Donne but famous in his field. She wouldn't talk about him. Never mind, he had more questions, burning ones. He finished off his beer and asked them. Was she married? No. Engaged? Not now. In love?—good God, he'd actually said it.

"No," she said, "not ever." Looking at him very straight and level for a second, then returning to her plate of Stilton. Blue and white.

He closed his eyes. One question left. He couldn't ask it.

"Carrie?"

"Hmm?"

He couldn't get it out. Why not? It wasn't anything so terrible. He wanted her. So little time. One day before the story broke and she'd be gone. She had to leave him, had to go. To save herself. This afternoon, for God's sake, just two hours from now, she'd drop him in South Cadbury and turn around, take off for London. She'd be crazy if she didn't. Over; done before it started.

"Carrie?" His voice: he was talking. "Look, I wondered, if you had the time, if maybe you were free for dinner, we could eat or something."

"Sure." The answer came right back as if he'd asked her for the salt.

The car whipped around curves. He didn't mind. The road was rising as it twisted now and they were roaring up into the Mendip Hills. The chalice, jammed into her purse, lay on the seat between them. They were making plans.

"Look, once we get to Hunter-Donne, how much time do you need?"

He hadn't thought. "I don't know; it depends."

"You think he's lying when he says he found the chalice?"

"I don't know."

"What do you know?"

A reasonable question, fair enough. Why did it irritate him? "Something's wrong, that's all I know, if I knew what it was—" He took a deep breath. "If you're Hunter-Donne and make a find like this, you shout it from the housetops, you don't keep the thing a secret. And there's something wrong with Kalman's story. Pieter thought so, too."

"If something's wrong with both, then everybody's lying."

"No." She hadn't understood at all. She had no grasp of scholarship. This kind of thing was commonplace, it happened all the time. Suppose old Berenson, let's say, identified a canvas as a Tintoretto and some other scholar just as famous said it wasn't. No one lied. Someone was honestly mistaken, misinformed, misguided and to find the truth, you went to them and talked and listened, hearing all they had to say. That's what a scholar did and that was all that he was doing.

He was going to explain it to her but they came around a curve and she said "Look at that" and there, below them, stretching on for miles, was a vast green plain. She pulled up, stopped, and they sat looking at the Isles of Avalon. King Arthur's country.

Melvil knew a bit about it, not a lot. King Arthur was fifth century; Melvil's period was earlier. Still, he did know that when William of Malmesbury wrote that Joseph of Arimathea had been given an isle in Avalon to build his church on, it had literally been an island. Which was why the land below was flat as a seabed. Here and there, islands no more, great hills rose up. On one of them—he couldn't see it yet—Cadbury Castle.

"Come on," he said, "let's go." She didn't answer. "Carrie?"

She was looking straight ahead and nothing moved except her lips. At first, he couldn't hear what she was saying. Then he could.

" '. . . the Grail's secret must be concealed
And never by any man revealed,
For as soon as this tale is told,
It could happen to one so bold,
If the teller should have a wife,
Evil will follow him all his life . . .' "

Her voice trailed off. Odd poem, medieval-sounding but he didn't recognize it. "Carrie?" Her face was blank, eyes motionless, out of contact for a second. Then, as if some hand had flipped a light switch, on she came.

"You looked enough?" She put the car in gear.

"What was the poem?"

"Oh, that." She shrugged. "That's 'Gawain and the Green Knight' in a terrible translation. Did a paper on it once." She gunned the motor and they roared off, winding down onto the plain.

Fantastic girl, a medievalist on top of everything. Most medievalists, the ones he knew, looked like old Graz of Arms and Armor. Did she know other medieval verse, was she a lover of it?

"No." And then, a sudden grin. "I know 'The Highwayman.'"

He knew it, too, and they recited it, some stumbling and some lines left out but no one minded and the highwayman came riding, riding as the tiny towns blurred by. West Camel—lovely name—a half a dozen houses and a store. Queen Camel next. Then Sutton Montis. Pleasant countryside but nothing special, winding road, some hills—South Cadbury.

They almost missed it. Easy thing to do. It had a pub, a store and, at a little distance from the road, a church. But they were looking for a castle and there wasn't one. The only thing of interest was a hill. It was an odd hill, rising in receding layers like a wedding cake.

She pulled up, stopped. "You think we've got the right South Cadbury?"

Could there be two? Impossible. "I just don't get it—where's the castle?"

"Let go ask."

They got out and started for the pub. The Red Lion, according to a faded sign, it was a little place; unpainted, worn. The doorknob was all rusted but it turned. Inside, and to the right, there was a tiny store. It looked like Appalachia: some flour sacks, a basket full of sad potatoes. Everything was quiet.

Down the narrow hall, ahead of them, there was a door.

The letters on the door said LOUNGE, except the G was gone. The room was dim. There was the smell of dust and beer. Along the far wall was a bar. Behind it was a lady, thin and middle-aged.

"Hello, luv." She had the saddest smile.

"Hi, hello," he said.

"Would you want a drink or are you looking for the castle?"

Melvil smiled back. "We missed it somehow. Is it near here?"

"Aye, and here's another for you, Chief Inspector."

Chief Inspector? Where? He spun around. The room was empty, wasn't it? A man was rising from a table in the corner, moving toward them.

"Drum," the man said. "Chief Inspector Drum." The man was tiny, five feet one or two and put together like a jockey; thin and quick, all bone and sinew. Narrow nose, bright eyes and ageless, anything from forty-five to sixty.

"Hi," said Melvil. "I'm—" He froze: what name, who was he; and those eyes were on him, knowing all. "I'm from America."

Drum nodded. "Take the way across the road, go past the Rectory and onto Castle Lane. You'd better hurry or the conference will be over. If it is, my men will stop you at the gate."

It was a dirt road, two deep ruts, a lot of rocks and they were bouncing past the schoolhouse, then the Rectory, the graveyard, bearing right on Castle Lane, around a bend. Cars. Carrie braked. The road was blocked with cars. A dozen; more. Reporters. Must be.

Hurry. He got out and looked around. From close, the hill seemed mammoth, artificial, as if giant hands had molded it. Those setbacks, strange concentric rings, each smaller than the one beneath.

"Come on," he said.

She nodded, didn't move, then took his hand. They hurried down the lane, past all the cars, around a turning. On their right, across a little field, they saw what had to be Sir Winston's campsite. He'd expected—it was hard to say but something grand, important-looking, proper quarters for so old and great a man. The only thing impressive was the fence: brand-new, bright shiny mesh, barbed wire at the top. Behind the fence was nothing much. Some tents, a shack that had to be an outhouse and a row of what the English used for Quonset huts.

They paused and it was then he heard the voices. Muttering, a lot of people. Around one final bend they went. The conference was breaking up; they'd missed it. Twenty, thirty men, reporters, milling, smoking, moving toward them. And behind them, standing straight and smart along the fence, were constables in uniform.

He stopped, uncertain. What to do?

"Come on," she said, walked straight up to the nearest group of men, held out her hand. "Hi. Condé Nast," she told them, asked them what the story was. The story wasn't much. Sir Winston didn't like these conferences, he'd kept things brief and all he said was he'd been on to the Prime Minister that morning, satisfactory talk and it was time for tea now, thank you very much. Aside from that, the most interesting news of the day was the arrival on the scene of CIA. In fact, if Condé Nast could do it without starring rudely, she could see him over there.

His stomach lurched. They couldn't know, be after him already. He pivoted and saw a man; aside, apart from all the others, normal-looking. Dressed in gray: gray suit, gray tie, gray hat, gray eyes—a gray man.

Carrie thanked the newsmen and he tried to nod and smile. Perhaps he did. Nerves; that was all he had. Of course they couldn't know. The State Department man had told him days ago the CIA was coming in. He must be calm, act normal, keep his head.

He rushed up to the gate. A constable was blocking it.

"I'm sorry, sir."

"I've got to see Sir Winston."

"Sorry, but the conference is over."

"I'm not a reporter."

"No?"

That wasn't very smart. Who was he?

"Are you an acquaintance then, sir?"

"No—I've come on business." That was better.

"May we know what kind of business?"

"It's about the chalice."

"If you'd write the matter down, sir, we'll convey it to Sir Winston."

"That's no good. I've got to talk to him."

"I'm sorry, sir. We have our orders."

"Listen." To what? What could he tell the man? He'd come so far. He'd risked so much. And suddenly, he had it. "Listen." It was brilliant. "Would you show him something for me?"

"No." That came from Carrie.

"Give it to me." He was reaching for her bag. The constable would take the chalice, show it to Sir Winston, they'd be with the great man in a minute.

"Hands off." Carrie snapped it out. The constable was looking and she wouldn't let the bag go.

"That's enough, now." The constable was talking. He was fingering his night stick and his face was set. "I think we'd better know the nature of your business here."

Christ, think of something. Were they going to be arrested? What, oh come on, was his story? Who, in God's name, was he? He didn't stop to think.

"Tell Hunter-Donne I'm from the Metropolitan Museum."

# XVI

*Disaster* was her first thought, followed instantly by *Wait a minute, sure,* and by the time the Constable said "Just a moment, please" and started off, she saw the brilliance of it, squeezed his hand and told him so.

He looked a little dazed. "It just came out, I didn't know what else to say."

They had a story to construct and clearly she was going to have to do it for him. Speaking low and fast—the other constables weren't far away—she shot her questions at him.

"Does VanWhoosis have a second in command?"

He nodded. "Three of them."

"Called what?"

"Associate Directors."

"Right, that's what you are, okay? Now, name one." He looked blank. "A real one, what's his name?"

"There's Ashton and there's—"

"Okay, Ashton, that's you, got it? I'm Miss Fredericks and I come from Press Relations and I'm here to help you write the statement that you're going to make." The thing would work; because if there was anybody in the world that Hunter-Donne would tell his story to, the works, the whole thing, it was someone from the Met.

He nodded as she spelled it out again and nodded when the constable came back and led them in and he was nodding now. Not talking much and looking awed but Hunter-Donne was talking quite enough for all of them. And charmingly. He sat there in his ancient armchair, head like Dionysus and a smile to melt the heart, and he was flattered by this visit and he understood the Met's position and was grateful for this opportunity to tell his tale, for surely, when the facts were known, the Met would give the chalice back and would they like some biscuits with their tea.

They were in Sir Winston's study, four of them. The fourth was Sanderson, Jock Sanderson, Sir Winston's Friday-man for fifty years. The perfect good-right-arm, his name was always there, on all the books; below, in smaller type. He was a natural scholar, born to be: mid-seventies and very Scots; tall, bony, out-of-doors, all creased and ruddy from the wind.

The room was small and cozy, piles of books and papers, full of findings from the digs. Bone awls and needles, knives and ax heads from the Iron Age, bronze ornaments from Arthur's time and Celtic coins and Saxon pottery and oil jars brought somehow into Somerset from Ancient Egypt. The old man was so proud of them.

"We found this fellow lying face down in the guardhouse." He was pointing to a man's head, fierce thing, done in bronze. "He's a god, of course, but Jock insists he was a Roman officer."

"No doubt about it." Sharp and quick from Sanderson.

"You're wrong, as usual." As sharp or sharper.

"We did find him in the guardhouse, Winston."

"We found saucepans in the guardhouse. Doesn't mean they cooked there."

Snap, snap; like two ancient boys at recess squabbling over balls and strikes. She liked the way they fit together, grooved to one another like the Jack Spratts, perfectly mismatched.

The tea was cold, high time to move things on, when Melvil came to life and started talking.

Hunter-Donne had made some passing reference to Herodotus and Melvil picked it up and he was off and running now on Classic Greece. He really knew his Periclean Athens, it had life and meaning for him and the old man started chiming in and they were good; not like the talk at Gardener's table, full of port and boredom.

But it wasn't what they'd come for so she frowned at Melvil and he noticed it eventually and took his cue.

"The chalice, yes of course," Sir Winston said. "I think . . ." He paused, then nodded briskly. "I think the story tells best if you see the site." He pushed up from his chair, shrugged on a heavy, shapeless sweater, bowed them out the door.

It was late afternoon and chill, but the old men didn't seem to feel it. They were moving at a good clip toward the hill. Sir Winston looked up at it. He owned it; it was his, this place, his treasure and his voice came low and full of life.

"It was no accident that Joseph came here with the Grail. Had all of England open to him. Ever think of that? What drew him to a hill in Somerset to put up Christ's first church in all of England? I say it was the souls that did it. And the gods. You mustn't leave the gods out." He was either very wise or senile. Six to five, your pick.

"When Joseph came to Somerset, it looked like Noah's flood. All water. Fifty miles in all directions, shallow water, flat as glass. And popping out of it like Ararat, two magic mountains; this and Glastonbury Tor. 'The Isles of Avalon,' says Tennyson, with geographical exactitude." Not senile: three to one.

"From the beginning, from as long ago as there were men in England, people lived here on this hill. Odd place to settle? Not at all. The hills were safe, best natural forts in England, miles of moat. And forts they were until the dikes went up along the channel less than a millennium ago."

"About the souls?" she asked. Important question. He believed the Grail existed. Was he a religious nut? It made a difference.

"I think I have one. Don't know what it's made of, energy or something. There were souls up on this hill for seven thousand years. The Druids knew it, felt it in the air and put their gods here. Other tribes before them did the same. Gwyn, son of Nudd, god of the underworld, inhabited this hilltop and the land was full of gods and souls and Joseph came here like a filing to a magnet."

Carrie wasn't a believer; not in gods or souls or spooks and there was sunlight, nothing spooky in the air but she stood close to Melvil when they pulled up at the trench. An excavation, actually, it cut into the hill six feet or more, exposing little piles and rows of stones that didn't look like much.

"The lower gate. You see?" Sir Winston on his haunches, pointing to a pocket in a pile of stones. "The pivot for the gatepost. Roman. Over there—" Another pocket. "That was Arthur's. Up we go."

The trench rose steeper than a stairway; almost vertical it seemed, cut down to rock, exposing ruined walls of stone. Crude work, like giant kids in kindergarten. And the ridges in the hill that made it look like layer cake were ramparts, old defenses; and for just a second she imagined men in skins with stones to throw, crouched down, and heard shouts in some strange, growly language.

"Melvil?" She was panting just a little, so was he, and they had fallen back a bit. Ahead, the two old men were bobbing up the hill like mountain goats. "Let's talk a minute."

"Have I been okay as Ashton?"

"You've been very good." He looked so pleased. She

felt like giving him a hug. Instead, she frowned. "What do you think?"

"I think he's a fantastic man, the real thing."

"Yes." She thought so, too. Yes, but. What bothered her? "You think he honestly believes the Grail existed?" Melvil bit his lip, then nodded. "What do you think?" He looked away and hunched his shoulders. "Come on, you're a scholar, what's your scholarly opinion?"

"You remember Heinrich Schliemann?"

Rang a bell. Who was he? Troy? "Was he the Troy man?"

"Right. No one believed that Troy existed, Homer made it up. But Schliemann took him at his word. He read the text as if it were a road map and he went where Homer said it was and dug and found the place. Most legends are like pearls; they start out with a grain of truth."

"Yes, but—the Grail, you think it's an obsession?"

"I don't know."

She didn't either, and they wouldn't find out standing there. "Come on," she said, "let's see the digs."

It was a funny sort of place, the hilltop. What it looked like was a mammoth putting green: thick grass with little mounds and gentle slopes. It was the digs that made it seem so weird. Scattered at what looked like random were these giant rectangles where they had cut the grass away and dug broad, shallow pits; a little like a sod farm in midseason. Mostly, what the pits disclosed were holes and trenches, little holes and big ones, and she thought of kindergarten once again; demented children digging senselessly.

The bigger holes were dug for storage pits, Sir Winston told them, and the smaller ones for posts. Cut into rock they were, from all the ages: Iron Age and Bronze and Roman and from Arthur's time—500 A.D. and some even later. Holes for posts that held up houses, churches, huts and feast halls and what made it look so crazy was that you were seeing all of them at once. The trick was sorting out the different ages, telling them apart, and when you did you saw the patterns and the shapes. And when Sir Winston pointed out which holes were there for Arthur's fortress, you could almost see it standing. Crude, rough wood, not very big, thatched roof, no windows.

Carrie blinked the picture off and looked up as Sir Winston threw his trowel down. "Jock, you're wrong."

"No, no; you *think* I'm wrong."

"I have some little reputation as a thinker."

"Did I see it first or did I not?"

"You did not."

They were all four sitting on the bottom of an excavation and the two old men were starting on the night they'd found the chalice. Carrie listened. They had been alone. No other witnesses. There were some locals, amateurs who came out regularly to the digs and worked for nothing, but they'd gone and it was nearly dark and Hunter-Donne and Sanderson were passing by the very spot where they were sitting now and one of them, it didn't really matter which, had seen a shadow or a shape or something and they'd dug it out.

"What happened then?" She drew her knees up, hugged her arms around them.

"Didn't know it was a chalice, not at first."

"I knew," Sir Winston said.

"You didn't. It was dark and bloody cold and we were kneeling in the mud and when we brought it up, it didn't look like anything, encrusted, stone and whatnot stuck all over it.

What happened then, apparently, was that they'd taken it to their laboratory—the building next to where they lived—and started working over it. The work was delicate and difficult but after two days, bit by bit, the shape, the contours of the thing emerged. A drinking vessel of some kind. First-century A.D.;

they knew that from the potsherds or whatever that they'd found around it. Still no inkling what it really was; and then a section of the encrustation fell away and they could see the base. Not clearly but enough to make out gold or silver as the metal of it. And enough to see, just barely, letters of some kind, engraving on the bottom.

"Last I ever saw of it." Sir Winston sounded bitter. "I was due in Glastonbury for a meeting of the Camelot Society. We have no funds, you see, and it takes money, so much money for a proper staff, trained archeologists. You know who comes to dig? Some locals when they can and students in the summertime and us, the two old skeletons. Look at the size of it. We have so much to do and darkness comes so soon. I haven't seven maids with seven mops."

He went on talking and his eyes were like ashen charcoal hit by sudden wind. Tomorrow was no good to him, you see. At eighty-five, next year was never. What had his life been spent on? Where was his achievement? Not his books; already out of date, his fine thoughts commonplace, just faded ink on yellowed pages. This would be his monument. To take this English myth—as great and deep a thing as Homer or the Bible, surely—and to prove it, make it real and true. And so he'd gone to Glastonbury questing funds and Sanderson stayed here at camp alone, still working on the chalice.

Sanderson had worked late. It was an important find, no doubt of it, and certain of the larger features of the piece were coming clear. The repoussé work, for example. Figures raised in gold or silver, human figures; he could see that much. No more, no details and he'd gone on working till he was exhausted, turned the lights out, left the lab and bent to lock the door. Whatever hit him—piece of pipe, the Yard men said—came crashing down. There wasn't any pain at all, not that he could remember.

The thieves—the Yard said there were two or three of them—had been professionals. Their work was neat, they'd broken nothing, left no mess. They'd opened up an old safe and two storage chests and taken most of what was there: some Celtic pieces and a lot of first-class Roman work; things, on the open market, worth perhaps a hundred thousand pounds. The pieces in the open, on the laboratory table, had been left alone. Except, of course, of course, the chalice. That they took.

He had been semiconscious when they left, heard footsteps on the grass, a car door slam, a motor. Somehow, he had gotten to his feet and made it back into the laboratory to the telephone. The operator put him through to Glastonbury—there was no constabulary closer. He had spoken to the sergeant and the next thing he remembered was the doctor working on his head an hour later.

"That's when you came home, Win."

"Thought they'd killed you."

"Burst out into tears, you did."

"Ah, that was for the chalice, not for you."

She felt a rush of feeling for them. They were absolutely dear, these two old coots: full of affection they denied. Warm and crusty; she thought instantly of pie, felt hungry, told herself to concentrate and got back to the mystery.

The motive. That was where to start. What was the motive? Why were treasures stolen? For the money they would bring. Who needed money? It was obvious: Sir Winston. Money for the digs. The man was driven, time was running, he was desperate. Which was how the thieves knew where the treasures were and what to take and she was really clicking now. An inside job, that's what it was. Sir Winston was the mastermind. He'd sold the chalice to the Met through What's-his-name, the movie mogul. Perfect; watertight—except he'd never give his chalice up. It was the keystone to his immortality, he couldn't bear to lose it. But he wasn't. He was claiming it was stolen from him, he was going to get it back. He'd end up with the millions and the chalice. Jesus God, the perfect crime.

She was going to try the theory on Melvil as they stumbled down the hill. The sun was gone, the land below them faintly touched by afterglow. She shivered from the chill, held close to him. There was a sense of souls about the place; old souls. Her bag was heavy with the chalice, bumped against her, and her theory seemed less brilliant every second.

Melvil stopped, turned toward her. "You know what I think?" His voice was low.

"What?"

"What I think is maybe what we've got here really is the Holy Grail."

"Come on."

His eyes were big, he looked about eleven. "He's as great a scholar as there is, Sir Winston, and that could be Camelot up there, it really could, and Arthur and his knights and Guinevere, they could have lived here, on this ground. It could have happened."

Something hooted in the distance and her foot slipped on a stone.

"There's something strange about this hill," he said. "You feel it. I can see it in your eyes."

She couldn't see his eyes at all. She had a good view of his lips, though. He had good lips. Sensuous, that's what his lips were, in particular the lower one. She turned her head to see it better which was when he tried to kiss her.

Missed completely. Got her jaw and bumped his nose against her cheekbone. And she grinned; because it always struck her kind of funny, like a golfer when he swings and misses, and it happened to her last when she was ten and Bobby Endicott had missed her on the porch and chipped his tooth and that was really funny.

"Sorry," Melvil muttered and she saw his eyes then, oh dear Lord, what was she going to do with him? She put her hands out, framed his face between them, fingers lightly on his cheeks. "It's all right," she whispered, "I'm your friend," and kissed him.

Funny; funny strange. Because he was so vulnerable, that's what he was and yet she felt so safe. It made no sense at all to feel protected by so vulnerable a man. She almost said so—just the safe part—but she didn't want the kiss to stop and when she shivered, he mistook it, thought that she was cold and hungry, took her hand and hurried down the hill.

She had to make a move soon. They were in Sir Winston's tiny kitchen setting up for dinner. It was seven. In an hour or so, back at the Met, they'd open up his safe and *blammo*. News would get to London late that night; by noon tomorrow, Melvil West would have his picture in the papers. Time was running; and the chalice, like a time bomb in her handbag, doing everything but tick. Explosive: if she took it out, she'd blow the place apart. Or would she? There was something wrong. What was it?

Dinner on the table. There was curry left from yesterday—Jock's recipe from when they'd worked those temple digs in Hyderabad in '38 or was it '39—and bread and butter, boiled sprouts. Suppose she took the chalice out and showed it to them. What would happen? They'd identify it; it was theirs. But how could they be sure? They hadn't really seen it, not in detail, it was still encrusted, all mucked up and that's what had been bugging her. How many details had they seen? And what if they described it differently, what if the details didn't jibe and even if they'd seen the photo in the *Times*, it only showed one side of the chalice. Easy now. She turned to Sanderson.

"Tell me, Dr. Sanderson, what's your opinion of the chalice?"

He looked up. "In what regard?"

Evasive? Hard to tell. "Well, as a work of art." She had to do this carefully.

"Quite beautiful, from what I saw."

"From what you saw?"

"We never finished cleaning it, impossible to see the finer points—"

"You've seen its picture in the papers, Jock," Sir Winston said.

"I've seen the photographs." He nodded. "Very beautiful."

Like perfume in the air; faint, faint, but definitely something. Melvil must have sensed it, too.

"We have a provenance, you know," he said.

"The devil take your provenance," Sir Winston snapped. "It's mine. I found it. Jock was there. He saw me find it."

Carrie kept her eyes on Sanderson. She knew what she was looking for. It had to be there.

"With all possible respect, sir," Melvil went on, "we have papers saying that it came from Corsica, from some collector there."

"You're something of an expert, Ashton. Tell me this. How rare is Roman plate?"

"Extremely rare."

"And chalices?" Sir Winston, leaning forward in his chair.

"They're even rarer."

"With engraving on the bottom?"

"Rarer still."

"Suppose you dig up such a chalice and it's stolen, gone, and four months later in New York a piece appears same size as yours, same shape, same age, engraving on the base—'Josephus.' And this Joseph lived upon the hill where you were digging. What, sir, what would be your scholarly conclusion?"

Melvil took a deep breath. "I would take it to be mine."

The little room was silent. Dead still. It was now or never. Carrie licked her lips. "What's your opinion, Dr. Sanderson?"

"Of what, my dear?"

She laid it on the line. "Is it your chalice in New York?"

"I haven't seen the chalice in New York."

"But is it yours?" She couldn't see his eyes well, couldn't quite see what was there.

"You heard Sir Winston."

"But I'm asking you." He turned his eyes away. "What do you think?"

"I think—" His eyes were on Sir Winston's; locked. "I think what Winston thinks. I always think what Winston thinks. That's right, Win, isn't it? If Winston says a thing is so, it is so, if he says a thing is not, it is not, if he says—"

He broke off and pressed his lips together, looking stiff and stubborn as an angry boy. Sir Winston shook his head and smiled. "I'm as bad as all that, am I, Jock?"

Silence in the room. Then knocking; someone outside knocking at the door. Sir Winston turned to Melvil. "Ashton, would you please?"

"Of course." He stood up, moved across the room and opened up the door.

Inspector Drum.

She blinked. Had things blown open in New York? It wasn't three o'clock there yet and she'd been counting on the time, so certain they had the night before the story broke. She put a smile on. Melvil muttered something with "Inspector' 'in it, moved aside. Drum came into the room with little steps.

"Sir Winston, sorry if I'm interrupting."

"Not at all. Miss Fredericks, Mr. Ashton, may I introduce Inspector Drum?"

Drum nodded to them—quick, polite—then turned back to Sir Winston. "Just been called by London, sir. News from New York."

She looked at Melvil. He was rigid, knuckles white, not breathing.

"It's about the Grail, sir."

"Yes?"

"It's gone, sir, I'm afraid."

"Gone where?"

"That's very much the question; no one seems to know."

A funny noise from Sanderson; you couldn't call it laughter, quite. "It's stolen?"

"That," said Drum, "is the presumption."

"Oh my God, Inspector, are you sure?" She'd laid that on a little heavy but Sir Winston might expect it, some reaction, they were from the Met and Melvil didn't much look like reacting. Anyway, Inspector Drum was sure but no one knew by whom, not yet. New York was keeping him informed and he would call Sir Winston and he wouldn't have a brandy, thank you very much and, by your leave, good night.

The room was very still. The chalice ticked but that was in her head. Then, suddenly, the last sound in the world she had expected: laughter. Sanderson was laughing.

"I fail to see what's funny, Jock."

"They've stolen it again." He barely got it out between the wheezes.

"Stop it, Jock." Sir Winston was distraught. "God knows what's become of it."

"And He won't tell." Tears, two of them, were trickling down Jock's cheeks.

"You want to know?" The words burst out of Melvil. He was striding toward her, fast, across the room. "I'll tell you where it is." He grabbed her bag. He fumbled with the zipper, pulled it hard. He had it open. Then he reached inside.

He stood there with the chalice in his hand. Nobody moved. Or spoke. Sir Winston's face was blank. No trace of anything; not joy or recognition or surprise, not anything at all. And then . . .

"My God." Sir Winston's voice was choked, unsteady, and his eyes grew full. "My chalice. It's my chalice. God has sent my chalice back to me."

"No." The word came out of Sanderson as if he hadn't used his voice for years. "No, it's not your chalice."

"Give it to me, let me hold it in my hands." Sir Winston's fingers shook.

"It's not your bloody chalice, Win."

"Not mine? I found it."

"No, you didn't."

"You were there. You saw me find it."

"You. It's always you. I found it. You were fifty feet away. I saw it and I dug it up. Mine. It was mine."

There was compassion on Sir Winston's face. "It's all right, Jock. There's no call to excite yourself."

"I found it. It belonged to me."

"Please, Jock, you know what happens. Here." Sir Winston held the chalice out. "It's yours."

"It's not. It's not the one I found."

"I'll get your medicine."

"You know what happened to the one I found?"

"It doesn't matter, Jock."

"I—I—I crushed it, I destroyed it, smashed the thing to pieces."

"If you say so, Jock."

"I did and I can prove it." He was on his feet. Face red from shouting, neck cords taut. "I fixed you, Win. I kept the pieces. Would you like to see your Holy Grail? What's left of it?"

The old man turned and scuttled to the door.

"Jock."

Out he went, into the night.

"Dear God." Sir Winston stood there, turning aimlessly, bewildered, lost as any child. "What has he done? He'll hurt himself. A light. Oh, Jock. We have to find a light."

They found one, two; two flashlights. Melvil gave one to Sir Winston. They were out the door. Then Carrie turned, went back. The chalice; she had left it on the table. She was shaking. It was terrible, these two old men, what they were doing to each other and she didn't want to see it, didn't want to know.

"Come on!"

Melvil shouting from the doorway. Damn the chalice anyway. She jammed it in her bag and shuddered from the touch of it; it felt so cold, like death.

He grabbed her wrist. "Come on, for Chrissake."

They rushed outside. Which way? He shined the light around. There. Toward the gate. Sir Winston, bobbing, jerking, starting up the hill. No sign of Sanderson. They ran.

They reached the trench, looked up. Sir Winston, way ahead of them; and, at the top, just for a moment, black against the grayness of the sky, the shape that would be Sanderson.

They started up. The trench was rough, uneven, full of pits and stones. He tried to keep the flashlight on their footing but it bobbed and wobbled, throwing shadows. Better off without it and she told him so. He flicked it off. Pitch-black. They kept on going, stumbling, slipping, breathing hard. The black was turning into gray, her eyes adjusting. She could see the low stone walls and ramparts where the trench cut through them. Far below, pale yellow light: Sir Winston's place.

They made it to the top. She went to one knee for a second; winded, and she felt a little shaky. He knelt beside her. It was like the dark side of the moon up there, all rocks and pits and craters and the earth was chilled. Ahead, they saw a light. It wiggled—that would be Sir Winston running—then it stopped. The two men were together.

Melvil helped her up. He looked so big. His hand was on her elbow; firm and sure she thought it felt. She let him guide her, take her where she didn't want to go. Nor did she want to hear; but there were voices now and she could see Sir Winston on his knees and, and for a second, there was Sanderson as if he'd been decapitated, just his face above the ground.

" . . . my whole life, Win, since I was nineteen, I was just a boy then when I came to you." All anger gone; his voice was quiet now and rueful as he talked about old times, old digs and old discoveries. He was standing, she could see now, in a pit. Could he be digging? Melvil moved her forward.

"All I ever wanted, Win, was sharing things with you."

"We've done that all our lives, Jock."

"No, not ever. You're a great man when it comes to thinking and the writing of the books, but when it comes to me you're very small and when you took the Grail and kept it all—I found it, Win, I was the one . . ."

The voice grew softer, muffled, muddied up with feelings and the wind was rising and she pressed in close to Melvil, arm around him. Would there be a chalice in the pit where Sanderson was digging; or rather, the remains of one and who was lying, which old man or both or neither?

She could hear again, heard Sanderson describing how he'd felt that night, alone, the lab light shining on that crusted piece of metal that would be Sir Winston's greatest glory. How he'd felt as if he held Sir Winston in his hands: there—at his mercy. It was in his power. He had crushed the chalice in a vise, had squeezed it, cracked it, mashed it into pulp. And left it there, out on the table, for Sir Winston to discover.

And had gone, gone out the door, been struck, recovered as the thieves went off into the night. And then remorse. His voice rose with the anguish of it. Criminal: what he had done was criminal.

"I couldn't tell you, Win, I couldn't face you with it; so I put the pieces in a bag and told the constable the thieves had stolen it and the next day buried what was left up here."

"It's all right, Jock."

"It's not, it can't be, it's beyond redemption."

"If it happened. But it never did."

"I didn't make it up."

"But, Jock, you saw our chalice in my hands tonight. It's down there now."

"It's here, I know it's here, I put it here. Oh God." Voice rising. "I can't find it. Which hole did I put it in?" He crawled on all fours from the pit, then stood. "They're all alike. Oh Win, please help me find it. Win—" He sounded like a little boy. "Win, you don't love me any more."

She had no business watching, shouldn't be there, so she turned away and didn't see them hold each other. And she had no business hearing, not such things as they were saying, not those whispers, no, and when Sir Winston started weeping, Carrie ran.

# XVII

The sign for Swindon shot by. Blurred. She had the pedal to the floor. The needle trembled at 130 kpm. The M-4 was deserted, dark.

"Go faster." Had he said that? Possibly: he felt a little crazy.

"What?"

The wind hissed and the car was rattling. Everywhere. He raised his voice. "Can we go any faster?"

"Not in this heap."

Ninety miles to London, Heathrow Airport. Everything depended on the time. The time Sir Winston took to call Inspector Drum, the time Drum took to get descriptions of them out to Immigration at the airport. That was all the Yard knew, what they looked like. No names yet. Drum hadn't heard of Dr. Melvil West. He'd hear tomorrow when the cops in New York started looking for him but by then they'd be in Corsica.

Unless, of course, Drum knew about their car. Sir Winston hadn't seen it: they had parked around the curve. But Drum had driven up the lane and down again, gone past it twice. Had it occurred to him to notice? Did he have a memory of the model or the color or the license plate? There would be roadblocks and patrol cars if he did.

So far, so good. He looked at Carrie. She seemed fine again; absorbed, at one with the machine. A very different Carrie from the one who turned and ran across the hilltop. He had held her when he caught her, very close, and whispered all the wise things people say to comfort one another: "No, no; there there; it's all right, it's all right." It wasn't, not all right at all but she grew calmer and he took her hand, held hard, and led her, stumbling, down the hill.

They hit the bottom, stopped. No constable on duty, not that they could see. No need to run, not really, nothing there to run away from but they ran.

It wasn't till much later—they were whipping down a nameless country road, the M-4 up ahead somewhere—that they tried taking stock of what they knew. Or didn't know.

It seemed at first as if they knew a lot. Not so. The more they talked, the clearer it became that all they knew for certain was that (1) there'd been a robbery at which (2) some objects had been stolen.

All the rest was supposition. Hunter-Donne or Sanderson, which one did you believe? It was a question of belief because there was no proof. If Sanderson had found the pieces—but he hadn't. Still, the holes did look alike, the remnants of the chalice could be up there, didn't mean that Sanderson was lying.

There was a likelihood—this was what made it so complex—that neither man was lying. When the passions and the strains are great enough, what can't a man believe? Take Hunter-Donne. How could he possibly identify the chalice when the final time he'd seen the thing it was encrusted with two thousand years of crud? The scientist in him knew better but the man of eighty-five, sustained and driven by his dream of Camelot, believed it absolutely. It was his: the one he found. Or Sanderson. His life spent for a pocket of short change, kept going by his feelings for Sir Winston, for his Win. Half-mad, if he destroyed the chalice; and he'd been half-mad tonight. He could have made the story up, invented it in front of them and still believe it to be true.

It all came down to this: the truth was somewhere but they weren't about to find it in South Cadbury. In Calvi, maybe; on the coast of Corsica. From what's his name, the man who said he'd owned the chalice—Stefan Kalman. Did this Kalman know the truth? And would he tell them if he did? And Adolf Mannheim, borders, passports, Scotland Yard, the French police. He shook his head.

Luck had been with them so far. No pursuit; no roadblocks or patrols. A sign said READING.

"How long to the airport?"

"Twenty minutes," Carrie told him. "Maybe thirty."

"What if Immigration knows about us?" No reply. "Or what if we do get by and afterwards they go around the airport asking questions and someone remembers us, what plane was took. They'll call ahead and when we land—"

Her voice shook. "Look, you got a better fucking plan, let's fucking hear it. I don't know what else to do."

"I'm sorry."

"Jesus Christ . . ."

"I said I'm sorry."

Very little else was said until they pulled in at the airport. Up the ramp. They picked a distant corner, parked the car and left it there for Hertz to find. He went to take the luggage from the back. She told him leave it, they were traveling light from now on.

They started for the terminal. Light traffic, not like Kennedy at night; some taxicabs and no police cars. They crossed the road, went in. Not much activity. Some porters stood about and there were passengers, a few; some wandering and some on benches. What did Yard men look like? Would he know one if he saw one?

Melvil took a deep breath, squared his shoulders back and headed for the Air France counter.

"Could I have some information, please?" He sounded very calm, he thought.

The girl looked up. "Of course, how can I help you?"

"When is the next flight to Corsica?"

"There isn't one."

She didn't look like a comedian. "We've got to get to Corsica."

"I'm sorry, sir, but I'm afraid you have a problem."

Swell: just what he needed. "Why is that?"

"There are no flights from here to Corsica. You have to fly from Nice or Paris."

Nice was nearer Calvi. "When's the next flight for Nice?"

"At nine tomorrow morning."

"Nothing sooner?" Jesus Christ. "Is there a flight tonight for Paris?"

"Ten-fifteen."

He checked his watch. An hour's wait. Too risky, wasn't it? He looked at Carrie. She was smiling, not a worry in the world. "Come on," she said, "let's have a drink and talk it over, maybe we should spend the night in London. Wouldn't that be fun?"

She giggled, took his arm and started strolling. Like two lovers, very casual, they crossed the lobby, up the stairs toward International Departures. Nothing wrong that he could see; just ordinary people waiting, filling forms. He felt her fingers tighten on his arm. He looked at her. What was it? Up ahead, there by the Immigration booths: two men. Nice-looking fellows, they were smoking cigarettes and talking.

"Goodness gracious." Carrie shook her head and giggled. "Silly me, I left my glasses in the car." She leaned close, kissed his cheek and whispered, "Give me sixty seconds and then wander out the front." With which, she straightened, giggled once more, clear and loud, and strolled away.

He watched her go and then—if she could do it, so

could he—called after. "Hurry back, dear." Fifty seconds. She was down the stairs and what to do? The normal thing, act normal. What was normal? Look at magazines. He saw a stand and wandered toward it, forty seconds, mustn't look to see if they were looking at him, browse around, stop sweating, thirty seconds, pick one up, look interested and don't—repeat don't—turn around and, twenty seconds, turn the pages, steady hands, they'll hear the paper rattling, get suspicious, come for him, ten seconds, maybe they were coming now. He spun around.

They'd seen him, they were looking at him, they were moving toward him. Jesus Christ.

He bolted. Ran like when he broke the window with the baseball and the big kids took off after him. Feet pounding, leaping down the stairs and skidding, which way, left or right, where was the door, across the lobby, people turning, someone shouted, out into the night.

Where was she?

"West!"

He saw her. In a sports car. Motor roaring. Door was open. In. Looked back. The men were coming. Slam the door. *Grazooomm!* She floored it. Tires spun, took hold. Shot forward. Like a bullet. He was riding in a bullet.

"Where'd you get the car?" They zoomed around a van, right up the wrong lane, what the hell.

"I signed it out."

He laughed. A bus was coming. Missed it clean, not even close. She was terrific. "Where we going?"

"First we lose them. Anything behind us?"

"Nothing much."

"Hang on."

She swung them off the highway somewhere west of Hounslow. Onto local streets. Kew Gardens, Chiswick, tearing up the night, around hairpin corners, left and right. Fantastic. Nothing in the world could catch them. Not a chance.

She pulled up in a dark stretch on the Fulham Road. Stopped, motor idling, looking straight ahead, not moving, hands still on the wheel.

He said it slowly, like they did in army movies: "Well, son of a bitch."

"Some fun." She took a deep breath, let the air out, flexed her fingers.

"Where to now?"

She shook her head. "I'll lay it on you, West: I haven't got a clue."

She didn't. Planes were out; that much was very clear. The same for boats across the Channel; they'd be watching all the ports. Perhaps they ought to lie low for a while. Lying low with Carrie; an evocative idea.

She sighed and shook her head. "I don't know, maybe we should go to Jasper's house. He'd take us in."

Who was this Jasper? Had to be a friend. How good a friend? Was Carrie having an affair? None of his business, was it?

"Who is Jasper?" Sounding very casual.

She smiled. "Oh, he's from long ago. He had this villa in Antibes, we used to go there all the time but Jasper wouldn't fly, he had this thing with planes so . . ." Her voice died and she sat there looking blank.

"What's wrong?"

"So every time we went to France we took the train."

The motor roared.

They tore through Chelsea as she filled him in. What made the whole thing possible was the security was terrible. The train was always set up on the last track in the station. The boarding platform had the train on one side and the Customs and Immigration offices on the other. The officials inside had no view of the platform. Nothing prevented you from walking up the platform and onto the train except a wooden fence. The fence was made of separate sections, portable. Sometimes there was an officer who strolled around behind the fence, sometimes he strolled away.

"So all we do is buy our tickets, make it through the fence and walk on board. The only hitch," she grinned, "is when it leaves. I think it's ten but I'll be damned if I remember."

There were other hitches, too, like Scotland Yard men. Odds were, it would be like Heathrow, they'd be waiting in the office by the Immigration desk. But what if they were on the platform, what if—Melvil shook his head: enough of that.

They left the car on Lower Belgrave Street and took off for the station. 9:45. If Carrie had the time right, they could make it. She was moving out ahead of him, the girl was really fast. He caught up and they ran together past the quiet houses, on to Buckingham Palace Road, then right and there it was. Victoria Station.

They skidded to a stop, went walking in. Brisk pace but not too fast; they didn't want to be remembered. Where was the Departure board? She spotted it, above the gates, stood squinting at it. Ten, it left at ten. He told her so.

"Come on."

They cut across the vast hall toward the Information booth. The station felt deserted. There were people scattered here and there, at random, like the candy wrappers on the floor. The place was huge, a ruin still in use, carved marble, vaulted archways. Running around the walls where rich arcades once stood were small tacky little booths of chrome and plastic, mostly closed this late at night, where magazines and ices, worthless souvenirs and other sad things were on sale.

The old man at the Information booth just pointed

when he asked which window sold their tickets. Carrie headed for the far end where their train was boarding. While he bought the tickets, she would scout around.

"Two tickets, please." Nice lady; no comedian.

"To where, sir?"

He had all the answers this time. "Paris."

"Second-class, sir?"

Did he look that shabby? "First, please."

"One compartment, sir, or two?"

It was the crunch. A gentleman would ask for two and he was one of Nature's gentlemen. "One. One compartment." Thoughts of Carrie danced like sugarplums. Long legs crossed, sitting on the bed. His hand reached out and touched the coolness of her thigh. She didn't mind. In point of fact, she smiled. Her eyes looked soft. She stood. His hand undid the button at her waist, unzipped her skirt. It fell without a sound. Her legs went up and up, like rockets, curving, smooth. He touched her where they came together, touched her there. Her lips moved and she made a little sound and he was going to do it to her and he would have but the ticket lady had his tickets in her hand.

"That's thirty-two pounds, seven pence in all, sir."

"Right." He reached into his jacket pocket, came out with a wad of bills, put them uncounted on the counter.

"I'm sorry, sir." Had she done something wrong? What was she sorry for? "I can't accept them."

Had the dollar sunk so low? "Why not?" And then it hit him. Dollars. He had never changed them into sterling. Pockets stuffed with cold cash and he couldn't buy a railroad ticket but he had to—five of ten, the train was leaving any minute and there was this pounding in his ears.

"Look, please, you've got to take them."

"It's not up to me, sir."

Not her fault, don't blame her. "Can I charge it?" Brilliant. "Can I use a card?"

She smiled. "Yes, of course."

He fumbled, found wallet, got it out, keep steady, here you go. He gave it to her and she took it. Saved.

"I'm sorry, sir."

He didn't scream at her. He felt it coming but he swallowed it. "It's good."

"I'm sure it is."

"It's mine, I didn't steal it."

"It's American Express."

He nodded, bet your life, and good at half a million airlines, restaurants, and shops around the world.

"I don't suppose you'd have a Eurocard."

A Eurocard? For Christ's sake. "Where's a bank?" There had to be one, had to be. "Is there a bank?"

"Just over there, sir, but—"

He turned and ran. Where was it? Magazine stand, souvenirs, a chemist's—there. There where the sign said FOREIGN EXCHANGE. No line, no people waiting; that was good. But why was it so dark? Another sign; all blurred, his eyes weren't seeing right. He squinted. OFFICE HOURS—OPEN DAILY 9:30 A.M. TO 4:30 P.M.

He kept his head. The Melvil West that used to be, he would have panicked, run away to his martinis, given up. This was the new West, desperate for a drink but hanging on. There had to be a way. Some kindly traveler would help him—that man there.

He tore across the floor. The man looked nice.

"The bank's closed and my train is going."

"If you're asking me to cash your check—" The nice man shook his head.

"No, nothing like that. Pounds for dollars. Change."

"If it's a question of a quid or two—"

"A hundred dollars."

"Yank, I haven't seen that much in one place since the Coronation."

You're not thinking, keep you head, it was a lot of

money, people didn't walk around with that much money. Who would have it? Magazine stand? Worth a try. He tried it but the guy was nasty, told him to piss off or something, and the bigger stores were closed, all dark, there had to be an open store, some place with money in it and his chest hurt from the running so he stopped, heard someone coming up behine him, spun around.

"What's been keeping you?"

He told her, let it boil out: the fucking money and the fucking bank. She left him in the middle of it, turned away and headed for the ticket window. When he got there, she was paying for the tickets with her Eurocard. He felt like hitting her. The girl was perfect, but goddammit there was such a thing as being just too goddam perfect and just once it ought to be his goddam turn to save the goddam day.

"Come on." She had the tickets.

"Give 'em here."

"What's eating you?"

He grabbed the tickets. She was talking. "No one from the Yard so far as I can tell. The cop on duty comes and goes, the way I said." Ahead, he saw the train. The fence. An old sign saying IMMIGRATION. No policeman. Steam was hissing. Something clanged. Ten on the dot.

They stood there by the fence. Last look around. All clear. He grabbed a section of the fence and held it like a feather, lifted it aside.

"Hey, you!"

He turned and saw him, there he was, the cop, the constable, the bobby, the policeman.

"Shit," she said. He looked at her and almost laughed. For once, she didn't have the answer. He didn't have the answer, either; not an idea in his head. It was the damnedest feeling: glorious.

"What do you think you're doing?"

"Me?" The answer sprang, God-given, to his lips. "What the fuck does it look like I'm doing?"

"You can't get on the train this way."

"I'm not getting on your bloody train, I'm getting off. I'm looking for my luggage." He waved his tickets at the constable.

"Where'd you leave it, sir?"

"With the porter. Took it from us when we got here."

There was another hiss of steam. Melvil started down the platform toward the train. Everybody followed.

"Look, all I know is we have got to take this train." He stopped, helped Carrie up the steps. "If I've been robbed and you're a cop, go find my luggage for me."

"Yes sir. What's your name, sir?"

"Paris. Melvil Paris."

"Right." The train was moving. "And the luggage, sir?"

"It's red." He hoped aboard. "Six pieces." Carrie took his hand. "And when you find 'em, send 'em on to Monte Carlo."

# XVIII

Unaccustomed as she was to thinking *Gee*, it was the only word that kept recurring to her.

They were having double whiskeys in the buffet car and he was looking like a little boy on Christmas morning, piles of packages to open. And the package in his lap, half-opened, was himself. It was all still pretty fragile, handle it with care, but gee, he'd been terrific back there on the platform. And he knew it. Couldn't quite believe it yet, nor could she, and his eyes were alternately either blank with wonderment or shining with surprise. She liked the look of it.

"I don't know what came over me." He shook his head. "I've never done a thing like that. Fantastic."

And a good thing, too. Because she'd drawn a blank. She'd been a gifted liar all her life, from back when she was three or four and fooled her mommy and her daddy. All the time. Nobody ever knew what Carrie really thought or really felt or, later on, what Carrie really did. The lies came, like Athena from the head of Zeus, complete; invention under pressure, she was Homer's equal but she'd seen that bobby coming and she hadn't had the wit to holler fire.

His story was a good one. It should hold, at least until tomorrow sometime when the bobby saw their pictures in the paper. By which time they would be out of England, safely in the South of France.

She took her eyes away from him and looked around. Plain place, the buffet car: Formica tables, menus worn and thumbed to gray, not much to eat. She wasn't hungry, anyway. The car was half full; quiet people dining on beef sandwiches in cellophane, and bottled beer.

The train had pleasant memories for her and she realized with a start—she hadn't give it a thought till then—that in a very little while she would go to bed with Melvil West. And what she found she wanted was, well, it was hard to say precisely and she wasn't having fantasies although she usually did, which was a little odd, and God knows bedding down was not an epochal event, but what she wanted was it should be wonderful. Whatever wonderful might mean.

What she was feeling must have shown. He looked at her, West did, and quickly looked away. Evasive was the word. He drained his glass, looked out the window, fidgeted. Like sixteen, like a boy of sixteen on a date.

The conductor was clicking his way through the car. West fished through pockets, found their tickets, held them out. The conductor punched them, smiled and wished them both a pleasant night.

West wiped his forehead. "Would you like another drink?" There was something almost hopeful in the way he said it.

"No thanks."

"Tired?"

Carrie smiled and nodded.

"Yeah." He wiped his lips. "I'll bet you're really tired."

"Come on, let's go."

"Okay." He nodded, drained his glass, paused, put it down. "Okay."

She reached across the table, squeezed his hand.

"What's that for?"

"Luck." she said and pushed her chair back.

"Wait." He frowned. "I haven't paid the check. What am I going to pay it with?"

"He won't mind the dollars."

"Are you sure?"

"Not if you leave him twenty."

"Isn't that a lot for four drinks?"

Carrie kept a straight face, shook her head, stood watching while he brought a wad of bills out, found a twenty, took his time about it, left it on the table, stood and bowed.

"After you," he said.

Their car was four cars back. He kept his distance, brushed against her once—by accident, the train lurched—mumbled something, eyes averted. She was going to have to treat him carefully, go slow. She liked that.

Their compartment door, of course, was locked. He trudged off, like a kid sent down to see the principal, to find the porter. Back they came. She watched the key go in the hole, she watched it turn. The door eased open. Shabby little room, gray-brown, all worn away. She liked it: warm and small and very private—it would be a good place.

She stood just inside the doorway watching as the porter made the bunks up. Nervous little man, a talker, rattling on and on. She wasn't listening. She was dreaming, in the lower bunk with West. Their clothes were off and she was seeing him for the first time. His chest was broad and deep, his flesh was firm, no muscles, none that showed. Men always wanted bulging muscles like the apes in action movies or the jocks in jockstrap ads. They didn't know, they didn't understand how much more beautiful they were without them, with their strength beneath the flesh. Like West. He didn't know how strong he was but she would teach him. He would learn from her.

The porter finished, put their key down on the little table. What was that he said?

"I'm sorry." Carrie frowned. "What's that again?"

"The Immigration forms, ma'am."

Christ, the Immigration forms. He had them in his hand.

"You fill them out and I'll be back to pick them up. And passports, too, of course."

How often had she made this trip? A dozen times? She heard the door close.

"I don't get it." West had the forms now, frowning at them. "Immigration? I thought we were through with Immigration."

"English, yes; French, no."

"Oh God." He sat down. "When we get to France . . ."

She nodded, told him what she knew. The forms West held were entry documents. You filled them out, the porter picked them up and took your passport, too. and kept them overnight.

"What for?"

"To give them to the French authorities in Calais. See, the boat train gets to Calais, I don't know, four, five o'clock, while you're asleep. They keep the forms and stamp the passports and next morning, when you're up, you get your passport back."

He nodded. "What you're saying is they nail us when we get to Calais."

"More or less."

He frowned. No panic; he was thinking. "There's a crack in every system. All we've got to do is find it. Take me through it step by step."

She shrugged. "They take your passport and you go to sleep and in the morning, when you're up, you get your passport back. This nice French waiter brings it with your coffee."

"Nice French waiter?" He looked tense. "Did you say French?" She nodded. "English crew in England, French in France. They switch." He stood, eyes shining with excitement. "What we do is hand our passports in and then, before we get to Calais, take them back."

She frowned. He spelled it out. There had to be a central place where forms and passports went, and if he slipped theirs out there'd be no trace that they were ever on the train. The French authorities would have no record of them. They would have to jump the train as it pulled out of Calais so that when the French porter came with morning coffee, there would not be two more passengers than there were passports. Just an empty room, a messed-up bed that anybody—why not kids from second-class?—had slept in. It could work.

They filled their forms out, like good children, signaled for the porter. When he came, they handed him the forms and passports, said good night. As he was leaving, West asked if they'd see him in the morning.

"No, sir. Leave the train at Dover."

"Good I thought to ask," said West and tipped him, showed him out. They stood together by the door. The train was rattling, banging down the tracks. He nodded brusquely. "Well, here goes." He opened up the door, "If I don't make it back, sneak off in Dover."

"West?"

He turned back and she kissed him, quickly, very lightly, on the lips. "Good luck."

He nodded. "See you in the funny papers."

He was gone. The funny papers? That dated him. She closed the door. Eleven-twenty and they got to Dover one-ish. Lots of time for what he had to do. No need to worry. Pass the time. But how? No books to read, no magazines. No clothes to pack or unpack. All those nice things, left behind with Hertz. Try counting dresses. Dresses were important to her. She knew why, she'd been to see the analyst. Six times and then the creep had tried to feel her up and she had kneed him, groined him good and left him on his couch. Down deep, she wasn't any good at all but if her dresses cost enough it wouldn't show.

Gone ten minutes. She got up, found a mirror. On the lavatory door. It had a crack. She grimaced; they had a lot in common, Carrie and the mirror, they had seen a lot. She took a deep breath, blew it out, relaxing, trying to. Good body. Everyone who'd had it said so, all those satisfied, contented customers. Try counting them.

Her face was dirty so she washed it. Hair like a bird's nest. She unzipped her bag. The chalice: in the way. No matter what you wanted, it was always in the way. Eleven-forty. West—was that him now?—not yet but any minute, soon, parading through the door, their passports in his pocket, pleased as Punch. It used to puzzle her, for years and years, how could a bowl of punch be pleased? Wrong Punch. And for Pete's sake; who was Pete? And Sam Hill, there were lots of them and maybe she should take a shower. Nice and clean all over.

Stupid button; stuck on something so she pulled it. Off the blouse came, then the skirt. No panties. Evil, dirty, bad, you naughty girl, Mom said so, so it must be so. Eleven-fifty. Nothing wrong. She faced the mirror, struck a pose. Fantastic. West would love it. Wouldn't he? What if he didn't? She moved closer to the mirror. What was that? Below the nipple. Not a blemish? Couldn't be. Try counting blemishes.

The water had to be just right. Lukewarm. Who was Luke? She'd called it lunk when she was little, Nanny had to make the water lunkwarm. Nanny did. She stepped in, drew the shower curtain. Heaven. This was how you got clean, not in the blood of the lamb, this way, the water hard, not hurting, almost hurting. Crummy soap, she always traveled with her own but beggers didn't choose and half a loaf was better and her hands were slippery, sliding, sliding.

Nice. That's how it felt and she was nice and sex

was nice and West was—what exactly? Big and good and gentle and sensational in bed. She closed her eyes and let the water play. Good lover. So was she; a lovely lover, loved it. Loving someone else, though, that would happen to her never. Loving was like Faith, you couldn't learn it, you were born with it or not, it came included in the package or it never came. She used to think "Poor Carrie" but she didn't any more. Beethoven heard the music in his head; she used her body. Lovely feelings, West would give her lovely—

"Hey? Where are you? Carrie, hey, it's me."

It was. He stood there, passports in his hand. He'd pulled the shower curtain back and he was getting wet and grinning. And he'd seen her. Looking terrible, all wet and soapy face, just one eye open. No. She must have said it. "No!" He turned away, his face all crumpled. Awful: she had meant to be in bed, all clean and sweet for him. He fled. The towels were worn and rough and didn't dry, no matter how you rubbed. Damp, like something in a fish store, clammy to the touch. She opened up the door a crack and asked him for a blanket.

Out she came, all wrapped up, feeling ugly. She was ugly and her hair, there'd been no time to dry her hair; it hung in strings. She meant to tell him she was sorry, that she hadn't meant to shout but it had been the first time he had seen her and he would remember.

She stood there in the doorway. He was sitting in the corner, trousers splotched with shower water and his eyes—he was so vulnerable and something round and hot was swelling up inside her.

"West?"

What was the matter with her? It was weird. No knees, that's how it felt, as if her knees were gone. She couldn't stand or feel the floor. The room was tilting and she tilted with it to the bed and went down hard and banged her bottom.

"What's the matter?" He was on his feet.

"I don't know what the matter is." She sounded seven and her head was shaking slowly side to side, like Gretel in the forest, lost. She looked up. He was there. He went down, close beside her, on one knee. Her hand, the right one, moved, came outside of the blanket and he took the hand and kissed it.

"Oh," she said, "oh shit," instead of bursting into tears.

"Oh, Carrie." And his lips were light on hers; moist, smooth and very gentle, barely moving. His hand still held her hand. They sat, like children kissing, for the longest time. Then she sank back, lips open, arms around him. She lay wrapped up in her blanket while he kissed her, drifting, floating, nude in sunny, shallow water. She began to press against him, little movements back and forth and everything she did, he did; as if he'd always known exactly how.

"West?" She had to say it twice. "Sit up?" He did. Her hand reached out, undid a button of his shirt. He shook his head. She spoke. "I want to. Let me." He seemed lost and then he nodded and she undid all the buttons and she took his shirt off and he stood—she didn't have to ask—and she undid his trousers. Then she waited while he took his shoes and socks off. Then she looked up at him, way up, and smiled. It must have been a funny smile because the way he smiled back was funny; nice but sort of crooked. Then, all by himself, no help from her, he stepped out of his underwear.

She didn't look. She kept her eyes on his and lay back. It was his turn and he took the blanket down, unwound her, freed her from it.

"West?" Her voice was dry. "Am I all right?"

"Am I?"

He smelled good. Men had smells; nothing to do

with soap or water, clean or dirty, not a thing you washed away but part of you. And firm. He felt firm—safe and solid, just the way she knew he would.

And where he wanted her to go, she went and what he wanted her to do, she did. Or tried to do because she didn't know, she wasn't sure, she wanted him to like her, wanted him to think she was the best thing ever in the world and should she move now? Would he mind it if she whimpered? Did he like it when she touched him there and if he didn't, what would happen? Couldn't stop her mind, stop worrying. She'd like it if he'd slap her bottom but she didn't want to ask because he might think she was kinky, which was true enough, God knows, but would he like that in his girl or would he not and she was so distracted that she didn't feel it coming. Out of nowhere. Blinding. Arched her back. Then nothing. Must have fainted.

He was shaking her, hands gentle, but he looked so worried. She was fine. She smiled and told him so, and he was wonderful, she said. He shook his head, she'd known he would, she'd have to teach him he was wonderful. He changed the subject, started telling her about the passports, trying not to sound too pleased about it. How he'd hunted for the porter, couldn't find him, couldn't find the place they took the passports to. All up and down the train.

"So what I did was figure out a story. Then I went straight up to this conductor and I said I'd left some money in my passport by mistake and could I have it, please. He took me to a little room that's fixed up like an office and unlocked the safe. They keep the passports separated, car by car. I took the ones for our car—he was going to do it but I told him not to bother. When I had ours in my hand, I dropped the others. He bent down to pick them up and while he wasn't looking . . . it was easy."

No, it wasn't and she told him so. He went on talking, soft and drowsy now. He said some sweet things so she said some, too. She didn't mean them, not a chance of that, no sir, but no harm done, what did it matter if she lied a little? Didn't say she loved him, never told that kind of lie. Just things like "I'm so happy." Crap like that.

From outside, there came noises: hollow clangs and ringing crashes. Train was loading on the ferry. Whistles, deep and long, and then the rocking of the water. Out of England. He insisted on looking out the window. Nothing there to see, she told him so; just the inside of the hull, flaked paint and rusted metal.

Then he slept. It was a gentle Channel; shallow, easy swells. She watched the way he breathed, the way his chest went up and down. And when she tired of that, she listened to his sleep sounds; he made nice ones, soft and comfortable. And for the longest time, she watched his face. Was it that interesting? No, surely not. A decent face, no more than that. She kissed it anyway. It needed shaving. Had she slept? She didn't think so. Five o'clock. They would be docking soon. She shook him.

# XIX

The train was moving, really moving now. He'd have to jump soon. He was crouching on the bottom step with Carrie just behind. The air was damp and cold. Still dark. He tensed his legs, got ready. There were things out there, dark shapes like posts or pillars, God knows what, and if he hit one, he was dead. He jumped.

He'd thought about it, worked it out. You tucked up, somersaulted when you hit, the way the Packers used to. Lew Brock and Tony Canadeo, early 40's, he had seen them do it, tuck it up and roll. He landed on his ass. The stones were sharp. They hurt. Another roll. He lay there all curled up. The train wheels crashed and clattered.

He uncurled. The arms and legs moved; nothing broken. Where was Carrie? Had she made it? "Carrie?" Couldn't hear, the frigging train. He stood, felt dizzy, went to one knee, looked around. The train was going, going, gone. Behind him, half a mile or so, he saw the faint lights of the Calais station, blurred by morning mist. And, closer to him, switches, signal poles, the stuff of railroad yards.

"Carrie?"

"Over here."

"I'm coming." On his feet. Where was she, where the hell was over here? "Where are you?"

She was sitting in a shallow ditch, not moving, but she looked up when he came. He helped her stand. She leaned against him, feeling heavy, holding on.

"You okay?"

"Fine." She shook her head. "Just got a little scared, that's all."

"Me too." A little? If she hadn't been behind him on the steps, a witness—like the girls at recess on the playground, watching who pushed who around—would he have jumped?

He held her for a moment more, then turned. They started up the tracks, back toward the station. Slowly, carefully, they walked across the ties. A little stiff and sore. No hurry; it was early, if they missed one train, there'd be another. They would buy their tickets, just like everybody else, and ride to Paris like commuters. They had no francs, which meant they'd have to use her Eurocard again. It didn't really matter, leaving Carrie's name behind. The Yard would find out who she was—the luggage in the Hertz car or the woman in the ticket window. Lots of trail to follow but the Yard would take a while, maybe days, to pick it up.

The station was a grim place, dimly lit and littered with remains of yesterday. 6:35. They bought their tickets, sat and waited for the 7:10 to Paris. Quiet, nothing going on. He longed for coffee, watched the tiny café open; fresh brioche and hissing steam. Then people started coming, gray and sleepy, and an old man tottered in with the morning papers.

Two neat bundles. Took them to the newsstand in the corner. News. He stood up, stopped. No money.

"Carrie?"

"Yes, I know." She held a hand out and he helped her up. "I guess we steal them."

It was after seven and their train was boarding. They headed for the newsstand. Paris papers: *Le Monde* and *Figaro*. Carrie asked the vendor for a magazine—up there, behind him—and he turned and Melvil grabbed and Carrie said she'd read it, "*Je regrette, m'sieur.*"

They boarded. Lots of empty seats. They sat down and the whistle blew. He opened up *Le Monde*. He had to hunt to find the article. Two paragraphs under International News. That was something to be thankful for: they weren't French news yet. *Le Monde* was statesmanlike, as usual. It took the long view, which was no mean trick in that short an article. Some stuff about the value of art to the nation and the need for cooperation between governments and how, when justice was done, the chalice would reside, *sans doute*, among the glories of the Louvre.

*Le Figaro* had more to say. The front page, toward the bottom. Quoting an official Scotland Yard release. The Yard had reason to believe the chalice had been brought to England, Dr. Melvil West was sought for questioning, there seemed to be an unidentified woman in the case, all ports were closed, the search was on. No photographs: not yet. It couldn't last. Somebody would remember—the bobby at Victoria Station, the porter on the train—and by the time *France Soir* came out that afternoon, he'd be all over it.

The train was racketing along. His stomach heaved a little and his butt hurt from the stones. He looked at her. She took his hand and patted it.

"It's not so bad," she said.

"It's not?"

She told him what she thought they ought to do. He liked the sound of it. They'd take the Blue Train to the South of France. It left, if she remembered right, at ten and they could make it easily. It was some train, the Blue Train: six-course lunches, private rooms. They'd take a room, keep out of sight.

"We'll leave the train at Cannes," she said, "and take a cab to St. Tropez."

"Why St. Tropez?"

She told him: yachts. She knew a lot of men who owned them. Private yachts. The harbor there was always full of them; bored men with boats, nowhere to go, and glad to take a pretty girl to Corsica. She knew because she'd cruised the Côte d'Azur—"on land and sea" was how she said it—years ago, when she was young.

He didn't like the thought of Carrie cruising; not one bit. "How old were you?"

"Oh, seventeen or so, I guess."

"Alone in Europe?"

"Sure."

"Your parents let you go alone?"

"They didn't let. I went."

"And all these men . . ." He couldn't say it.

"What about them? Do you want to know did I put out or how old was I when I lost it?"

"No." He really didn't. "I don't want to know about it."

"Any time."

"Forget it." But he couldn't. Rich men—were they young or old or both?—with polished nails and alligator shoes. And she was just a kid and they had used her. "Carrie?"

"It's all right." She gave a little grin and took his hand and held it all the way to Paris.

Busy station. The Blue Train left from the Gare de Lyon, a twenty-minute taxi ride but they could make it easily enough unless the cab got stuck in traffic. Carrie seemed to know her way. She hurried down the platform, threading through the crush of people. Almost nine and all the world was on its way to work.

The air was warm, a spring day for the books. He'd been to Paris several times before but never once for pleasure—meetings or research, Museum affairs. Lord, all the time he'd wasted and the things he'd never done: the Bateau Mouche for dinner, candlelight and Carrie.

They were in the lobby now and she was just ahead. The crowd was thick and someone shoved him and he got stuck for a moment behind some nuns. He'd lost her, where the devil was she? Over there, near those two gendarmes, standing at a newsstand.

Could that be his picture in the paper? Gray face, stiff and stodgy-looking, was that him? He blinked. His name was there, too, in the headlines. London papers. DR. M. WEST, WEST AND MYSTERY WOMAN, CURATOR AND UNIDENTIFIED FEMALE ACCOMPLICE.

He felt as if all movement stopped and everyone was looking at him, in particular the two gendarmes. He grinned at them, at least he thought it was a grin, and tugged at Carrie. She was talking gaily to the news vendor as she piled up London papers: *Times, Express, Observer*. Fluent French, it came so fast he couldn't follow. Did she mean for him to steal them? She unzipped her purse—the chalice; could the gendarmes see it?—took a ten-spot out. The vendor frowned. She smiled. He shrugged. She winked. He took it.

Carrie turned to him, still smiling, handed him the papers. Were the gendarmes watching? "Slow and easy," Carrie said and took his hand. They headed for the exit through the crowd. He had to think. The train was out, they couldn't risk it. He'd be spotted if he hadn't been already. What to do?

They made it to the street. He turned, looked back. No gendarmes.

"There's an empty," Carrie said.

He turned and saw the taxi, hailed it. They got in. She rattled off instructions. They were moving, traffic everywhere, horns honking.

"Where are we going?"

"To a bank. We've got to get some francs."

"Then what?"

"I don't know yet."

"That's great."

She turned on him. "You know what you can do? Go—"

"Sorry." It was up to him to think of something. The cab was at a standstill. There was shouting now, fists out of windows. Impossible to concentrate. Besides, he had to see those papers.

He was big in London. Front-page articles in both the *Times* and *Observer*. Quotes from everywhere. (1) From New York: there was a warrant out for his arrest, they'd picked up the American Express charge on his ticket, knew he'd gone to England. (2) From Washington: a report of a formal request to Whitehall for assistance in his apprehension and for prompt return of the chalice to American authorities pending its rightful disposition. (3) From Whitehall: a formal reply to the American request, promising full cooperation in hunting him down but getting very vague and diplomatic as to what Her Majesty's Government would do with the chalice once it had it in its hands. (4) From Scotland Yard: a full report of yesterday's activities up to and including their escape from Heathrow, detailed descriptions of them both, assurance of a quick conclusion to what seemed to be developing into a nationwide manhunt. (5) From South Cadbury: a telephone interview with Sir Winston who was sticking to his story—or the truth or what he believed to be the truth—that the chalice West had stolen was indeed the Holy Grail which he had found.

Some small things to be thankful for. Nobody knew they'd gotten out of England or who Carrie was; at least, not last night when the papers went to press. But she had used her Eurocard and they would find it, find her name. They might have found it out already and for all he knew, she was as hot as he was. He was looking at his picture when it came to him. A blinding flash.

"Carrie?"

She read faster than he did and she was looking out the window, frowning, thinking as the cab oozed down the street. She didn't seem to hear.

"I've got it, Carrie."

"What?" She turned.

It sort of dried up on him, and he didn't want to say it. It was just that he'd been looking at his picture and he thought, Well, Paris—Nazi-occupied, behind the lines, Krauts everyplace and he was Errol Flynn and what would Flynn do? Tie a silk around his neck, clap on a beret, light a Gauloise; wouldn't fool a seventh-grader but the Krauts all took him for a Frenchman.

He told her—not the Flynn part, just the general idea—and forty minutes later, after stopping at the bank, he was in a boutique on the Boulevard St. Germain. According to the mirror in the dressing room, he looked sensational. Starting at the bottom, he was wearing boots. Then blue jeans—faded-looking; how could they be new and faded-looking? Then a broad black leather belt with a terrific buckle and a sort of sweater-shirt with horizontal stripes in red and blue, a faded denim jacket and—be still, my heart—a silk square at his throat.

Her outfit was the same as his: boots, denims and a silk. They stood together for a second, looking in the mirror. She was frowning, tugging at her jacket. She was his. His what, exactly? Mistress, friend, accomplice? What a world.

They paid and went out to the boulevard and down two blocks to Le Drugstore where they bought a pocket radio and lunar-looking sunglasses. He felt unrecognizable.

And hungry. They crossed the street and took a table at the Deux Magots, out on the sidewalk in the sunshine, ordered four ham sandwiches and two

Camparis. There was much to talk about. The problem was their transportation. Planes and trains and buses, all the public means were out. They couldn't buy a car or rent one, not without filling in forms and that meant names and driver's licenses. Hitchhiking was a possibility but not a very good one; there were risks, like standing on the road for hours getting nowhere, anyone might recognize them.

No solution yet. The sandwiches were good. He ordered more Campari and they sat and thought and watched the people come and go. Young people, mostly; students, scruffy, dressed in blue jeans. The Ecole des Beaux Arts was around the corner and they drifted in for coffee or a drink: on foot, on bikes, and lots of them on Vespas, Hondas, motorbikes, all kinds.

He looked at all the motorbikes and shook his head. "You know," he said, "I wouldn't get on one of those, not if you paid me."

Carrie turned, looked at him hard. "Just stay right here," she said. She stood up very straight and, looking good enough to eat, strolled over to the bikes. There was a shiny red one and she stopped and touched it, looked at it admiringly. It must have taken twenty seconds for the guy to get there. Beard, long hair and blue jeans, toothy smile. She smiled back. He offered her a cigarette. She took it. In a minute, half a dozen guys were out there, all jammed in around her.

Then there she was, back at their table with her hand out and he came up with a wad of bills. "We paid too much," she told him when he joined her at the curb. She'd bought the red one and no questions asked. She got on, kicked the kickstand back. "Let's go."

He had to do it so he did. He sat behind her, reached for something to grab on to. Nothing. He was terrified of horses and at least they came with saddle horns.

"Hold on to me."

She didn't have to tell him twice. He closed his eyes and wrapped both arms around her.

"Ready?" As he'd ever be. The motor coughed. The whole thing shook. Unsafe at any speed. He risked a look around. Her hands were doing something with the handlebars, her foot moved, they were off. He put on ten years getting out of Paris.

It was a little better on the highway; no more sudden stops, U-turns, trucks inches from his knees. The A-6 was six lanes wide and they were whipping down it toward the Riviera. Her purse was on his lap, the chalice—he could feel it—tight between his knees. His eyes were slits, the wind sang in his ears. There was a little traffic, not much scenery to speak of; superhighways look alike. The sun felt warm. They stopped for tolls and once for gas. No chance to talk while they were moving. They had gone, he guessed, about one hundred fifty miles. Almost two o'clock.

Signs up ahead. She slowed, pulled off the highway at a Jacques Borel—gas and food. Like Howard Johnson's, but exactly: clean and bright and fundamentally depressing. Didn't matter; anything to get him off that damned machine.

They found a booth and sat. She ordered. Soup and sandwiches, some fruit and cheese. She'd brought in the transistor and she turned it on.

"What for?" he asked.

"The news."

Pop music for the moment, soft and tinny. She looked wonderful. Her cheeks glowed from the sun and wind. She took their road map out—they got it when they stopped for gas—and looked it over. They were near Auxerre, she said, and showed him. Little dot about three inches south of Paris.

"Where's St. Tropez?"

She unfolded the map, ran a fingertip along the blue at the bottom. "Here."

"How far?"

She shrugged. "Four hundred miles, maybe more. That's eight, nine hours on the bike. We may not make it, not today." She frowned. "Could be we'll have to find someplace to spend the night."

"When do you think we'll get to Corsica?"

"That's hard to say. Tomorrow night, the next day. What's your guess about this fellow, What's-his-name, in Calvi?"

"Kalman. Stefan Kalman. I don't know." He frowned. "We know what Kalman's story is; we've read it in the papers. How his father was an archeologist and dug around the menhirs and the monoliths; and how his father found the chalice and some other gold and silver plate; and how the chalice has been sitting in his home, in his collection, all these years.

"That's all we really know. It's not enough. The story could be true; I've heard some stranger ones. It raises questions, that's all. Questions like, well, Kalman's a collector so he knows he's sitting there with a Pasiteles. It's written on the bottom, all he has to do is read it. So he's got a treasure worth a fortune and he knows it. But he keeps it secret. How? Does he stuff it in a shoe box, take it out at night? And why? He doesn't tell a soul, he can't have, anyone who'd seen it would have talked, it's too important. Why behave like that? And why, after he's kept it secret thirty years, why turn around and sell it?"

"Money. That's why people sell things. But you're right about—" She stopped because the soup arrived, the music ended and the news came on.

He leaned across the table toward the radio. The French was fast but some of it he couldn't miss. Like "Docteur Malveal Vast" for instance, or "Mlle. Cahroleen Gardnair." They had identified her. Swell. What else did they know? *"Echappé,"* he heard, and *"Angleterre."* Escaped from England, must have found her Eurocard. And more. They had been seen in France. The gendarmes at the station? Disappeared in Paris. Still presumed to be there. Then descriptions of them. Both of them.

Carrie flicked it off and said lightly, "You might at least say welcome to the club."

How could she sit there eating? "Let's get out of here."

She took another bite. "Don't worry. They don't know about the bike and even if they did, they don't know where to look. It's a big country, France, with lots of Vespas in it. Eat your lunch."

He paid at the cashier's desk, bought some chocolate bars; quick energy, you never knew. The sun was still warm as they crossed the parking lot. Some kids ran past, a couple with a dog, then two policemen. Highway patrol. He didn't stiffen, didn't tighten up. Just nodded and they nodded back and strolled on, slow and easy, to the restaurant, two nice guys on their way to lunch. And all he'd heard as they went by, the only phrase that caught his ear, went something like: "*. . .ah, oui, un Vespa rouge.*"

He told her not to worry, that it didn't mean a thing. The cop could have a cousin with a red one or he'd seen one in a window and admired it and even if they knew in Paris, France was big, they couldn't cover all the roads. She looked at him and nodded.

"Sure," was all she said.

They got off the superhighway at Auxerre. The country roads were safer. Biking through the Côtes del Beaune was not a thing that fugitives were apt to do. He'd dreamed for years of doing Burgundy, but not like this. A bottle at a time, a little open car, a girl; just drifting, gently buzzed, from town to town. He watched the signs go by: Clos-Vougeot, Nuits-St.-Georges.

The time went quickly as they rolled along through little towns and open countryside. There was some local traffic and he saw some farmers in the fields. The green of spring was everywhere.

There were long shadows suddenly. The sun was sinking. It was five o'clock, the air was cool. They stopped for coffee and some cognac in a country town, St. Something, east of Lyons. After that, the darkness came. A clear night, stars and moon and cold. It felt like winter and the day had been so warm. Off to his left, there in the east, a strange horizon: jagged, rough, what looked like white stuff on the top. A sign went by. Grenoble. Where they held the Winter Games? He felt her shivering in his arms.

She slowed down, pulled up on the shoulder, stopped. He pointed east. She nodded.

"Alps," she said.

"You didn't tell me."

"I forgot."

"A detail like the Alps?" She shrugged and smiled. "We've got to get a room."

"We can't."

He felt insanely angry. He was in his denims in the Alps and he had money. Why, why couldn't he seek shelter? She explained. The inns of France were tigers when it came to passports, *cartes d'identité*, police forms. Didn't matter who you slept with, you could take your sheep to bed but not without its name and address on the register.

The wind cut through his clothes. A car went by. It's headlights touched her face. Her eyes were watering. Exhausted, drawn, thin cheeks, dead white. He put his arms around her.

"Carrie?"

"I'm okay."

"I'll drive."

He sat behind the handlebars. He felt her close behind him. He'd been watching her all day and he could do it. This thing turned and that thing pushed. The motor farted—had he killed it? No. It coughed and held and they were moving, wobbling, Jesus keep it on the road.

He saw the situation clearly. If you couldn't stop, you kept on going. And he was going to go the fastest way. Back to the superhighway and the hell with it. He took a right. Farmland, deserted. Sign ahead. St.-Etienne-de-St.-G. Could that be what it said? He kept on going. There were lights. A town. More signs. Valence—he thought of curtains, was it curtains for them?—and another sign. A-6. 10 kilometres.

Out of town and into dark again and then, dim light ahead. A little more and he could see, what was that, tollbooths? Absolutely. She was clinging to him, trembling from the cold. He had to think of something. Shelter. Had to find some. He slowed the bike down, stopped it more or less where he intended, fished for change and looked at her.

"I'm fine," she said.

"You look it." He handed her a chocolate bar and drove up, hardly wobbling, to the tollbooth, paid his toll and revved the motor. It was then he saw the trucks. Huge vans, three or four, pulled up along the sides, the drivers catching sleep. Familiar, they were always stopped by tolls at night and he was almost past the last one when he thought of it.

He braked, pulled over, stopped, got off. "Come on," he said. "Just stay a little bit behind me and look shy."

He stepped up on the running board, peered in. The driver—huge man, bald and powerful—was sleeping. Not the kind to take it kindly, being wakened up. He hesitated, made a fist and rapped.

The driver wasn't happy, you could hear him grunting through the glass. He pulled the window down, growled something. Melvil didn't understand. No matter, he was going to do this Carrie's way: her stories worked because she used her feelings. So he looked embarrassed, shivered from the cold, put on a man-to-man face, leered at Carrie, didn't speak a word. The driver grinned.

He turned to Carrie, nodded. Then he went back to the Vespa—couldn't leave the damn thing on the highway overnight for any cop to see—and wheeled it around the van. He heard the driver grunting as he wrestled with the loading door. He hurried to the rear. The door was open, he could make out wooden crates inside. He gave a hand to Carrie, helped her up and heaved in after her.

The door clanged shut. They felt their way around and found an open place. They sat and pressed against each other, holding tight. He felt a little warmer. In a while, when her shivering stopped, they stretched out close together, side by side. She clutched her bag—the chalice: his or was it theirs now?—with one arm. He held her very close.

It was funny, life was. You were sure—because you had a good mind and you thought about it—what your choices were. They disappeared as you grew older, life was conical, the walls closed in. Then one day, someone took you through a door you hadn't seen and you were young again with possibilities. He tried to put it into words for her. She told him he exaggerated, kissed him lightly, lips still cold. Not cold like Dido's lips; that was another kind of cold. Poor Dido. Poor in what way? Poor in husband; what a poor one he had been. Afraid and angry and dishonest; God, the lying, all the lies he'd told. The worst kind: lies about his feelings. He must never do that any more. No lies to Carrie.

"Carrie?" Was she sleeping? It was pitch-black and he couldn't see a thing. "I love you."

Silence; then a whisper from the darkness near his

ear. "If ever, if I ever for a minute think you do, I'll leave you."

"No." He shook his head and kissed her hair. "You'd never do that."

"Try me."

No more talk. He held her tighter, that was all.

The driver woke them up at four. Still dark. Still cold. The sky was gray though, in the east. There would be sun soon.

ST. TROPEZ—QUINZE KILOMETRES. Carrie sat back in the taxicab and watched the ragged beauties of the *Massif* roll by out the window. Wondrous countryside: sharp, sudden drops of rockface to the sea, stands of twisted pine and wild brush, strung through with rows of saplings, the legacy of summer fires. She liked her scenery stark. Those picture-postcard-sunset-through-the-palm-fronds scenes were pretty, if you cared for pretty. This was beautiful.

It was a little after twelve and she was feeling good. Excited, tense and good. She was entitled to. The day had started, it seemed days ago, at four o'clock. The truckdriver woke them. It was dark and freezing cold and as she stood there looking at the bike, one thing was crystal clear: they had to ditch the thing. A man and woman riding on a Vespa *rouge* down empty roads: they might as well send up a flare.

The driver was an easy mark. She smiled at him and shivered, said a few well-chosen words. The driver listened, grunted—"*Oui, d'accord.*" He even gave a hand to Melvil, helped him heave the Vespa up inside the van.

They all three settled in the cab. The driver's name was Guido and he came from Naples and his French was terrible. Which didn't hurt: no need to talk, no stories to invent. His destination was Toulon. Terrific. St. Tropez was down the coast, just sixty miles or so.

She longed to play the radio, to catch the morning

news. No way, not with a red Vespa in the back. They stopped at six, another Jacques Borel. Eggs, coffee and brioche. No morning papers yet.

It was ten o'clock when they pulled in to Toulon. The day was warm and sunny. Guido dropped them in a warehouse area. They thanked him, got the Vespa started, drove around until they found a junkyard, left it there. They walked to *centre ville* and bought the morning papers: two from Marseilles and a *Nice-Matin.* The front-page stuff was local news but they were featured toward the back. The boy they bought the Vespa from had spotted Melvil—they had left their London papers at the café: that was smart—and he had gone to the police. The hunt was on, all ports had been alerted, there was no escape and *Vive la France*. She dumped the papers in a trash can and they got the taxicab.

It was warm in the taxi and she yawned. She hadn't slept much in the truck and when she had, bad dreams. No matter, normal, par for Carrie's course, she had them all the time and they were gone now, brushed away, forgotten; just about.

ST. TROPEZ—DIX KILOMETRES. Didi's villa wasn't far away. Except in time; a million years ago. She'd paid her dues at Didi's summer place. How many bedrooms? Seventeen? Had she been laid in all of them? It felt like that but it had only been the yellow room, bright chintzes, bed complete with canopy. Ah, what a smart young thing she was. Was there a smart young thing she hadn't done? Her first and only overdose, her one and only pregnancy. My goodness, yes, a lot of memories of St. Tropez. A lot of drinks and pills and boys and girls and fun and games and wasn't she a lucky girl to be alive. She shivered and he asked her what the trouble was. It wasn't anything, she said.

ST. TROPEZ—CINQ KILOMETRES. At least she knew the territory: what to do and where to do it. All the action was along the port. The little harbor on the left, a pleasure boat at every dock. And running by the docks, the promenade, the main drag, thick with nuts and creeps and dykes and fags and millionaires and movie people. What a groove.

And facing on the promenade, the bars and restaurants. All bulging, stuffed like sausages with people on the make and makers; givers, takers. Getting picked up was like catching cold in London: unavoidable. The trick, no pun intended, was to know what you were looking for and where to find it. At cocktail time, La Pinède wasn't bad and late at niqht, the club up at Byblos. But if a girl were on the make at lunchtime, she would take the merchandise and park it at L'Escale. But not just anyplace inside. You had to know which tables, know the right ones from the wrong ones. Those tables on the right just by the bar, that's where the boys with big boats took their pleasure, listing into their martinis.

ST. TROPEZ-CENTRE VILLE. The taxi took the turn, moved slowly toward the edge of town. The sun was something and the sea, what you could see of it, was glittery and blue. The port itself—they couldn't see it yet but the *vieux port* was really rather beautiful except for all the people always mucking up the view. Where they were now was dumpy, though. Shabby cottages, shops with marine supplies, a monstrous parking lot, some tacky modern buildings by a small, depressing square. She told the driver this was it. They got out. Melvil paid. It cost a fortune.

Simple-looking soul, the driver. Still, he was a risk, you didn't get a fare like this one every day. And Guido, too. This afternoon, tonight, tomorrow, one of them would see their photos, put it all together. What the hell, they'd be long gone by then.

She stood up tall and stretched. Joints cracked: her fingers, toes, knees, elbows, like a pan of popcorn.

Glorious. She scrunched her eyes closed tight, threw back her head and let the sun pour over her.

"So this is St. Tropez," he said.

Could that be wonder in his voice? She looked at him. His eyes were big and he was looking like a kid again and it was sentimental of her, being touched by all this kid stuff, and she made a note to cut it out.

"Look, here's the thing." She pointed down the narrow street ahead. It ended in a little wharf and water. "Just around the corner to the left, they've got this dandy art museum, so why don't you go have a look and I'll come get you when we've got a ride." He shook his head. "Oh, come on, Melvil—"

"If you think I'm going to let you pick some guy up in a bar and not be there in case—"

"In case what?"

"Just in case."

It was embarrassing enough, she didn't want him watching from across the room. "Oh, come on, I'm a big girl." But he wasn't having any and the best she could do was get his promise that he wouldn't interfere.

"Okay," he mumbled, hands jammed in his pockets, "I don't like it but okay."

"Let's go." They started down the little street. No noise. The air was full of sea smells, fresh and good. They turned right at the corner, stopped.

"Oh shit," she said.

"For God's sake, Carrie, where are all the boats?"

The port was empty. Not a yacht in sight. A half a dozen fishing boats in from the morning's catch, nets drying in the sun. And not a creep in sight. No crowds, no fags, no nuts; just one small French boy running home with bread for lunch.

A bad dream? No, it wasn't. Time of year, that's what it was. The end of April, start of May, she'd lost the date: it didn't matter, all that mattered was that no one came to St. Tropez this time of year. Oh God, she'd brought them here, dead end—

No, wait. The date did matter. Easter was a week or so ago and people came at Easter. Not a lot of people, mostly just the very rich. As for the yachts, they might be anchored at some other port nearby: Ste. Maxime, Port Grimaud. And they would come, the yachtsmen would, to St. Tropez for lunch.

She told him all about it as they walked along the port. "We'll be okay. The only thing is, I won't have a lot of men to choose from and I've got to find the right one. It could take a little while, that's all."

They passed another couple: Germans, middle-aged. Mic-Mac was open. So was Choses. Last year's resort wear, next year's prices. Tacky T-shirts, poorly made, and why for God's sake did she like them? Was there time to shop around, pick out a thing or two? She tore her eyes away.

L'Escale was coming up soon. There were people to be seen now eating lunch alfresco in the other restaurants along the port. Not many people: some. They looked like locals, on the whole: shopkeepers, farmers, fishermen. At one table, a family group, four generations; old and toothless down to young and toothless and she felt a sudden wash of memory, as if in some life she'd been a member of a family.

She stopped and nodded. This was where they split. "Five minutes, give me five; then you come in. But not before."

"Okay."

"And sit across the room."

She turned and left him there. He really liked her. Like was fine; but love—had he said love last night? No time for that. She paused and for a moment, like an actress, she prepared. Tensed the muscles in her bottom, bunched them up. The proper movement of the butt was vital. Never jiggle. Round and proud and unavailable: that was the look it wanted. Posture next. Straight, very tall, the shoulders imperceptibly thrown back so that the breasts—and this was delicate, vulgarity was just around the corner, must not thrust—so that the breasts displayed themselves. Then head erect and eyes straight forward, never any movement of the eyes; you never looked like you were looking.

In she went, not seeing much of anything. The key tables by the bar—that much she saw—were empty. Moving at the proper speed—that is to say, as slow as possible without creating the impression you were up for sale—she headed for the tables. Paused, as if it mattered which of three she chose; it didn't.

She sat and flung the glance she used at "21" to summon waiters. None in sight, of course, but expectation, the assumption that one's wishes would be granted, added to the ambience. What one expected in this life, one got.

Everything smelled good. Food was being served around her: *soupe de poisson, loup grillé*—she loved it—*steak et pommes frites*. Ravenous, she wanted everything in sight. Her stomach grumbled and the waiter came.

A vodka tonic and a package of Gitanes, a slice of pâté and a steak and French fries. All time-tested choices, pick-up food. The drink because it helped the man to think the girl was high. The cigarettes—they always made her slightly ill and dizzy—were for openings. E.g., "You smoke my brand, I see," or "Want a light?" or "Never tried that French tobacco. Is it blah blah blah?" As for the food, you had to order simple things. Not simple cooking; simple eating. Soups or fish or sauces, out. You had to watch the pickup, concentrate on him.

The room was fairly empty; fifteen, twenty people. Mostly locals, here and there a tourist. Any live ones? Still too soon to tell. Her drink came and she drank it.

She was thirsty and it tasted good. She signaled for another one and West came walking in.

If you could call it walking. Thudding was more like it, stomping to a table right across the room. He sat and stared at her. There was a local next to him, a farmer or a fisherman. It wasn't fair: no yachts and out of season, zero action in the room and he kept staring. She took a good rip at the package of Gitanes. It didn't open.

"*Fräulein, wollen sie eine cigarette?*"

She turned. Von Stroheim to the teeth. Bald as a mothball, beady eyes. She gave him her myopic look, the one that read, "I can't make you out yet but hang in there."

"*Bitte?*" Von Stroheim's hand came forward. Held between two fingers like a claw of bratwurst was a cigarette. She examined the hand for signs of wealth: rings, cuff links, bracelets, wrist watch. Nothing, but she reached out for the cigarette—not sure about him but she mustn't let a live one get away. She was about to thank him when a voice she knew well called, "*Garçon!*"

West. He didn't have to shout the walls down, did he? Could have killed him but her German stood there and she had to smile, she had to or she'd lose him. Naturally, the smile came out wrong and all he did was light her cigarette and go away. Her hand was trembling: rage, or was it nerves? Her glass was empty so she signaled for another. Did he think she liked what she was doing? Feeling like a piece of meat? That's all the men there thought she was: prime tenderloin. Her eyes began to sting. She wiped them, didn't see the new one coming.

"May I offer you a drink?"

"Yes-no-I've-ordered-one." It came out like one word. She bit her lip. This one was English, fifty-five or so, a little limp but you could never tell with Englishmen. Big diamond ring, one of those thick gold

I.D. bracelets that she hated and a Piaget watch. Terrific.

"Didn't catch that." He was smiling. "May I?"

Her drink came. "As you see . . ." She smiled contritely, oh so sory that she had one.

"Ah." He smiled as if defeated and for just a second Carrie wondered who was conning whom.

She paused—the right pause at the right time could be critical. "Some friends are coming . . ." Thoughtfully she put out the cigarette, which was making her sick in any event. Time for the quick, shy smile. She let him have one. "Do sit down."

He sat and snapped his fingers, ordering champagne. A little much, but times were desperate and she mustn't lose another one. His name was Monty and he'd come down over Easter and she drank her drink and tried to pay attention but she kept on darting looks at West. What was he going to do next, what new outrage? He was talking to his fisherman and scowling at her. Why was he so mean? Her pâté came. She couldn't touch it, had a cigarette instead. The waiter poured champagne, she drank it and her Englishman was playing kneesies, for the love of God, and it was time to bring the subject up. With subtle skill.

"I love boats and I thought for certain there would be some boats here." Sigh and smile. "Big ones."

Which reminded Monty of the big boat he'd been asked to lunch on. Adolf Mannehim's boat, you've heard of him of course, but it had steamed off early morning, no one bothering to call, and he had driven down from Ste. Maxime for nothing, shocking lack of manners, only now he'd met her and that made the day worthwhile, don't you know.

She knew it was important, Adolf Manehim was important. Mannheim knew important things, it was important that they see him, talk to him. She tried to clear her head, she couldn't think about that now, she had a fish to catch.

She sighed, a sad one, "Such a lovely day and I'd give anything to go out sailing." Not very classy but she didn't care, past caring, everything depended on her. One more sigh. "Just anything." Small shrug. "You know . . ."

He knew all right. He had a boat. With sails. Three masts, a crew of eight. He licked his lips. She'd landed him. His hand was on her knee, ascending, and she reached across the table, just to touch his cheek and West kept staring at her: daggers.

The champagne. Someone spilled it. Carrie spilled it, look what Carrie did. All over, on the table, on his shirt and jacket, oh dear God. She reached out for her bag, grabbed at it, spilled the other glass. It didn't matter, nothing mattered, Kleenex in the bag, to wipe him off. The zipper stuck, it wouldn't open, and her Englishman—where was he? Getting up, all full of napkins, napkins everywhere all over him. And leaving, he was leaving her. He looked so funny but it wasn't funny. Was she crying? Were those tears? She touched her face. Her hands were sticky.

"Carrie?"

West. She looked up. There he was. Right by her table. With his fisherman. His arm around his stupid fisherman.

"You're so mean." It wasn't what she meant to say. Her lips were quivering. "How could you be so mean."

"Jesus, Carrie, what's the matter?"

Red. Red was what she saw, she actually saw it. Up she stood. Straight up, shot up like a rocket. Knocked the table over. Knew she'd done it, saw it go. She didn't hear it, didn't feel it, either. All she felt was dizzy. Drunk? She wasn't, she was sober, absolutely sober and her head was clear. She felt a little queasy, that was all; because the room was turning.

She was lying down. She'd fallen. God, the last indignity. She felt like dying. West was there, his arm around her, holding her.

"Are you all right?"

"I hate you."

"I've got news, great news."

"You do? Well, fuck you and your news."

"This is Jean-Paul."

The fisherman bent over her. "Well, fuck him too."

*"Allô, bébé."*

Jean-Paul was stoned. Out of his mind. Kept weaving back and forth as if he stood on stormy seas.

"Jean-Paul is a fisherman."

*"Ça va, Jean-Paul?"*

"His mother's birthday is tomorrow. She'll be eighty-nine."

*"Joyeux anniversaire."*

"His mother lives in Corsica."

It registered. *"Vous avez un bateau, Jean-Paul?"*

*"Oui, oui, bébé."*

She laughed. Their boat—they had their boat.

The *St. Etienne*. Jean-Paul's *bateau* looked older than his mother. Fifty feet, high in the bow and stern, pure Provençal. And moored across the street. Too much.

The sun, the sky, the laughing, everything was too much, they were laughing, all of them, and West was kissing her or trying to and Jean-Paul was careening back and forth, a bottle of marc in one hand, unmooring the boat, more or less.

Then Jean-Paul crouching, poking at his motor, got it started. Fabulous. It sounded like Camille. The thing was moving. On the sea. The *St. Etienne* was moving. Someone ought to take the tiller. Jean-Paul took it. Didn't hit a thing. He missed the dock, he missed the buoys, the sea wall. In the clear. They made it.

Harbor looking smaller, smaller. Lots of talk from

Jean-Paul. Gravel voice. Like Gabin, Jean Gabin; he even looked a little like him: short and stocky, gray and tough, kept calling her *bébé,* she loved it. Loved West, too, the way he felt, his arm around her and she felt like purring, wasn't she his kitten? She rubbed up against him, let the sun drift down. Jean-Paul was singing something Corsican. It would feel nice to sing. She said so and West asked her if she knew "Ninety-nine Bottles of Beer on the Wall." She didn't but she'd learn it if he liked. He taught it to her. Stupid song. They sang it for the longest time.

# XXI

He woke up feeling good. A quiet, lazy kind of good; all soft and drifting, wrapped in cotton. No confusion; knew where he was right away. On wooden floorboards, that was where. On Jean-Paul's boat. And that was Carrie's bottom, her adorable, her perfect bottom pressed against him. And his rod, his ramrod, stiff inside his trousers, flagpole straight. Could Jean-Paul see it? Did it matter? No, not much.

He made his body long and tense and then relaxed it. Nothing ached, not anyplace. Except his dick. He grinned and let his eyes come open. Mist, that's all there was, mist everyplace. Faint light. The sun, apparently, was up, just barely, blanketed in mist. The motor chugged, like coffee bubbling in the next room, warm and comfortable.

He sat up slowly, looked out. Nothing anywhere but haze. The sea was flat as bed sheets, had been all along, the whole time. In the stern, Jean-Paul sat, tiller nestled in his armpit: awake, asleep, you couldn't tell. And Carrie—looking at her almost felt like pain—deep-sleeping, head against one arm, the other arm around the brown bag, all curled up; around the chalice.

He wriggled toward the rail, not far to go, and put his elbows on it, then his chin, looked out into the mist. It would feel wonderful to pee. He thought about it, then he stood and watched the arc he made. Amazing; Melvil West was peeing in the ocean.

The trip across the sea had been a dream. A small

dream, little things, no great events. A lot of singing and a lot of drink and Carrie, like the sweet-sixteen she'd never had the luck to be, on holiday, that's how she'd seemed; as if real life were closed for summer vacation.

They had sailed along the coast, steep cliffs, the little islands with the ruins on them built by Richard *Coeur de Lion* on crusade, then villas, great hotels, Maugham's house. All this came from Carrie; Jean-Paul talked mainly about the fish beds. In and out the coast curved. Cézanne never did it from the sea; he should have come and looked at it.

She had mentioned Mannheim, brought up how his yacht had been in St. Tropez and gone off suddenly. A subject worth investigating. Not the yacht: nothing odd about it being there or taking off. The man. What did he know, if anything? If Kalman's story didn't hold, what did that do to Mannehim's? Plenty. He must think about it—but some other time, when Carrie wasn't in his arms and all that sun and brandy in the air.

They left the shore behind at Monte Carlo and Jean-Paul produced another bottle. *Myrte,* he calle it. Made in Corsica. A kind of brandy; myrtle-flavored. Myrtle grew there in profusion and his people gathered it and made it. Raw and rich and fiery; like Jean-Paul, like the man himself. He'd never met a man like Jean-Paul, not to sit and talk to, and he'd always felt a little bit afraid of them.

Jean-Paul had talked for hours. Heavy accent but the words came slowly and with feeling. All about his island and his family and how hard it was to be away so much. His mother lived near L'Île Rousse. Tiny town. A little harbor, not much fishing—which was why he lived and worked in France—a railroad station, two hotels, a Citroën garage, a marketplace and 1,800 people. *Two* hotels—the way he said *deux*—as remarkable as if the people had two heads. And there were statues in the square—but they would see them—and Calvi was 24 kilometers away and they could get there by a train that came *de temps en temps* or by a bus that came a little more occasionally.

His mother's house was just outside of town. It had a tile roof. His grandfather had built it; stone by stone. A mighty man, his grandfather. Came from a tiny village in the wild central highlands where Jean-Paul's relations—uncles, aunts and countless cousins—lived. Came down to the sea and built a farm; some olive trees, some lemons and some oranges and some goats.

You had to understand that Corsica was very poor and life was very simple. Everything was mountains and his family there were mostly shepherds; raising goats and kids. The land was hard and little grew except the pine trees and the chestnuts and the *maquis*. *Maquis* everywhere.

What was the *maquis?* Undergrowth: hard, thorny, tough—you couldn't kill it which was why the Underground that fought the Nazis called itself *le maquis*. Nothing like it anywhere. It wasn't just one kind of plant but many, tangled up together. Juniper, arbutus, heath, bay, myrtle, box, rosemary, lavender and spiky climbing things and cactus. Dense, too harsh for walking through but every spring, each May, there was this miracle. It blossomed. All at once, in all the colors—white and lavender and red, blue, yellow: everything was flowers and the scent of it, the perfume was—Jean-Paul had hunched his shoulders and belched—it was too beautiful for words.

And Melvil thought he smelled it now. Out in the mist. A wind was rising and the boat rocked gently and Jean-Paul was right: it was too beautiful, as if some master chef had worked for days to give him all the flowers in the world for breakfast.

He heard the sound of Carrie stirring. She came out of sleep as if it were a nightgown she were slipping off. She eased into his arms and smiled and they were holding one another when the mist around them thinned and faded, disappeared, and there, a mile or so away, was Corsica. The land rose sharply from the sea, a wild place all blanketed in flowers.

Jean-Paul was showing signs of life. He cleared his throat and stretched and spat and pointed to the marble island off to starboard—actually marble, rose-red stone that gave L'Île Rousse its name. And sheltered by it was a little bay, the harbor and the town. Orange roofs, a little curve of beach, a boat or two at anchor, houses right down to the water's edge.

And people. Tiny figures now but coming closer; people on the quai. "*Ma famille,*" Jean-Paul said, jumped up and started waving, shouting to the shore. Arms waved back to them and shouts and all at once the trip was over, they were there, boat tight against the quai, hands reaching down to help them up, harsh laughter, cries and smells of garlic, brandy, flowers.

There were fifteen, twenty people. Mostly older, mostly dressed in black. Black shawls and shapeless dresses on the women, black suits and black hats on the men. Short, stocky people, faces lined and lean, eyes dark and very bright, sharp smiles, missing teeth. All talking in some language neither he nor Carrie understood. Italian-sounding more than anything; but not Italian. Full of *oo* sounds, fast and rhythmic.

Two trucks were pulled up on the quai. Small, open farm trucks; prewar, battered. Everyone was piling in. He looked for Jean-Paul, sad to say goodbye, he didn't want to but they had to get to Calvi.

"*Non, non, non.*" Jean-Paul refused to let them go.

Because the bus began at nine or ten and God knew when the train came, if it came at all, and it was only seven and the food was cooking at his mother's house and it would be an insult if they didn't come along. With which, he bounded up into the truck, reached down a hand for each of them. The motor had no muffler; it was like New Year's Eve in Chinatown. The gears engaged, teeth gnashing. Carrie winced. One lurch. Another. They were moving.

Off the quai and up a little street and into town. Jean-Paul, fresh bottle in one hand—where had it come from?—shouting, waving, pointing out the glories of the town. The Place Paoli—tiny square, small fountain, marble bust of Pascal Paoli, the great but temporary liberator of the island. A little convent and *l'hôtel ancien Napoléon Bonaparte*—there were *rues, places, avenues* for Corsica's most famous son all over the place. Then on past L'Hôtel Le Grillon—*10 chambres, sans restaurant*—and out of town.

The road—this was the main road, highway N.199, the best in all of Corsica—was like a washboard. Two lanes wide, no shoulder, cactus, palm trees, homeless goats. You had to clench your teeth to talk or else you bit your tongue. Kissing was impossible but he was holding Carrie, nuzzling and the jiggling made it feel sensational, when she whispered in his ear.

He had her whisper it again because he thought she said, "They've all got guns."

He looked around. She had a point. He thought of jumping off the truck but they were doing forty, maybe fifty, and the road was full of rocks. He held her tighter and they stood there with the chalice pressed between them. No one knew they had it and Jean-Paul was friendly. If he were a thief he would have thrown them overboard or something. They were fine. He told her so. She nodded but she held on tight.

He didn't hear the singing till the motor died. They hadn't gone a mile when they turned sharp right onto a narrow drive, two rocky ruts that ran downhill. The driver cut the motor and they coasted. The singing came from up ahead.

They heeled around a curve and there it was: the crude stone house, the twisted olive trees, the tiny citrus grove, the rocky field, two other trucks, much smoke, more relatives. Another twenty; like the first, all dressed in black, all armed. The singing—strange archaic music, angular and menacing—cut off and shouts went up.

He didn't like it, not one bit—what had they gotten into?—but he turned to Carrie and was putting on his reassuring smile when someone pushed him off the truck. He tumbled, too surprised to cry out, straight into Jean-Paul's arms. Much hugging, kissing, squeezing, laughing, meeting all the family. *"Bonjour, ça va,"* keep smiling, where was Carrie? There. He reached out for her, kept her close.

He was Flynn—the name had popped out on the boat when Jean-Paul asked him who he was—and she was Baby. Fleen and Bébé. Everyone was glad to meet them. Gave them little mugs of homemade brandy, *marc de résine* this time. Like a house afire, scalding all the way, but you got used to it.

Then Jean-Paul's mother. All in black, a black shape sitting in a crude oak chair. Bright eyes, a mug of *résine* in one steady hand. Then off to see the food. The smoke rose from a long low bed of coals and over it, on rusted metal, golden brown, fat crackling, there was meat. Strange meat: too big for lamb, too small for beef. Boar: wild boar. The woods were full of them; whole herds, if you believed Jean-Paul, stampeding, fierce and snorting, through the *maquis.* And finally, something to eat. Vast, chipped enamel pans filled with *pâté de merle,* of blackbird, piled on slabs of fresh baked bread.

He couldn't eat, he had to know.

"Jean-Paul?"

"*Oui, oui?*" Pronounced *way-way*, eyes bright, good smile.

He got it out: why all the guns? Terrific guys, his family; why was it everyone looked like a bandit?

Big smile. For good reason. They were sons of bandits, sons and grandsons. Jean-Paul said it proudly. But there were no bandits left, not any more. Departed; gone. Since 1918, when the war was over and the bandits, all the great ones, fled the island. As for the pistols, Jean-Paul shrugged. Up in the mountains, all the men had pistols. In the tiny villages, old places where his family came from, life was cold and hard and people drank and lost their tempers and there was a little shooting now and then but no one bothered them. The gendarmes left the villagers alone.

Fantastic. In the mountains, fifty miles away, vendettas still went on. His boyhood books came back. *The Corsican Brothers,* clan against clan, murder in the mountains. But they were so nice, such friendly people, all the laughter and the brandy and the blackbird pâté was delicious. Nothing bad was going to happen—was it?—and he looked at Carrie. She was eating, too.

Hands full, they followed Jean-Paul, sat down on the grass. A circle of them, all the elders of the tribe. The sun was higher, warming him and there was Carrie, mouth full of this gorgeous pâté stuff, lips wet with brandy. He had everything: the bread, the wine, the thou. Pure paradise, except for the knots in his stomach.

The Corsicans were speaking French now—thoughtful of them—so their visitors could understand. They spoke much slower than the northerners in Paris. And more musically; up and down, half sung. He tried to relax, just let the sounds wash over him. No luck. He listened.

They were talking, if he got it right, about the Foreign Legion. Days of Brian Donlevy and Gary Cooper. On alert, they said. The French Foreign Legion was, at that moment, as they sat there, on alert. Not possible. There wasn't any Legion any more. Disbanded years and years ago.

Not so. It still existed. Only here; on Corsica. Where else? Just scattered outposts, two or three. A tall, thin man was doing all the talking. Loulou was his name, or nickname, and he had some kind of job with the police—a janitorial position, more or less—in Corte. Corte was a big town, forty miles away, up in the mountains. The Legion had its headquarters there, in an ancient citadel that perched, alone and isolated, over Corte on a cliff top.

Anyway, the Legionnaires were on alert. A crisis there must be; some great event. He knew because—here Loulou dropped his voice—because while he was waxing his lieutenant's floor in the Gendarmerie, the phone had rung. Last night.

"*Allô, Dufresne ici.*" Loulou was doing his lieutenant. Bitterly, with great derision; no love lost on the police in Jean-Paul's family. "*Quoi?! Mon Dieu!*" Stupidity and panic mixed on Loulou's face and everybody laughed. "*Oui. Oui, oui. D'accord.*" More laughter. Phone call over. "*Sergent!*" The sergeant waddled in, his weak eyes lost in folds of flesh, saluted. "*Oui, mon Lieutenant?*"

Loulou got caught up in his story. Nothing funny any more. He hated the authorities, they all did, and he was excited and the words came faster, hard to catch. What Melvil thought he heard was everyone on duty, all leaves canceled, trouble was expected down in Calvi. Loulou wasn't certain what the trouble was but he could guess.

As which point, Loulou stopped abruptly—he was looking straight at Melvil at the time—and spread his hands, no point in guessing, story over.

Instant chill. He looked at Carrie. She was smiling blandly. Either she was really good at this or she had missed the look. He took a long pull from his mug. The men were standing, circle breaking up. He leaned toward Carrie, touched her arm. It felt like taut rope, tight around the chalice.

"You okay?"

"Sure." She sounded calm. "A lot of money floats around in Calvi. There's a good hotel or two, the yachts come in." She smiled slightly. "Maybe Lady Guinness lost a necklace."

"Maybe so." He stretched—he didn't want to worry her—and checked his watch. Near nine. O.K. to go. He drained his mug, wiped his hands on his trousers, stood, held out a hand for Carrie, looked around for Jean-Paul. Had to say goodbye. With smiles and hugs. Where was he? Over there, half covered by the smoke, there where the boar was crackling. Huddled up with Loulou; talking, talking.

Great goodbyes. A beefy hug from Jean-Paul and a bony one from Loulou. Then farewell to Jean-Paul's mother and much waving as they moved across the rocky ground, past all the trucks, onto the rutted little road. It was a long walk.

At the curve, he stopped—he felt like running but he didn't—turned and waved. A lovely picture: bright blue sky and bright blue sea, green grass, white house, red flowers and the people dressed in black.

They waited by the roadside. He could hear the singing; very faint, a zither with the voices and what sounded like a jew's-harp. At that distance? Most improbable but he was listening hard. He jumped a little—hoped she didn't see it—when he heard the bus.

The thing was rattling slowly down the road, about as modern as the trucks. She took his hand and squeezed it.

"What's that for?" he asked, as if he didn't know.

"I didn't think we'd make it."

"Why?" The bus was creaking to a stop.

"Because they're on to us," she said.

He didn't feel like shrugging but he did. And helped her up.

# XXII

They ambled side by side along the water's edge; shoes off, pants rolled up. Honeymooners. Just the look she wanted; dreaming, talking, nothing on their minds but one another and the morning. All an act and she was Queen of Acts. The sand felt good between her toes.

Not many people on the beach. Still early. Calvi up ahead, around that bend, beyond that little hill. He stopped, picked up a shell. Orange mixed with white. He gave it to her. Good: she'd given him the honeymooners image, told him how to play it. How the way you walked, your posture and your speed, the things you looked at and the things you didn't made a difference. They were going to wander into Calvi looking like they'd been there for a week; it was the best she could think of.

To make it look right, they had left the bus outside of town and headed for the beach. They hadn't spoken on the bus. Not possible. The rattling and the babies and the chickens and the dogs. But she had clicked the racket off and done a lot of thinking.

Loulou knew about them. She was sure. But how much had he overheard in his lieutenant's office? Enough to know that a big man in his forties who spoke French with an American accent and traveled with a tall girl and no luggage were wanted by the cops. But did he know why? Did he know what they'd done or that they had the chalice with them? Maybe; maybe not. And either way, she didn't think it mattered very much. They'd slipped away, the sons of bandits hadn't followed. It had been a long wait for the bus and nothing happened. File it and forget it.

Others knew they had the chalice, that's what mattered; others, starting with Sir Winston. And if he knew, so did Chief Inspector Drum. Was Drum in Calvi? Was the Yard? The Corsican police were there, that was for sure. Who else? The CIA? Why not? and Interpol? and Papal representatives? She had a sudden flash of all of them, in uniform, all lurking under beach umbrellas. Broke her up.

But it was serious. How had they figured Calvi? Had she slipped up, left a clue? Most likely, someone had a hunch. It didn't take much hunching when you got right down to it. They'd gone to Somerset: where else would they go next? She wondered, for a moment, what the outside world thought they were up to. Gardener, sitting with his books in Boston, what would he think? Never mind: what mattered was there would be people watching Kalman. Had to be. What else made sense?

Some kids ran past them. Out at sea, at anchor, was a pleasure yacht. A big one, too big for the port, a crew of thirty, maybe more. She wished to hell they were on it. Having breakfast under a blue awning on the upper deck, men in white jackets serving omelets and muffins.

"So with all those people watching Kalman, how do we get in?" She squinted at him.

"Yeah." He kicked a stone. "It's tricky."

"I don't know." She shook her head.

"Why don't we call him on the telephone?"

She stopped. Not bad. "What could we tell him?"

"Oh, some kind of story, have him meet us on the beach or someplace."

"Nope." It wouldn't work. "No good."

"Why not?"

She told him why. They had to get to Kalman in some natural way. He had to talk and not know he was talking. They weren't cops, they couldn't cross-examine him; he had to spill his story out in human terms, the things he thought and felt.

"Okay." He picked a rock up, sent it skipping. "No phone. You think of something."

They started up the beach again. The sun was warm. She took her jacket off. She had to find a natural way and she was looking for it, deep inside herself, mind whirring; which was why she didn't notice Calvi till he touched her.

Enchanting. Almost too enchanting, almost sweet; something a sixteenth-century Disney might have built. The Bay of Calvi circled to their right, a gentle arc of white sand. Then, at water's edge, the little houses and the quai, all curving. Then, thrust up on jagged rocks, an ancient fortress town: steep walls, old houses, ruined towers. And beyond it rose the hills, all flowers, all the colors, blanketed. And in the distance, cutting up like broken glass, a mountain topped with snow.

"Is that a picture."

Yes, it was and wouldn't it be nice to loll around and touch each other in the sun. Another day; it would be nice to come some other day. The chalice rubbed against her leg. She started forward.

There were people on the beach now. Not a lot, the remnants of the Easter crowd. Some beach umbrellas, red and yellow, and some lounge chairs. Small yachts bobbing in the harbor, four or five of them, and fishing boats along the quai. A normal day, no ripples of excitement, nothing odd. No fuzz. Not on the beach. She hadn't really thought there would be.

"Now what?"

"We'll see." She smiled, held out her hand. He took it and they started slowly strolling. Very slowly, take it slow because she didn't have it yet and something had to come to her. The kids splashed by again and one boy stopped and suddenly she had it.

Sensuality is not acquired; nor does it come, like second teeth or pubic hair, with time. No, sensuality is there from the beginning and you have it or you don't. And those who have it recognize each other—just like homosexuals or Jews or any other sensitive minority. It didn't happen often and she loved it when it did because it felt so nice; not sinister or dirty, nothing bent. Just saying "Good to see you" to a fellow member of the tribe. He stood there, eight or nine, this boy, brown skin, brown hair and big brown eyes, all wet and glistening in the sun: their passport.

"*Ça va, ça va?*" She wandered over toward him. Things went well enough, *merci*. What did he call himself? Gian-Carlo. Did he live in Calvi? Yes, at 27, Rue Alsace-Lorraine. Did he know of a Monsieur Kalman? Big frown, deep thought. Monsieur Kalman who sold antiquities on the Rue Clemenceau, was that the one she meant? It was, it was, that very one. And would Gian-Carlo take them to this shop? O.K., *d'accord*.

So far, so good. This was the crunch. She went to one knee, met him eye to eye. He looked straight back. He would be something twenty years from now. She didn't smile because what happened next depended on their being equals. Was he interested in earning fifty francs? Too much: she should have offered ten. He stepped away, alert and wary, looked to left and right. Then back to her, head on. What would he have to do to earn so much? She told him.

Hand in hand they went, straight down the beach, the three of them. Gian-Carlo in the middle, skipping. Chatter, chatter: it was *Maman* this and *Papa* that, the boy was perfect. And she chattered back, in French she hoped was good enough, about the things they'd do that afternoon, a boat ride if Gian-Carlo was a good boy and *langouste* for supper, think of that.

They drew the kind of looks they should have drawn. The women looked at West, the men at her and now and then an aged face would smile at the boy. On past the last umbrella, off the beach and onto pavement, by the tiny railroad station, then the chapel. Houses now; old, whitewashed stone. A shop with native oranges, olives, fish. The quai began. A boat or two, like Jean-Paul's, scarred and beaten.

Chatter, chatter, on and on. She had to keep it going, what to talk about? She came up with a little sister and the boy caught on, called her Cecille and she was five and ugly and he hated her. And still no fuzz. Not anyplace. Where were they? Had they called it off? Had Loulou heard a false alarm? No; it would be a stakeout. All the cops were there, inside someplace, behind the curtains in the little windows. West was smiling. Good for him.

*"J'ai faim, j'ai faim, Maman, Papa."* Gian-Carlo stopped, dug in his heels.

*"Tais-toi."* The kid was overdoing it. And then she saw. Rue Clemenceau. And near the sign, a little shop that sold soft ice cream. The boy was either really smart or really hungry. Either way, she felt like hugging him. He grinned and hugged her back.

*"Trois glaces vanille."* If Gian-Carlo and vanilla ice cream didn't fool them, nothing would.

They marched off, side by side, each with his ice cream cone. Rue Clemenceau was—well, what could you call it? A typical main street in a small seaside resort in Corsica? She grinned; some typicality. Dark, narrow, straight, then left and straight again. All very old. A little traffic: battered Citroens and Simcas—local; three or four Mercedes—tourist. Murky shops, fresh produce, workers' clothing, shoes, a travel agency, a really rather nice charcuterie—dear God, she wasn't hungry, not again—a place with papers and tobacco and a store called Pour le Sport with snorkels in the window.

"*Voilà, Maman.*"

They stopped. Across the street. A pleasant-looking window filled with china, bits of silver, decent-looking things. Two signs. A large one, done in faded gilt, all weather-beaten: BELA KALMAN ET FILS. ANTIQUITÉS. MAISON FONDÉE 1927. And in the window, propped against the glass, a small sign, done in ink: "*A Vendre.*"

Up for sale. Was Kalman moving down the street or moving out? No time for speculation, check the street. No hopeless drunk alert against a doorway; no one dozing, eyes wide open, in a car; no cafe customer not drinking coffee. Clear, the place looked clear. She nodded, led the way across the street.

"*Au 'voir, Maman; au 'voir, Papa.*" The boy was leaving, running down the street, without his fifty francs, without a hug or anything.

"Gian-Carlo!"

"*Oui, Maman.*"

"*Viens ici.*" He came. She went down to one knee again. She had the franc note folded up, a tacky little wad of paper, and she pressed it in his hand. He had a warm hand. So she kissed it, touched his cheek and told him she'd be back in twenty years. He grinned and took off, waving, calling *'Voir, Maman, Papa, Maman . . .*" Off down the street.

"Nice kid," he said.

She nodded.

"Never had a kid. It's just as well, I guess."

She didn't think he meant it but there wasn't time to think. One last look down the street. No cops. No boy. She turned to West. He had his shades on, couldn't see his eyes; she could put in them anything she liked.

He reached out to the door. He had it open. "*Après toi.*"

The store was dimly lit and, coming from the outside glare, she couldn't see; just shapes, dark things to hide behind. But with the tension came a sense of something civilized, the sounds and smells, a feel of natural refinement. There were flowers in the room somewhere and there was music. Mozart in the distance. Slow: sonata for piano. Nice sound—not professional but sensitive.

The whole shop, as it came clear, looked like that: not professional but sensitive. Some lovely china—Meissen, KPM—and silver pieces—Viennese?—and no one in the shop. No clerks, no customers, no cops. If cops there were, what were they waiting for? The Mozart stopped. Some clocks were ticking. West picked up a silver pitcher, turned it in his hand—then stiffened.

"*Bonjour, madame, monsieur.*"

The girl was ravishing. Just barely in her teens, ash-blonde, skin tanned to caramel, eyes blue as cornflowers. And bones. The girl had bones—like who? Like Garbo possibly; but more refined, more delicate.

"*A votre service.*"

With a start, she looked at West. Who were they this time? Were they from the Met again or what?

"I've been admiring this pitcher. It's a charming piece," he said.

"Thank you." Her smile was enchanting. "I am very pleased you like it." Perfect English with the slightest accent.

"My name is Flynn and this is my associate, Miss deHavilland. We have come a long way to see Mr. Kalman. Is he here?"

"My father may not be at home. He visited with friends this morning in the harbor."

"You expect him soon?"

"He may be upstairs now. It is a most peculiar house, you see. Its back is front, it looks upon the water. If I may?"

A fleeting smile. She was moving up a narrow flight of stairs. Then gone.

"West?"

"Did you ever in your life see anything like that?"

"She's very pretty. What's our story?"

"Very pretty? She's exquisite, she is probably the most—"

"Okay, she's exquisite. What's our story."

"It's a good one."

"Care to tell me what it is?"

"I'm sorry, it was just that girl, I mean I've never—"

"Mister Flynn?"

They looked up. Exquisite was there at the top of the stairs.

"My father wants to know what is the reason that you wish to see him."

"Certainly." His eyes—revolting—they were eating her alive. "I'm a collector, in my own small way, of Greek and Roman plate and I was hoping Mr. Kalman might have other things in his collection that he cared to sell."

She had to hand it to him. Not that she was in the mood to—but he even stood there like a rich American. Not what you'd think of ordinarily as a collector but she'd met some pretty odd ones; millionaires in Keds and blue jeans, there were lots of them.

"Miss deHavilland, Mr. Flynn?"

She stared up at Stefan Kalman. Stared and stared, she couldn't stop. Exquisite got her looks from Father. Over fifty, with a young man's body, gray-white hair, eyes large and deep.

"Please come up, won't you?"

"Thank you." West was smiling so she smiled, too, and trotted up the stairs. She was a little nervous but she didn't think it was a trap. They'd gotten in and later, when the time came, they'd slip out.

"This way, please." Kalman moved along a narrow

balcony, then stopped. He opened up a door and bowed them through.

The sunlight in the salon made her blink. Large windows opened on a terrace and the sea. The walls were stone, old stone, natural and bare. The floor was tile, native-looking, primitive with polish. All the rest—from large to small, from secretary down to crystal whatnots on the coffee table—came from home. Ancestral home. In Budapest? The leavings from a little palace.

"Please sit down. You'll find the sofa comfortable."

It was. West settled next to her. Kalman was pouring something lovely-looking into lovely-looking glasses.

"Sorry if we look a little ragged," West was saying, "but we've only just arrived."

Kalman brought the glasses on a little silver tray. "I know, I know, you couldn't wait. Collectors . . ." He looked at West and made a face; a charming face, it made her smile. "In any case, I've been expecting you."

West didn't blink. "You have?"

"In just a general way. I've sold one piece from my collection, it makes news around the world and here you are, the first collector to appear." Vague accent, like his daughter's, not from anyplace.

He sat across from them, back to the light, and chatted idly. Were they staying long and had they come by plane or ferry, they must rent a car and do the island, most extraordinary place, *maquis* in bloom, pâté de merle. She sipped her drink and listened, found him likable and charming. It was odd because she never cared for handsome men. Distrusted them, on top of which she found them unattractive. There was more to Kalman, though, than looks. Talk of pâté led to native customs. Did they know about the *signadori?* Kalman asked.

"Extraordinary," he went on, these *signadori.*

*Signa*—sign; they know the secrets of the evil eye. You doubt me? Forty miles from here, it can be fatal, I have seen it make men die. Fantastic island, Corsica. The pity is, I've lost my taste for fantasy."

He made it seem a foolish thing to lose and West began to talk about the things back home in his collection: bowls and saucepans, jugs and dishes. Why so roundabout, she wondered. Did it always take this long to buy and sell? Then West began to talk about simpulum handles—swell; a lecture on simpulum handles—and what did Kalman think of the ones in the Hildesheim Treasure? Kalman liked them, in particular the handle shaped like leaves and branches. And it dawned on her: credential time, the boys were testing one another. Kalman sounded genuine; but what did she know?

Certain things. She got up, wandered to the window aimlessly, looked out. Where were the watchdogs? Had to be there; that she knew. Reporters, at the very least. They had been covering Sir Winston; they'd be here. But there was nothing on the quai that didn't look as if it lived there. Mamas heading home for lunch with baskets full of bread and onions; fishermen, a few, out mending nets. Some kids, just doing kid things. Anybody else? A man, his felt hat covering his face, lay sleeping on a bench.

All normal, just what you'd expect to see. Some cars, a white Peugeot sedan, old Citroens, the corrugated ones, all parked and empty in the sun. Way out at sea, miles off, the pleasure yacht she'd seen that morning. Didn't feel right but the view was beautiful. Just to her left, the ancient fortress walls soared up and could that possibly be France on the horizon? West was talking to her.

"Sorry, Mr. Flynn." She turned. "Daydreaming."

"We've been asked for lunch."

She wanted out. The quiet was too much and

something she had seen or felt or heard was very wrong. "How nice."

"And while I'm setting table," Kalman said, "you must come see my small collection."

In his bedroom. Funny place to keep it. Didn't look like much to her. Some pottery, some knives, a jug, a drinking cup. Not many silver pieces and the ones there were looked broken, incomplete. The French vitrine that held them was a beauty, though; bronze doré on the door that Kalman opened.

She kept her eyes on Kalman's face; she couldn't judge the silver but she could the man. He loved these things, he really cared about them. They were precious; not because of what they'd sell for but some other reason.

"Nice simpulum," West said, picking up the remnants of a ladle. So that's what simpulum was. Or were.

"I'm pleased you like it."

"First-century?"

"I think so, yes. The Romans in those days were much in Corsica. There was a settlement, in fact, at Calvi; gone without a trace." He turned. "Examine what you like. I must tell Margit we are four for lunch."

She liked the way West looked. She hadn't seen him lost in things before, the things he knew about. His field. He really was a scholar: but with feelings, that's what mattered. He was putting down the ladle and she felt a wish to see it with his eyes.

"West?" He looked at her. "Is it a good piece?"

"No," he said, "not very."

"Show me which the good ones are."

He shrugged. "There's nothing, really."

Carrie frowned. "What does that mean, exactly?"

"Just that all the things are real enough, they're genuine, but not Museum quality."

Her heart was beating. "What's it worth? The whole collection?"

"Hard to say. Ten, twenty thousand."

Was he being dense or what? "That blows his story, doesn't it? I mean, how could he own the chalice if the rest of it is junk?"

"It isn't junk and isolated finds are commonplace. What happens is the site gets plundered. Back a thousand years ago or two, whenever, someone stumbles on the site. He takes what's good and leaves the rest, he's in a hurry, things get left behind. It happens all the time."

"You think he owned the chalice? Was it his?"

"Could be." He closed the vitrine door. "Too soon to tell. We haven't heard his story yet."

They got it after lunch.

*Salade niçoise*, a local wine—white, clear and cold—some really lovely *chèvre*—lots of goats on Corsica—and fruit. Margit turned out to be the kind of girl you couldn't hate. Shy, sensitive, intelligent; a lot of life behind those eyes. An only child; had to be, you felt that special Daddy-daughter thing that only only children seemed to have.

So it came as no surprise to hear that Margit and her father played four-hand sonatas together, went out watercoloring together, read poetry together. Fathers and their little girls; she could have done with some of that herself.

Her orange was eaten. Was the story never going to come? She started feeling edgy. Every sound, each time a car went by, each voice that reached them from the quai, each door that slammed on the Rue Clemenceau, the radios—Kalman said the island was a paradise for birds and all you heard was radios.

She suggested coffee on the terrace. Maybe it was paranoid of her, but when they came at least she'd see them coming. There was sea breeze, very light. The sun was warm. West sat beside her. Nothing moving on the quai—life stopped for lunch, no action—and she missed the way the conversation started.

"Most extraordinary man, my father"—Kalman talking—"but the Great War superannuated him. He was an amateur. Musician, archeologist, philosopher, historian, collector—all those things. A Doctor many times; from Heidelberg, Vienna, Budapest: eternal student. In the old days, there were many such: the finest thing the nineteenth century made, the Amateur. Too rich to work, too gifted not to.

"But the nineteenth century stopped in 1918. All life changed. My parents fled from Budapest; took all they could and ran. The running lasted many years because, you see, there was no place for Amateurs and students studied now to gain some end, no eternal students any more."

She sat back, relaxed a little, felt the chalice in her bag and listened. They had lived in Rome and Florence, many cities, aimless and displaced, until the day that Kalman's father read about the menhirs. Passing reference. In some book. Extraordinary things they were and most extraordinary was the fact that they were unexplored. No digs, no excavations. Which was how they'd come to live in Calvi, Dr. Kalman and his wife and little boy of five.

That was in 1926. He had driven with his father on the very day they docked in Calvi up to Calacuccia to see the menhirs. High up in the mountains. Cold. They looked like stones to him, old stones, not very interesting, though he had rather liked the ones with faces. But his father found his life's work on that day and studied them and excavated, all alone, year after year, and put his findings in the monographs that no one read and dug up all the treasures they had seen. The treasures came to be the old man's life and when he died, the son had vowed to keep them always, as the father asked him to. So they had been there in the bedroom, not for show and not for sale, for all these years.

"What makes you sell them now?" West beat her to the question.

"My wife died in November." Said it easily, no emphasis, but she was sure she saw it in his face; real grief. Behind the eyes, inside, all torn apart. "I do not like it much in Corsica, not any more; and Margit grows. So big. An interesting girl, much promise, and there must be more for her in life than this, this shabby little shop here in this shabby little place. There really must, you know."

"*A Vendre*"—the for-sale sign in the window. Any man who had the taxes on three million six to pay had reason to be moving out. Right out of France. Still, sentimental of her, but she wanted to believe that he was doing it for Margit. He would do, she knew it, anything to help his little girl. She liked that: there was danger in him. They were the best, the gentle men with violence. Her West was one, though he didn't know it yet.

She sat there full of questions. How could Kalman prove he owned the chalice? Did he have a photo of his father holding it? Or what about those monographs? His father would have written all about it if he found it, wouldn't he? And why, after so many years, why sell it now? She turned to Kalman and she asked him.

"I don't know." He smiled sadly. "Greed? It's possible. We do mad things sometimes and my wife was dead, I couldn't think and Mannheim came, he often does, he likes my shop. He sits and talks of Budapest; it interests me. We sat here on this terrace looking at the chalice—it was on the little table—so much money, it would mean so much, a whole new life . . ."

She read it on his face: regret. A man who wished a thing could be undone. But he had done it,

Mannheim sold it, yes, and now the press, the questions, the insinuations: it was terrible.

She asked about the photos but there were no family pictures. None? Not one of anybody. What about the monographs? No mention in the monographs of any of the plate. How come? Collector's greed: his father thought there might be more, more treasures to be found. And now, he went on, now today how could he prove the provenance? Of anything he owned? How could he sell his other pieces? Who would buy them? Mr. Flynn. Would he?

West hesitated.

"Come." Kalman stood abruptly. "Would you come? I'll take you to the menhirs. You must see before you buy. I saw my father find these things, I sat and watched and helped a little, I was there the day he found the chalice, I can take you to the very place."

True or false? So much about the man was real: his grief about his wife, the daughter thing, his love of his collection and his feelings for his father; and regret. She looked at West. What did he think?

He nodded, rose. They went.

Downstairs, they told Margit they were going, left the back way—or the front—into a little garden, walls around it. Nervous-making. Walking out with Kalman was like playing hide-and-seek with bells on. Every cop in Calvi would be watching him—if cops there were—and maybe they had squeaked by on the way in but there were no ice cream cones this time around.

She did it very nicely. "Oh," she gasped, just loud enough, and fell, not hard enough to hurt, and held her ankle. West came down beside her.

"Is it bad?"

"It's nothing, just a twist, fine in a minute."

"Sure?" She nodded. "Mr. Kalman, would you bring the car around?"

Of course he would and awfully sorry, all his fault,

the walk should be repaired, he wouldn't be a minute, right back. Out the garden door.

No time. Talk fast. "About this ride," she said.

"We've gotta go."

"You think?"

"For one, we can't stay here; for two, he wants to get us out there and, for three, I want to find out why."

They heard the car door slam. The engine started.

"West? You think it's his?"

"I liked his story, most of it."

"Same here. What bothered you?"

West frowned. "I don't know, does he strike you like a man who's got three million in the bank?"

He didn't. Carrie shook her head and wanted very much to talk to Adolf Mannheim. Would his version jibe with Kalman's, would—

"He's here."

"Be careful, West."

"Let's go."

She went out, low and limping. Kalman had the car door open. She slid in, West right behind. He closed the door. They started forward. Someone had to shout or shoot or stop them; something. On they went, the quai still almost empty. A lady shrouded all in black, all you could see of her was black, sat dozing in the sun. A tourist, small and trim, a wiry little man, was buying fruit or something at an open store. So far, so good.

She looked out the rear-view mirror. They were turning at a corner as the man in the felt hat sat up. Gray hat, gray suit—a gray man. They'd been spotted by the man in gray. Christ, and the tourist buying fruit was small and trim, built like a jockey: Drum. Inspector Drum. He knew them by sight, he was the only one who did. He'd seen them and, oh shit, the lady all in black, like Jean-Paul's mother, one of them.

The car was moving past the railroad station, down along the beach. Kids playing, beach balls, bodies browning in the sun. A waiter served a drink. So normal. Life was going on. Unreal. How could life just go on like that when she had seen—hold on. Just what exactly had she seen? She hadn't seen the gray man's face, a lot of people dressed in gray, it wasn't lavender or something and the man who bought the fruit wore tourist clothing, had his back to her, the sun was in her eyes. And every crone in Corsica was shrouded up in black. Oh Lord.

She ran a tense hand through her hair. She'd be seeing rapists underneath the bed next. Even so, she kept an eye on the rearview mirror as they drove along. Same road they'd bussed down earlier, along the coast, all curves and turns and they were near L'Île Rousse and all they needed was a flat in front of Jean-Paul's place. The mirror—mustn't look too often—didn't show much. Farm trucks now and then. Jean-Paul's? She couldn't tell, all old and battered, looked alike. And now and then, white cars. The police drove white cars; Citroens, or was it Peugeots? So did everybody else. Four cars out of five were white. She had to stop it, cut it out. The road was never straight, though, and for all she knew, they could have an armada back there; all they had to do was keep a curve behind.

A little past L'Île Rousse, they left the coast and started inland. Up into the foothills. *Maquis* everywhere. So beautiful, the perfume flooding through the open windows, flowers, flowers. Narrow roadway, really treacherous, all twists and hairpins. Over there, a shepherd; sheep or goats, she couldn't tell, it was too far away. No farms now. Only *maquis* grew and blossomed here and stands of pine; tall, strong and straight, like Roman soldiers still on guard.

Where were they now exactly? On the road to Corte, Kalman said. A lovely village and they really ought to see the Citadel: magnificent. Oh swell, the Citadel and Loulou and the Legionnaires.

"Tomorrow, if you're free, I'll drive you up. Today, we take a different road. To Calacuccia and I must get you home again before the sun goes down. These roads at night—well, you can see how dangerous they are."

She saw, sat back and tried to figure Kalman out. To start with, did he swallow West as a collector? Loulou had caught on to them and Loulou was no genius. So, assume he knew who they were. Why was he dragging them up here to see his menhirs? Maybe, if she got him talking . . .

"Mr. Kalman?"

"Yes, my dear?"

"About these menhirs—"

"Fascinating." He was off. She heard a lot about them, some of which she knew. The early ones, huge rocks, transported somehow back in neolithic times and placed, just so, in circles. Circles for the dead, a marking off of sacred ground. Later, things got more sophisticated and they started making dolmens. They were coffin-like and stood above the ground, not buried under. Massive slabs of stone, they weighed tons. No one knew how people who could barely shape an arrowhead had done such things.

The menhirs were the last development. Stone posts was all they were. The stone was carved, sometimes with faces, sometimes not. But to the people then, these posts had life and power. They stood guard, they watched the dead and there were prayers and sacrifices. Legends grew up. There were stories about gold, great hoards of it, hidden in the sacred ground. And evil spirits, too, of course. Ogres, fiends and monstrous animals; one still heard talk about it in the villages.

"And so," said Kalman, breaking for a turn, "if you had been a Roman at the time of Christ and enemies had come to plunder, steal your silver and your gold, you would have buried it at such a place. You weren't afraid, they weren't your gods; but island gods would keep the islanders away. And even the invaders, who had gods at home a lot like these, would see the menhirs and would feel afraid.

"In time, of course, the old gods died and there has been much plundering since Christ. Still, much was buried at these places, finds are made and you will see."

They turned. Another road. Just past Francardo; tiny village, four or five stone houses, sheep, some dogs, no people anyplace. They were well into the mountains now. Not Alps but there was naked rock above and snow. The big peak, rising miles ahead, was Monte Cinto. Altitude of—Kalman hesitated, putting meters into feet—around 8,000. Second highest mountain in the Mediterranean, after Etna. There were clouds around the top of it.

Things were starker now. They drove through Calacuccia, a grim town, houses made of stone. There were a few goats on the street and little carts, a nice church on a hill. The land beyond the town looked really bleak. No farms, no people; rocks and *maquis*, that was all. Some birds flew by. Buzzards. Carrie didn't know a bullfinch from a condor but those things were buzzards.

They were slowing down. "We're there," said Kalman, nodding to the right. They left the road and bumped around a little on a rocky field, then stopped. In nowhere. She had seen a lot of nowhere in her time: the Grill at the Savoy; the north of Iran; Gary, Indiana. Couldn't touch this place for good old-fashioned nothingness. Just rocks and grass you couldn't get a goat to eat.

She looked at West. He rubbed his hands together, made a face intended to convey collectorish excitement. "Are we there?" he asked. "Is this it?"

"Very nearly. Up the little hill, then down and up again. Not far." He made it sound like to the corner for a Coke.

West got out, leaned in. "Be careful of that ankle."

"I'll be fine." She took the hand he held out for her. It was cold; but steady. Out she went, stood close to him. A car went by. White Citroen. It kept on going, didn't mean a thing.

"I think you ought to stay here, in the car." He squeezed her hand hard, really crunching it.

She let him have her best go-fuck-off smile. "The walk will do me good." If he thought, for one second, that she'd let him go out there alone. Without her. He bit his lip, looked furious.

"This way." They turned. A smiling Kalman.

The field was easy, all you had to do was watch your footing. Going up the hill was harder, clumps of *maquis*, patches of it and the rocks were larger, so you picked your way and went around the rough spots. The chalice rubbed against her thigh. She took one last look back: the field, all desolation, Kalman's car, a battered farm truck coughing down the road.

She turned. Ahead of them, a little valley fell away beyond the hill. Two hundred yards across. A sea of *maquis*, waves of color. How bad could it be? She waded in. Blue murder. There were vines and tendrils, thorns and thistles, everything as tough as cactus. Dense and thick, the damn stuff came in waves; deep, shallow, waist-high, kick those knees. She needed both hands and her bag was in the way and there were noises, scrabbling noises down there on the ground. Rats? Were there fucking rats in fucking Corsica?

She anthropomorphicated—was there such a word?—the *maquis*, thought of it in terms of people she had hated: Mr. Dench in second grade, the bastard, laying hands on girls of eight; and Mrs. Clean, that can't have been her name, who taught

Phys. Ed.—and it was over. She came stumbling up out of the little valley onto the plateau.

The plateau sloped and tilted, rose and fell; but, by comparison, the land was flat. She brushed her denims off as Kalman started to apologize. He hadn't been there in the spring for years and he'd forgotten all about the *maquis*.

There were scratches on her hands. West's too. She took his carefully and, Kalman leading, they started off across the plateau. It wasn't far, perhaps a quarter-mile: across a tiny stream—one running jump—over a rise and then around the corner. That was how it felt, as if she had to turn past something sharp to get there.

The stones lay strewn about, not really in a circle but there was a pattern to them, something secret that she couldn't quite make out. The dolmens, two or three of them still standing, looked enormous. But it was the menhirs that were most disturbing. Some stood straight, some leaned at crazy angles. There were faces on them, eyes cut deep, eroded, washed away so that you saw them but you didn't see them.

"Over here." Kalman stood behind a row of menhirs. "See? The digs were here." The ground was all grown over, weeds and grass and wild things. "I was a little boy then; seven, eight, and it was Easter time with festivals and singing and the people dressed up strangely. I was on vacation and we came here every day. My father was so big a man, so tall and strong and I would sit and think of stories all about the stones and he would dig. When it was time, he stopped and we would eat: bread, cheese and wine. He let me drink the wine but *Maman* wouldn't and it was our secret. Some days, he would lie beside me on the grass and tell me much about the people who were here once; how they hunted, what they did all day.

"I liked the things he found. Spearheads and points

for arrows made of stones. And metal things, all rusted so the shape was hardly there; but Father knew and they were knives or ax blades and if I was careful, he would let me hold them.

"The chalice was all covered over, too, no shape at all. Another tool, I thought, but he was so excited, speaking in Hungarian—we never did, we lived here and he wanted us to speak in French. It was the greatest moment of his life; he told me so when I was grown but I knew then. He stood right here and cried—he thought I couldn't see because his face was wet with rain. I never should have talked with Mannheim; it was wrong of me."

He looked up. There was anguish on his face. "I brought you here, I showed you this and told you everything because you must believe me. All I've said is true. I need the chalice, Dr. West. I ask you, please, to give it to me."

Nailed; he knew them . . . and the man said please.

"I'm sorry but I haven't got it." Not a blink from West: he even sounded sorry.

"I must have it, Dr. West. Miss Gardener, if you will? It must be in your bag."

She looked at West. He shook his head.

"I don't want any trouble." Kalman said it softly.

Which was when she knew he had a gun. Which pocket was it in?

"You make a puzzling thief." West sounded like he meant it.

"I'm no thief. I don't think you are, either."

"No?"

"I ask myself, he steals the chalice and he goes to Hunter-Donne and then he comes to me. Why would a man do that? It makes no sense unless the man is looking for the truth. And you have found it."

"Yes, I see; but what I don't see"—West bent down, picked up a blade of grass—"what baffles me is Margit."

"What about my daughter?" Sharp; dangerous territory.

"How much money does she need? What kind of new life are you buying her? You got three million six. She seems a modest sort of girl. I would have thought—"

"I didn't get the money."

"Oh, come on."

"Ten thousand dollars."

"That's a lie." Be careful, not so hard, don't press too hard.

"Ten. What can I give my little girl with—"

"Where's the rest? Who got it?"

"Mannheim. Mannheim kept it all. I want the chalice now, please."

He was stretched tight, a nice man in a corner and he wasn't used to corners. Anything could snap him. There would be no please the next time. Carefully—she didn't want to startle him—she brought the bag around and tugged the zipper. Stuck. It wasn't funny but she felt like laughing.

Kalman wiped his forehead. "Take your time. There is no hurry. No one ever comes here."

Was that why he brought them here—nobody comes—and would he shoot them once he had it?

West was talking. "Look, if Mannheim kept your money, why not go to the police?"

"How do I prove it? Mannheim doesn't keep the money in his pocket. Money like this disappears, it vanishes in Switzerland. He told me so today, he said I couldn't prove it."

She kept tugging. Maybe, if she threw the chalice—what would West say if she dented it? But if she threw it carefully, Kalman would try to catch it, be off guard—The zipper gave and everything got very quiet.

"Now."

She reached in, felt the chalice in her hand.

"Describe it, Kalman." West was crouching. "If it's yours, describe it, is it cracked along the bottom, where it's signed, is there a crack?"

The gun came out. Right jacket pocket. She was almost glad to see it. One good throw, that's all there was. She held the chalice in her hand. It glittered in the fading sun.

There were tears in Kalman's eyes. His voice was high and sharp. "I never should have done it. Mannheim said to, his idea, the chalice, I could buy a new life for my Margit, take her everywhere and buy her everything and I believed him. Oh, my God . . ."

"Give it here." West held his hand out for the gun. "I'll take it, you'll feel better then." Wrong move, it wouldn't work. West started forward, Kalman made a funny noise, there was this ringing in her ears.

She threw the chalice and a gun went off. One shot.

She wasn't hit. Was West? He stood still, frozen. Only Kalman moved, a sort of lurching turn, like drunken dancing. There was red, red there on Kalman's arm.

Kalman was falling down. She heard a voice. A new voice. Who? She looked around. That tall man standing by the menhir, skinny as a menhir. Carrie knew him, knew his name, how did that song go, *dum-dum, Loulou's back in town.* Loulou was walking toward them, rifle cradled in one arm. She felt cool, cool all over. She had faced armed men before. One time, in Iran—she'd been in her do-good period and went there with these missionaries, doing good—this Arab had come at her with a knife. No reason, out of nowhere and she got his knife and cut him with it, left him cursing on the ground. She'd walked off like a zombie, vomited and cried all night.

She moved to West. "It's Loulou, Loulou's coming."

"Get behind me."

"Fleen?" Loulou waved. "*Ça va?*" A smile like a shark.

"You know him?" That was Kalman, voice hoarse, sitting crookedly, hand on his arm.

West reached down to him. "Can you stand?"

"I think."

Would Loulou shoot them? Absolutely. Put the scene in Hatfield country, they'd be shot; and this was Corsica and no one ever came and there were shootings in the mountains all the time. She didn't feel like dying. Loulou moving, coming closer, talking. He was hunting, up here hunting and Jean-Paul and all the men, they felt like hunting, too, and they were in the *maquis* there, behind the rocks.

Loulou was twenty, thirty feet away, and West was talking at the same time, low and fast. Their only chance was scattering, different directions, all at once. He'd give the signal. O.K., but he'd better give it soon, Loulou was asking for the chalice. Standing there all smiles, all teeth like a piranha and asking for it.

She felt angry. Deep-sixed by a janitor. This fucking primitive was going to kill her. For the chalice, for the money it would bring. Not right, not fair. He wasn't going to get it, put his mother-raping hands all over it. Where was the damn thing? Which way had she thrown it? On the grass, five yards away, she'd grab it when she ran, she'd save it.

West was talking to her. "Meet you at the car."

She nodded. "See you there."

"I got you into this, I'll get you out."

"Be careful." What a stupid thing to say, not what she meant.

West sounded shaky. "Don't forget I love you. Hit it."

She took off, heading for the chalice first. She ran—a step a minute, like a dream, forever—dig in, there it was. She scooped it up, she had it. Faster. Go. She'd done the hundred once in thirteen flat; good runner for a girl.

She heard the shot. It didn't hurt but something turned her right around. What was she turning for? And falling. Why fall down? The ground was hard. Her hip hurt but her arm felt fine. Her left arm, just a little numb. Below the shoulder, she could see it, blood was trickling.

"Carrie!"

West was calling her. She turned, saw Kalman running slowly, sort of tilted, over the plateau. And West—he hadn't scattered, hadn't run away. He'd gone for Loulou. He was crouching, not ten yards from Loulou. Fool.

"I'm okay," she shouted. "Run!"

He didn't run. He stood up and his face was weird. A sound was coming out of it. A scary sound, some other voice; not his at all but like an animal, a big one, like a lion in a corner. Then he turned away from her, toward Loulou, noise still coming out of him. He started forward heavily, not fast. Loulou was stepping back. He aimed at West. No shot, it must have jammed. He swung the rifle like a club. It hit West on the shoulder, staggered him. He kept on going, grabbed for Loulou, had him. Had him in his hands and raised him up. Straight up, right off the ground, and crashed him down.

Loulou was screaming. West was on him, arms like clubs, she heard the sounds they made. He'd kill him, West was going to kill the man. She got up, had to stop him, murder was a bad thing, terrible. She grabbed him, yelled his name. Again. He heard the second time. He turned and looked. He saw her.

"West?"

His voice was strange. "I saw you bleeding."

"Doesn't hurt." It didn't much. She moved her forearm, just to show him. "Nothing broken." Moved her fingers. "Just a scratch." Loulou was moaning. Fuck him, let him moan, it was vendetta time in sunny Corsica and any second now his family would even up the score. She put her arms around West, held him close, went flat against the ground.

The shooting started. Sounded like the Battle of the Bulge. But funny shooting, bullets should be kicking up the dust around them and they weren't. Some shots, these Corsicans. And there was shooting in the distance, too; a lot of it.

"What's going on?" West raised his head. "Son of a bitch."

She looked. The plateau stretched before her, half a mile or so of it. The valley with the *maquis* they had come through was way down there on her right, at the far edge of the plateau. Men were coming from it, shooting, shouting, fanning out. A lot of men. In uniforms, gendarmes and Legionnaires. A hundred of them? Hard to tell. One flung his arms up, staggered, dropped. Jean-Paul's relations weren't such bad shots after all. There—close by, on their left, at the near edge of the plateau—Jean-Paul's people. She could see them now: black hats and jackets, running low and shouting, taking up positions, crouching down behind the menhirs and the stones.

"Come on." West sounded like himself again. He nodded toward a clump of bushes twenty yards or so away. "Okay?"

"Okay."

They made it. No one noticed, everyone too busy shooting everybody else. The arm hurt when she ran; a little, nothing much.

"Look," West was panting, "here's the thing." He pointed to the edge of the plateau. The ground sloped all along the edge, it fell away, and there was brush, good cover. "What we do is slip along below the edge of the plateau and when we hit the valley, we cut through it to the car."

The sun was sinking, lots of shadow, and there was some cover for them to the plateau's edge. A lot of *maquis* and some trees. Some open spaces in between, though, and she didn't like the thought of creeping through the valley, all-fours in the muck and how about those rats, let's hear it for the rats, please.

He tended to her shoulder, more or less. He helped her take her jacket off and ripped her jersey by the wound and said it wouldn't scar, he thought, as if he knew, and made a sort of bandage with his handkerchief.

The pattern of the shooting changed: long silences, then lots of banging. Saving ammunition? She didn't know and didn't care. The thing you did was wait until the bursts and then, while they were plugging at each other, you took off.

They made it to the brush below the edge of the plateau. Good cover, lots of undergrowth. They started toward the little valley, keeping low. Her hip hurt when she ran. The ground was rough. The undergrowth began to thicken, more and more of it: tendrils and vines and cactus—*maquis*. They were in the valley, just below the plateau's edge.

She went down on her hands and knees, then stretched out, panting. West tumbled down beside her. There was shouting up above on the plateau. In English. Someone shouting English. It was Drum, Inspector Drum. She knew the voice and she'd been right, it was Drum in the market doorway. Then another voice. American. The man in gray? What was the shouting all about? New battle plans, first shouted out in English, then in French. Get West and get the girl. Forget about the locals now, they'd keep. Spread out, start hunting, comb the place.

Terrific.

West was touching her. His hand was on her cheek. "We've got to do it on all fours. Okay?"

"Okay," she said.

He started crawling. "Take it slow and easy."

Slow, for damn sure. Inch by inch. No noise, careful, mustn't move the stalks or branches and the rocks were sharp and thorns and there were bugs and little crawly things. Her arm hurt—Carrie didn't mind pain, even liked it—but it hurt. The thing to do was think of things. Like shoes and ships and sealing wax. What imagery. O.K., she was the Walrus and the Carpenter said, "Lay it on me: sealing wax" and what was that?

Was something coming? Scratching through the *maquis*. Did she hear it? Claws? No, not claws; nails, the sound of horrid feet. Not rats. Boars? Wild boar with pig-red eyes and filthy yellow fangs? She felt an urge to stand and scream. Not help-me-save-me screams. Mad screams. She hadn't felt this mad since Mother sent her friends home in the middle of her seventh birthday party.

"Boar?" She started talking to it, just a whisper. "Fuck off, boar." She crawled on, straight ahead, right at the sound. She meant to bite the bastard if she saw him but he went away. Then more things went away: the feeling in her knees and then her hands and, by and by, not knowing how she made it, she lay stretched out on her back, a sunset sky above her.

"You okay?" West panted.

Never. She would never be O.K. again. His head moved into view. He looked a mess. She moved an arm and murmured, "Come here, baby," and he put his head down on her breast. Not long; just for a minute.

They had come out of the *maquis* dead on target. Just ahead, beyond the little hilltop, was the field where Kalman parked the car. Keys didn't matter, she was good with wires but—

She sat up. "What if the car's gone, what if Kalman got here first?"

"We walk."

They stood; not straight up, crouching low. Her knees were agony. The air was cool; not cold yet but it would be when the sun went down. The sun was hanging, darkish red, above the peaks of Monte Cinto; sky already shot with color. Their shadows, long and black, stretched out in front of them. They reached the hilltop.

Kalman's car was there. And then some. Parked around it, scattered, in no pattern, were—how many?—twenty shiny white police cars. Also scattered in no pattern were a half a dozen gendarmes, left behind to man the radios or some damn thing. Two of them were playing with a pocketknife, a game. Another lit a cigarette.

She dropped down fast and started swearing. Dirty, filthy words, the worst things she could think of.

"I'm with you." West shook his head. Then, suddenly, he grinned; a tight grin, not a funny one.

With which, he took a deep breath, opened wide and started bellowing. "They're in the *maquis!* Move it! Move, you dumb fucks! Down the road! Toward Calacuccia!" He sounded like a sergeant.

The gendarmes stiffened, guns came out.

"Okay," he said, "give it to me in French."

She gave it to him.

A minute later, she was underneath the dashboard, panting, fishing for the wires. West was at the wheel, foot on the gas and mucking with the gear stick.

"Cut it out, you'll flood it."

"Sorry."

She was thumbs, all thumbs, her hands kept shaking. There. The motor kicked, then died. Again.

The thing was wheezing, then it caught. He gunned it and the motor roared. She got up on the seat. He slammed the clutch in, stripped the gears. The car shot backwards. "Where's fucking first gear on this fucking car?" She showed him.

They banged across the rocks and gullies, made it to the road. He swerved left, back the way they came. She took a last look out the rear. All peace and quiet. No pursuit. Not yet.

He had it up to sixty. Citroen; the French police used Citroens. A few years old, well cared for, ninety horse, twin carbs; not like a sports car but not bad. The thing could hit a hundred twenty on the straight-away but if there was a straight half-mile on Corsica, she hadn't seen it.

They tore past Calacuccia. Dark shadows. Twilight. Not a car, no traffic. Rotten road: all dips and curves, loose gravel cracks, no banking on the turns, no shoulders. Sixty-five. He took the corners wrong. She told him so.

"Stop braking on the curves."

"Stop braking? I'll go off the road."

"Shift down."

"Shift down?" They didn't shift down when he was a kid, his father had a 1940 Nash, last one before the War, kept it all through the forties and he drove it, West did, drove it plenty, took it up to sixty all the time and what was all this shifting-down crap? She explained. He wasn't bad.

Five miles or so and they would hit the road that went from Corte back the way they came. She took a deep breath, checked the mirror; nothing on the road behind them. They were in the clear. Home free.

But where exactly were they going? Corsica had water all around it. Steal a boat and sail into the sunset? Possible. Or ferries; surely there were ferryboats and they could slip on, stow away. An answer would provide itself and she was feeling hungry, a sure sign of life. She was imagining a steak when West asked her to check the chalice.

Had she hurt it, had it landed on a rock? She took it out: no marks. She held it in both hands and turned it slowly, staring at it. Was it Hunter-Donne's or Kalman's? Both their stories could be true, though there were details in what Kalman said that troubled her. Like wouldn't he have asked for a receipt from Mannheim, something down on paper? They were dealing in the millions. Wouldn't Mannheim, wouldn't any honest businessman have drawn a document? But was he honest? Kalman's story, if you bought it, meant that Mannheim was a thief. Was it conceivable: He was a rich man, famous; yachts and movies. Could a man like that do—what had Kalman said exactly? Disappearing money, vanishing in Swilzerland, "he told me so today."

She had it. That was Mannheim's boat, the one she'd seen, the big one, crew of thirty, omelets on the deck. It all made sense. Mannheim had been in St. Tropez and Kalman must have called, demanding money, something, which was why the boat took off so suddenly. And Kalman had been—Margit said so—in the harbor with some friends when they had come that morning. Mannheim was in Calvi, on his boat. They had to get there, get to Mannheim. There was something rotten and she knew it. Why? Because Mannheim had come when Kalman called, changed plans, and steamed off in the middle of the night and—

"Carrie!"

"What?!" Bolt upright. "What's the matter?"

Men, a line of men across the road. The junction of the road from Corte. Uniforms, the men wore uniforms with epaulets and flat hats. Legionnaires. The Foreign Legion. Radioed: that's what they'd done. To Headquarters in Corte. Army trucks, police cars parked along the sides. There wasn't any way around. She should have guessed or thought ahead, she was so smart.

"We've got to stop."

"The hell we do." West's voice was flat. "I'm going through." He floored it.

"West!" The car was rattling: eight-five.

"They'll break and run."

"What if they don't?"

"Tough shit."

"It's murder."

"They've been shooting at my ass all afternoon."

He came down on the horn. They broke. The line broke and the car shot through. Nobody hit. The turn, hard left, the Corte road, he shifted down, gear's screamed, the back wheels floated, no control, like ice, don't fight it, rifle fire, shooting, they were shooting, window shattered, broken glass. The car was weaving, crashing sound, they bounced off something, straightened out, the motor roared, went faster, held the road, he'd done it, brought them through. Sharp curve ahead. And more curves. Sirens now, behind them. Squealing tires. Sun down, darker, getting dark. No end. It was the longest road.

She looked at West and wondered what their life would be like if they had one.

# XXIII

It was freezing, icy air in through the broken window. Noise; the motor and the rattling and the sirens behind them. Sometime soon, they had to hit the coast road, couldn't keep on going down forever. She was sitting close to him, curled up against the cold, and looking small. He felt enormous, nothing bad would happen, he could put her in his pocket, keep her safe from anything.

The road was wild; rocks and pits, loose gravel. But the trouble, the real trouble, if you didn't count the mountain goat—he hadn't seen it, just two glowing spots three feet above the road, what was it, glowing things were eyes, the animal just stood there, swerved and missed it, left the road a second, scraped the rocks—and if you didn't count the truck he didn't hit, the real trouble was the mist. It came in patches. Light stuff, gray; and when it came, the road got airbrushed. Like the dirty pictures when he was a kid; you couldn't see it but you knew the thing was there.

They hadn't talked much. She had given him her theory about Mannheim and his yacht and how important Mannheim was and she was right. He was the middleman, he sat between the buyer and the seller and there were a lot of questions but the burning question was: Was Mannheim's yacht still there? The shore was where they had to get, a boat was what they needed and they'd passed by villas on their walk that morning, someone would have left a skiff, a rowboat, something on the beach. But if the yacht was gone, how were they going to catch it in a rowboat?

Signs ahead. The coast road. Left toward Calvi. Melvil took it on two wheels, went faster, roaring now, past Jean-Paul's place, ten miles or so to Calvi, really making time. They'd leave the car outside of town, make for the beach—

The motor died. Just coughed and went, came back, then went again. No gas? For Christ's sake, were they out of gas? He listened for the sirens. They were there, not gaining, hadn't gained the whole way down; not losing, either. How far back? He asked her.

"Hard to tell. Two miles, give or take."

How long was that in time? The motor went again, the needle dropping, down to fifty, forty-five. They had to ditch the car. Just get the damn thing off the road and out of sight. Dark, hard to see much. Trees, the trees showed in the headlights. Any rocks? Was there a ditch? He couldn't tell. The motor coughed and farted; pick a spot, he had to risk it.

"Any tricks to this?"

"Don't hit the brakes too hard, just ease it off."

He braked. The needle dropped to thirty, twenty-five . . . Was that a clearing through the trees? There? Twenty, fifteen . . . brake it easy.

"Hold on, here we go."

He edged it off the road. Rocks right away, then thudding down, a lot of trees, they glanced off one and into underbrush. A ditch, he bounced up, hit the roof, held on, just held the wheel. Big rock ahead, a huge one. Bigger than the car. The steering wheel came at him.

Something buzzed. A tiny sting. A buzzing thing was biting him. He ought to slap it but he didn't feel like moving.

"Carrie?"

"Hi."

She sounded far away. Where was she? "You okay?"

"Fine."

She was fine. He slapped the buzzing thing. He must have missed it. There was whinning now. Like sirens. Getting louder. He sat up.

"It's them," he said.

"I know."

The sirens. He could hear the sirens, coming closer, howling down the road. How far away? Where was the road? He turned. He saw headlights, faintly, through the brush. Right by, they went by, went right by.

"We made it." Safe. He felt like moving, tried the door. It opened. He got out, felt dizzy, leaned against the car. His chest hurt where the wheel had hit him. Otherwise—he checked; the arms, the legs, the neck—not bad. He felt his way around the car. Dark night, no moon, some stars. She was standing when he got there.

"Totaled out." She shook her head.

He looked. Big gash along the side, hood all banged up and they were in one piece and standing.

"Beginner's luck," he said. "You want to rest?"

"No time." She shook her head. "There's bound to be a roadblock, probably in Calvi. They'd have radioed ahead and set one up. They'll get there, turn around and come back looking for us."

"Yeah." They'd find where he'd gone off the road. He used the road to get his bearings. It wove along the shore, sometimes right on it, sometimes inland. They were inland now, a little, but the sea—he couldn't hear it yet—was close. It had to be. He took her hand and felt her wince; that arm must hurt. They started off. A lot of stumbling, hard to see and there were gullies, rocks and cactus. Nothing like the *maquis*, though, and they would hit the beach soon, find a boat. If Mannheim's yacht was gone, they'd sail along the shore, keep going, maybe try for France, depended on the weather–

"Carrie?"

She was panting, just a little. "What?"

"Is that the sea?"

They stopped and listened. Bugs and birds and sirens. Not too near but near enough. The cops were coming back. Pick up the step. A fallen tree. He helped her over it. A clump of bushes. Go around them, keep on moving. Sudden drop, four feet or so, and there it was: the beach. He went down first, held out his arms. They stood there close together, listening to the sirens and the lapping of the waves.

The beach was rocky and the sea looked gray. Which way was Calvi? Left. The sirens died; they'd found the marks along the road. They would start pouring through the woods now, dozens of them. It was faster wading through the water. Clammy, cold. They came around a little point. Lights glimmered in the distance, tiny. Villas? Cops with flashlights?

"Villas," Carrie said. "We're going to make it."

Moving faster, splashing through the shallow water. He was good with boats, the same way he was good with cars: he hadn't done it yet but he was going to be terrific. Around another little point. A little bay, more lights and voices.

There were voices.

Calm, don't bolt. He reached for Carrie, held her. Voices coming closer. What to do? Slip back into the woods? Hold still? There was a ridge of something–shrubbery?–between them and the voices. Use it. Duck behind the shrubs.

They crouched. Cold feet, cold hands. He crossed his fingers.

"Bored?" A girl's voice, not ten feet away. "I'm bored to fucking death. It's zombie time out there."

He couldn't catch the answer. Murmurs. Then the girl again.

"The old fart, playing rummy with the living dead all night, it's all he does."

She had a nice voice. Slightly smashed but very nice. He knew it, didn't he? Impossible.

"The *Samovar*? It's Buchenwald with servants."

Yes, he knew her, absolutely knew this girl. Who was she? Other voices, then the girl's again. "The tender's on its way to pick me up. Good night and thanks."

He'd met her. Where? At work? A friend of someone's? No, it was her voice he knew. He'd spoken to her. When? He knew her name, too. When it came to him, he said it.

"Nancy!"

"Hi. Who's there?"

He straightened up and moved around the shrubs and into wonderland. Vast rolling lawn, a swimming pool and formal gardens and a villa, far off, glowing in the night.

Nancy was glowing, too. Soft blonde hair, pale skin, sweet features and a long white dress that clung and fell away and clung again. She held a highball glass, half full, and didn't seem the least bit startled. She handed him the drink and told him he could use it, asked him where she knew him from. Antibes, the phone call, Mannheim on the *Samovar*, she'd liked his voice and asked him over.

"Better late than never." Nancy took his arm and smiled. He was looking at her cleavage when a voice that sounded more or less like Carrie's asked him who his friend was. "Carrie-Nancy." It came out like one word, mumbled. Carrie said hello to Nancy in a funny sort of way, unzipped her bag, got out a brush and mirror, took one look and threw them in again.

"The tender's coming," Nancy said.

And so it was, putt-putting toward a little dock. There was a rowboat tied up at one side: they wouldn't need it now. They had to get invited, that was all, and he was wondering how to bring that off when Nancy did it for him.

"Look," she said, big smile. "You'd be doing me a favor. It's like Forest Lawn with caviar out there and if you'd come, just for a day or two, there's lots of room. Come on."

There were two sailors in the tender, dressed in snappy whites. They got on board. The motor thrummed. The boat moved slowly, curving from the shore, then roared away. He wriggled over, close to Carrie. It was misty and the sea was calm. Pale lights from villas glimmered on the shore, then faded out. They curved around a point of land, sent up a sheet of spray, and just ahead, at anchor, lit up like the Crystal Palace, sat the *Samovar*.

The first mate waited on the deck. He helped them up, went with them to the stern. They stood among the bamboo chairs and cocktail tables, just outside the lounge. The doors were glass and through them he could see eight people, maybe ten; long gowns and black ties. It was after dinner: there were brandies and cigars. And suddenly, he wondered what would Mannheim do? He'd recognize them, certainly. Their pictures must be in the Paris papers, he'd be following the case. If he were honest, if his hands were clean, he'd radio to shore and turn them in.

He turned to Nancy. "Look, if Mr. Mannheim wants to meet us—"

"He won't care. I'll tell him you're old friends of mine."

She grinned, went in. He watched her cross the room to Mannheim. He looked different from his photographs. Much older, and his eyes—the photos didn't catch his eyes at all. Half-closed, half-open; like a gila monster watching flies.

Two words and Nancy came out smiling, led the way downstairs and rang for Cecil. He appeared. A black man in a spotless steward's jacket; elderly, a face of great refinement and an English accent. Nancy said to wash and rest and ring for food if they were hungry. As for drinks, there was a little bar inside and they could help themselves. She blew them each a kiss and left them there with Cecil.

It was some room he showed them. French, done to the teeth, bronze doré on the built-in chests and make-up table, crystal fixtures, walls and curtains done in matching toile. A whore's dream and he loved it and two bathrooms, one for each of them, with faucets plated gold and there were nozzles in the showers all up and down the sides. Too much. He made them each a double double and headed for the shower.

Water. Cool and fresh. It showered down all over him. He ducked and let it rain and rattle on his head, then on his back. The soap was fine, the lather felt like velvet and the dirt of England, France and Corsica was flowing, peeling, running off of him and down the drain.

The water, as it guzzled down, was changing color, lighter, almost clear. He was beginning to be clean. He raised his arms, his fingers touched the tile ceiling, tingling spray. All over. Tingling in the groin. He looked. The thing was standing up. Fantastic. After what he'd been through. Standing up for Carrie. For his woman. What a world.

The towel was thick and soft. He dried all over. Carefully. Colognes and powders on a shelf. He never used them. Well, why not? Where did you put cologne? All over, only here and there, just on your wrists like womern did? He poured a palmful, splashed it on his chest. It smelled good. Then the powder. Armpits first; then balls. Still standing up: you beast, you dirty old man. At your age.

She was lying on the bed, as clean as he was and as naked. On her back, not moving. Oh, the whiteness of her skin, long dancers' legs converging at the private place. His throat was thick, felt solid, and he couldn't swallow. He went on stiff legs to the bed, sat next to her. Her arm, below the shoulder, looked red and raw: a cruel line, like an angry burn. He kissed it, barely touching.

"Carrie?" No response. Her eyes were funny-looking, sullen. "Carrie?" Did she see him? What was wrong? He took her shoulders and he shook her. "Carrie?"

Shook her gently and she came apart.

Literally, as if she were made of many pieces. Like a crystal rock, formed under dreadful pressures, held together, shattered at a single tap. No tears, no weeping till the very end when all of it was over, out, and there was nothing left.

He learned a lot about her. Heard it in the strangest voice: a dry voice, merciless, no pity. Not for Carrie. Carrie was a bad girl and she should have died a lot of times, a car crash, pills, so many of them, stomach pumps and vomiting and vodka, like the ads said, didn't smell, the teachers never knew and Sandra—that was Mother—never home and Gardener, he was disappointed in her, Carrie was a disappointment; but Cissie and Joanna, sisters, they were big and they were good and did right, pretty sisters. Carrie never did right which was why you couldn't love her. No one ever could or ever did or ever had, you couldn't blame them, not their fault: not Jacques or Philip, Dick or Dieter, Bob—it sounded like the roster of a football team—and he had heard enough names so he slapped her.

She smiled as if it were a victory and told him he could beat her if he wanted to, she didn't mind. He stroked her but she told him none of that, she didn't want it, not from him and she was leaving, leaving now. She sat up, warned him not to try to stop her, she would hurt him, she could do it. She stood up. He reached out for her and she warned him in a whisper, let her go. He held. It was about then that the weeping started.

It went on quite a while, convulsively at first, then softer, very soft. He rocked her: Carrie was his baby, Carrie was his little girl and nothing bad would ever happen to her any more. She said she loved him, in a tiny voice. He said he knew she did and he believed her and he kissed her in a brother-sister sort of way. He felt such tenderness, it filled his chest. They lay back on the bed, hands moving, his and hers, all over, everywhere.

At which point, someone in the hallway started knocking at the door. If he ignored it, it would go away.

The knocking stopped. Then Cecil's voice: "Miss Gardener, Dr. West?"

So Mannheim knew them. No ignoring that.

"What is it, Cecil?"

"Mr. Mannheim hopes to have the pleasure of your company at dinner, sir."

"Now?"

"If it please you."

The subjunctive, if you please. He looked at Carrie. "Clothes." She whispered it. "No clothes."

"We've nothing to wear."

Cecil had thought of that and if Dr. West would be good enough to open up, he had some things that might be suitable. The things turned out to be a smashing dress of Nancy's and, since no one else on board was quite his size, a uniform, compliments of the ship's first officer. Melvil took the things, sent Cecil off for gauze and some adhesive tape, kicked shut the door.

She bounced up from the bed, eyes bright. "He lets us know he knows us and then asks us out for dinner. Don't you love it?"

"Not especially. It could be just to keep us quiet till the gendarmes come."

"No way." She shook her head. "He figured on a quiet deal, no names, no questions asked; and what he's got is international hysterics. Nervous-making and he's full of questions; what we're up to, what we know, what we've found out. After dinner, he might call the cops in, there's a chance of that. But not before."

She had a point. He slipped his trousers on. "We ought to be prepared. What do you think he'll ask?"

She shook her head. "Attack, always attack. What do we want to ask him?"

"I don't know, about the provenance."

"You bet about the provenance. The more I think, the more I feel there's something wrong with Kalman's story."

"I believed him."

"To a point. I think the things he actually said are true. It's what he didn't say . . . Look, put yourself in Kalman's head. Assume he owns the chalice, that it's really his. He wants to sell it, for the reasons that he said. Why go to Mannheim? What does he need Mannheim for?"

"Same reason that you always use a middleman: to keep yourself a secret."

"Right. You don't want your name involved. Why don't you?"

"To avoid the taxes."

"That's what gets me. Kalman's leaving Corsica, he planned to all along, he only sold the chalice so that he could get away. French taxes aren't a problem for him, not if he's in Switzerland or someplace. I don't think he needed Mannheim. I think it's the other way around."

"You're guessing."

"Sure I am. It could be Kalman went to Mannheim because Mannheim knew the market and could get the highest price. But just suppose it was the other way around. Suppose it all began with Mannheim, that he needed Kalman. What would he need Kalman for?"

He looked at her, stopped buttoning his shirt. "The provenance?"

"And why does Mannheim need a provenance? Because his chalice doesn't have one and what kind of chalice doesn't and who do we know who's had a chalice stolen?"

Could it be? Fantastic? It was logical enough and Carrie, as they talked about it, sounded more and more convinced. Somehow, Sir Winston's chalice must have found its way to Adolf Mannheim.

He felt absolutely great and Carrie looked sensational. Her dress was silk with swirling colors, mauves and lavenders. It had a jacket. She decided it was best to leave her arm unbandaged and he helped her slip the jacket on. Her eyes were shining, no sign at all of what she'd just been through.

His uniform was navy blue. The shirt was white, the tie was black but what he loved about it was the braid, three rows of gold braid at the bottom of each sleeve. There was a hat with gold stuff on the visor, too. He popped it on for just a second, tossed it to the bed and took her arm. The time had come to go and lay a trap for Adolf Mannheim.

They followed Cecil to the dining room. Done like an English mansion, everything mahogany. Thick carpet, red; thin waiter, white. There were two places set, one midway down each side. The china and the crystal were exquisite. Not a thing to eat in sight. They sat. Champagne was poured and Cecil and the waiter left the room.

No Mannheim. Did he want to make an entrance, get them nervous? Melvil sipped his wine and looked around and felt his stomach tighten; not with nerves so much as with a kind of hopelessness. The wealth of what he saw—two first-class Miros, a Cézanne—the money and the power Mannheim had. A great, maybe the greatest film producer, a distinguished man. Not very active any more. Why should he be? He had his houses and his yacht, his art collection and his famous friends. The man knew absolutely everybody in the world, from royalty to politicians, millionaires, celebrities. Would such a man do something criminal? It made no sense. At all. He looked at Carrie.

"Yeah," she said. "I know. But think how much it costs to keep it up."

He shook his head. "If all of this were mine—you'd have to be a fool to risk it."

"Or a knave."

He was about to answer when the motors started. Deep vibrations, humming. They were moving.

"Carrie—?"

She was grinning. "I was right. No cops till after dinner. If at all. He would have kept us here at anchor if . . ."

She let it trail away. She'd heard it. In the hallway. Someone coming.

Mannheim. Moving through the doorway toward the table. Heavy, short and thick and oddly graceful. Coming stomach first; hard stomach, clearing all that stood before it, like a prow of an icebreaker, slicing things away.

He sat; the seat of power, at the head. His face was serious and thoughtful. He didn't speak, just looked at them, first one and then the other. They were being judged, that's how it felt; as if the man were searching them for values, weighing them before deciding what to do. Weird, sitting there in silence, watching, being watched; but what he said was even weirder.

What he said was, "May I see it?"

"Certainly," said Carrie, easily as if she'd just been asked what time it was. Unzipped her bag, she did, and took the chalice out and put it on the table.

Mannheim looked at it and sighed and shook his

head. "So beautiful. What it has brought us to." His eyes, what you could see of them, were soft and sad. They wavered, left the chalice. "I am sorry to have kept you here so long. I have been listening to police calls. They continue searching for you in the woods and there is much confusion. When it lifts, they will begin to think of boats and so we sail a little while we talk. You must be very hungry."

Mannheim rang a little silver bell and Cecil and the waiter came with caviar and more champagne. He looked at Carrie. She was smiling at the caviar. How could she eat?

The waiter left. Then Cecil. Mannheim cleared his throat. "You mystify me, Dr. West. Miss Gardener, too. You strike me as unlikely thieves. It feels wrong, out of character, and when I think of what you've done these last few days, you make no sense to me at all. And yet, you stole the chalice—there it stands. How mystifying."

"No, it's really very simple." Why not say it? "We've been looking for the truth."

"The truth, of all things." Mannheim smiled. "And have you found it?"

"Not yet but we're coming close."

"When you arrive, you'll find it's what I've said it was. We must be frank with one another, very frank. Did Stefan Kalman tell you . . ." Mannheim sighed, looked at the chalice. "Beauty is the cause of so much ugliness. How pure our chalice is and yet it's driving Stefan Kalman to destroy me. Did he tell you I had cheated him?"

He wanted frank, he'd get frank. "Yes."

"I banked it for him, all three million, every penny. In Geneva."

"Can you prove it?" That was Carrie, on the attack.

"Only Kalman can. He has the papers. Greed." He shook his massive head. "It is a dreadful thing, the wish for more. I have been driven by it and I know.

Poor Stefan. I have been his friend for more than twenty years. I knew his father and his wife, Jeannine, how beautiful she was and it has shaken him, the loss of her. His world is torn apart and he has come to be half-mad, I think."

A sigh, a sip of wine. "He called me when she died. November. I was on the boat. We sailed at once and I was shocked, the change in him her death had made. We sat, two old friends, on his terrace. He had put the chalice on a little table. I had seen it in his bedroom many times, I knew its meaning, how he loved it. How I wish to God I'd said no when he asked me, begged me, please to help him sell it. Parting with it was so painful, he could not endure the meetings and negotiations, I must do it for him. He was weeping when he put it in my hands.

"And now, he threatens me. How is that possible? To say I cheated him. And worse, he has much worse to say. Perhaps he hates me. Many people do, I have been turned upon before. Did Stefan say to you—" He swallowed, couldn't get it out. "Did Stefan say the chalice wasn't his? To me, this very morning, standing here, that's what he said he'd say. Do you know what my friends would think, what that would do to me? My God . . ." His voice broke. There was perspiration on his forehead and his cheeks were flushed.

"I don't believe it." Carrie sounded shocked. "You mean to say he got his money and he wants three million more?"

"I don't believe it either." Mannheim wiped his forehead. "It's a madness, it will pass. Perhaps—he didn't say to you it wasn't his?" She shook her head. "Perhaps he has forgotten it already."

Cecil came and took their plates away. More food appeared. A silver platter, steaks or something, Melvil didn't really notice, he was busy sorting out what Mannheim said. It sounded good. He didn't want it to but all the points that Carrie made seemed wiped away. Kalman did need a middleman and they had only Kalman's word he never got his money and he had seemed mad or half-mad up there in the menhirs.

"Mr. Mannheim?" Carrie talking. "Tell me, I've been wondering. I don't suppose you know Sir Winston Hunter-Donne?"

Mannheim smiled. "Old Hunter-Donne? Delightful fellow, most amazing grasp of things. I know him well, good friend, I saw him last in—was it January?"

Melvil's heart stopped, absolutely didn't beat, but all he said was, "Really?"

"Yes, in January. We're preparing a new film you know, *The Loves of George the Third,* and I was looking for locations down in Bath. His digs are nearby—but of course you've been there."

Carrie nodded. "Awful thing, what happened to his chalice."

"Dreadful." Mannheim nodded. "Didn't mention it to me; perhaps it hadn't happened yet. I didn't know about the theft till last week when I read the papers. You don't think—?" Full stop. He looked at Carrie, eyes wide open. "My dear young lady, you don't think this chalice is Sir Winston's?"

Carrie met him head on. "It's an academic possibility."

"My dear, I had the chalice in my hands before Sir Winston dug his up. I told you Stefan gave it to me in November. I had been in Rome to raise some money for the film and I was resting on the boat when Stefan called and I went straight to Calvi, then home to Geneva with the chalice and I wrote to your VanStraaten all about it and he came to me at once, I saw him in Geneva Christmas week, and then to Paris, money, money, London, down to Bath and back to London, polar flight, Los Angeles—" He stopped, a little out of breath. "My God, I'd be a lunatic to sell Sir Winston's chalice to the Met. He's sure to claim it."

Carrie nodded. "If you knew the thing was stolen when you sold it."

Mannheim's eyes came down to half. "Young lady, I have been accused of many things but . . . This is not Sir Winston's chalice. I am not a thief. I do not roam the countryside at night to rob distinguished men. If this is your idea of truth, if this is what you are pursuing, heaven help you both."

He shook his head, stood up. His face was grave. He leaned across the table, took the chalice, held it in his hand. "To steal a thing of beauty is a wickedness. I want no part of it." He sadly put it down. "The boat is sailing to Alassio. I'm meeting friends there in the morning. When we dock, I shall myself call the police and I will stand out on the deck and hand you over to them personally. I have done no wrong. Think what you will of me, my hands are clean. May God forgive you."

That was it. He turned and went. Without another look.

Dead silence. Melvil watched him go, then turned to Carrie.

"Bullshit." That was all she said until they got back to the cabin.

# XXIV

Cecil saw them to their room. He had the brandy that she asked for on a tray. He put it down, asked courteously was there more that he could do and, when there wasn't, bowed, wished them a good night's sleep, went out and locked the door.

Big click. She laughed at that—delicious—flopped down on the bed and burst out with it. "What a rat. 'May God forgive you.' Boy, who writes his dialogue? I knew we had him when I saw the caviar." She'd had her share of caviar from other Mannheims; always meant they wanted something. Usually her tail. What did this Mannheim want? She knew, she knew—

"We have got him?" West sounded angry, hands stuffed in his pockets. "We're locked in and when we get to shore he's calling the police and we have got him? And where the hell's Alassio?"

"Italian Riviera. It's a little port not far from Genoa. And as for Mannheim, it's like this." Be careful, watch it: it was dangerous sometimes to know too much, men got resentful. "What I think is maybe—I said maybe, okay?"

"Okay."

"I don't think he wants to make that call. That's not to say he won't. He's on the spot, he looks extremely fishy if he doesn't turn us in. But West, that chalice is Sir Winston's and the last place Mannheim wants to be is in the spotlight handing West and Gardener to the cops."

He frowned. "I don't know . . . "

"Oh, come on. Why does he wait till morning? Why not radio from sea? He needs the night to think. He's got a lot to think about."

"Well, maybe. Maybe so." He nodded slowly, started for the brandy.

"What I think is, he's running scared. He made this Kalman story up, he's stuck with it and what that whole scene was about was making us believe him. What a story." And she poured it out. Believe that Kalman was obsessed by greed? No way. Believe he had three million in the bank and wanted more, for God's sake? And that line, had Kalman said the chalice wasn't his? You bet your ass it wasn't his. "I mean, believe that Kalman had a genuine Pasiteles and kept it in his bedroom, never talked or bragged about it, never showed it to a living soul for forty years except to Adolf Mannheim? Shit for brains, that's what you've got if you believe it, you've got—"

"Okay, take it easy, I'm with you."

He handed her a brandy. She was angry, really mad. It was a little crazy but she couldn't help it. All the Mannheims of this world, their endless women, Nancys on each arm; and hating them, they hated women, and the things they made them do because they couldn't get it up. She took a swallow, felt the brandy burning.

He sat down by her on the bed and started talking. Organized and sensible. The chalice was Sir Winston's. Reason said so. How—Sir Winston had been right about it—how could there be two chalices? How, after two millennia, could one pop up in Somerset and one in Corsica? And both first-century, both with repoussé work, both with writing on the bottom? It didn't matter if Sir Winston thought it was the Grail; the Grail was legendary but the chalice wasn't. It was real and it was stolen. January. But if Mannheim had his chalice in November—

"It's the dates." West bounded off the bed. "If we could prove that Mannheim didn't have it in November, didn't have it until after it was stolen—"

"Right." The timing was the key. Mannheim had spelled it out. In detail, every place he'd been and when he'd been there. "Right, let's take his story step by step."

"He was in Rome, he said, for money for his movie. Then he's on his boat and Kalman calls and he takes off for Calvi. Right so far?"

She nodded. Then what? Mannheim had been talking fast, what was it he had said? "Geneva next. He went home to Geneva, didn't he?"

"That's when he wrote to Pieter. Pieter came and saw the chalice—when? When did he say it was?"

"Christmas week."

"That's right and then he went to Paris, London—"

He stopped absolutely cold, just stood there, frozen. Then his lips moved and he said it. "Pieter saw the chalice first in February."

"What?"

"I saw the correspondence. Pieter showed it to me, brought it to my office, I went with him to the Board and Jesus, Carrie, it was February. Mannheim lied about the dates. He panicked when we got him on Sir Winston and he tried to change the dates. VanStraaten in Geneva Christmas week? It never happened. It was February."

That was it. They'd solved it. He was guilty, Mannheim didn't have the chalice in November. He had blown it, given it away. He'd even told them what his motive was, why he had done it.

"You know why? she asked. "Because he hasn't made a film in years and now, *The Loves of George the Third*? There's one the world is hungry for. The rat can't raise the money."

It struck her funny. She was laughing and he caught it from her, picked her up right off the floor and started swirling her around. They were like that when the phone rang.

"What the hell?" He frowned and put her down.

"Beats me," she said.

The phone was on the bedside table, an elaborate affair with rows of push buttons. He picked it up.

"Hello? Oh, Nancy. Hi. A party? No, no thanks. We're just too tired. That's what Manny said? Who's Manny? Oh. Did Mr. Mannheim have anything else to say? About us. That's all? Sure, I'll tell her. See you in the morning." He hung up.

"Well?"

"Nancy says she hopes you liked the dress."

"And that's all Mannheim said about us, that we're tired?"

"That's all."

She grinned. "I wonder if he's figured out he's blown it yet."

They talked a long time after Nancy's call. At first, about Sir Winston and poor Sanderson. Poor bastard; had he made his story up or had he been so frantic with his feelings for his Win that he believed what he was saying? Either way, there was no ruined chalice on that hilltop: he could search his pits till doomsday.

Mannheim fit the story perfectly. He was a natural choice to bring the chalice to. Whoever stole it from Sir Winston—anyone who knew enough to rob an archeologist—would know of Mannheim's reputation as a middleman. She got a real charge thinking how excited Mannheim must have been. Just one look at the chalice and he must have dropped his teeth. He knew about old plate because of Kalman's things. He knew how valuable the chalice was and Kalman was the cover story of all time.

After they got in bed, there was some talk about New York. They had to get there, God alone knew how, and see VanStraaten. They would tell him what they knew and with the letters dated February and VanStraaten at their side, they'd meet the press and so long, Charlie, that was that for Adolf Mannheim.

It was almost two and they were getting drowsy when he turned to her and said, "Look, Carrie, how the hell do we get off the boat?"

She shrugged. "We'll see."

"I mean, we're locked in. What if there are guards outside?"

She didn't think there would be. "Look, a lot depends on when we reach Alassio. If it's still dark and everyone's asleep, that's one thing. If it's noon and everybody's up . . ." She yawned, she was exhausted. "And a lot depends on if we anchor out at sea or tie up at the dock." She yawned again. "I'm sorry, I can't cope with it, I'm beat."

"Okay."

They made a deal to spell each other through the night: two hours on, two off. It was important one of them be up when they arrived. She kissed his hand and that was all she knew until he awakened her at four.

It was—she held her watch close, squinted at it—almost five now. She was up and pacing. West lay stretched out on his left side, making sleep sounds. Pacing helped her think. There might be problems getting off, a lot of them. She stopped and frowned. Something was wrong. No motors. They had cut the motors.

She hurried to the porthole and peered out. She saw a string of faded yellow lights along a dock. The dock was long and L-shaped, broad and flat on top. The sky was getting lighter and it would be dawn soon. Some of the crew were up and moving, she could hear them now. A muffled call, a gentle bump, then whirring as the winches doled the cables out.

She knew the drill. She'd come into a lot of harbors in her day. They would secure the ship, connect the hose lines up to take on water, hook into the electric outlet to save the batteries. What else? She heard a car start. A little van was moving toward them down the dock. Supplies of some kind. What else would they do now? Not much, but if the harbor was equipped, they'd plug the phones in.

Jesus Christ, the phone. She spun around, three steps, and fumbled with the bedlight, got it on. Those buttons on the phone. She read the labels: Captain, Steward, Master's Cabin, Lounge, Library, Dining Room. Then Staterooms, nine of them and, at the end, the one she wanted: Shore.

They wouldn't have it plugged in yet. She'd have to wait. She tugged her skirt on. Backwards, Pucci always did things backwards. Then the blouse. Her hair was hopeless and her arm still hurt. Outside, the sky was getting brighter. Shoes. She blessed Nancy for wearing sevens and went back to the phone.

She pushed Shore. Nothing much at first, then snaps and crackles. "*Pronto?*" Carrie said. No answer. Louder. "*Pronto, pronto?*" Not too loud, don't wake the boat up.

"Carrie?" West was blinking at her.

"*Pronto?*" Nothing, only hissing on the line.

"What the hell are you doing."

"What does it look like I'm doing? *Pronto?*" What was that? Was that a voice? She thought it said, "*Aspetti un momento, per favore.*" She answered it. "*Vorrei un tassì. Per favore, mi chiami un tassì.*"

"Who are you calling, for the love of God?"

She looked at him. "I'm calling us a taxi."

Which was not as easy as it sounded, not in Alassio at five-fifteen. The operator was an angel, kept on trying numbers—"*Non risponde, non risponde, signorina.*"

"Look," West said, "what's going on?"

In principle, it was extremely simple. "We walk

straight down the gangplank, just like we were guests. It happens all the time, guests take off early, catching planes, I've done it—but you do not leave on foot."

West got up, started dressing. "What about the crew? They'll know about us, won't they?"

"Odds are, no." She sounded surer than she felt. "Look, Mannheim didn't tell his guests about us, Nancy said so. My guess is, he's kept it from the crew. He might have told the captain, Cecil knows, but yachts this big have rank and discipline and all that Navy stuff, you don't go cluing in the crew. So if the captain's not around and—*Che cosa?*"

There was a taxi, it would come. *Quando?* In fifteen, twenty minutes. West was ready, looking nervous. No sense going into what they'd have to do if there were guards outside. She checked herself, one quick look in the mirror. Dressed for evening but it didn't matter, she'd walked off of yachts at dawn in ball gowns. West stood beside her, cap on, frowning at his uniform. He shook his head and started taking off his jacket.

"What's the matter?"

"The crew knows what their first mate looks like, right? They'd spot me in a second."

She watched him fold the jacket so the gold braid didn't show. He put his cap in one hand, jacket folded over it. Dark slacks, white shirt, black tie: he was a businessman in shirt sleeves.

"Come on," she said, and headed for the door.

"It's locked."

"I know its locked." She yanked her Vuitton open, reached inside. The frigging chalice lay there, always in the way. She fished around. Her charge cards wouldn't work; the door swung inwards when you opened it which meant the flange would be the wrong way around. Something long and thin was what she wanted. There it was. She pulled it out, a—

what did you call the thing? She bent down to the lock and slipped it in the keyhole. It was what you used for cleaning fingernails, to scrape the muck out. Did it have no name? She felt the tip of it engage. Suppose she needed one, what would she ask for? Press it harder: there. The lock went click.

The click was loud enough to raise the dead. She took the knob and eased it, very, very slowly, pulled back on the door. An inch of corridor appeared, the stateroom door across the hall. All clear so far. Another inch, another, almost wide enough to slip through.

She turned to him, smiling, and nodded. "Here we go."

The corridor was empty. Tiny corridor, one exit; up the stairs. That's where the guard would be; up, waiting, at the top of the stairs. She moved on tiptoe, slow, tense, down the corridor, stairs just ahead, around the corner.

Clear. Night lights burning and gray dawn outside. She straightened up. No creeping from here on. She started up the stairs as if she owned them. Up and out the door, onto the deck. Lounge chairs in a stack, two sailors mopping. No one else. They looked up and she nodded to them, not too friendly, kept on going. She could hear West just behind her, and some voices in the distance; normal conversation, no one shouting. The gangplank was just ahead. She held the ropes and didn't stumble.

There were on the dock. The little van she'd seen was way up at the bow. A sailor with a crate was looking at them. Natural curiosity? She turned away, looked down the dock and toward the port, the way the taxi had to come. The sun was coming up. Alassio looked pink and dingy. Good-sized harbor, fishing boats, some pleasure craft. The stores and houses by the port looked old and poor. Steep cliffs rose up along the shore, and high above there were some houses and a road. She checked her watch. Five forty-two. The taxi was a long time coming. But it came.

*"Alessandro, quanto siamo lontani la stazione principale?"*

*"Dodeci, tredici chilometri, signorina,"* Alessandro answered.

It was Alessandro's Fiat they were riding in and the Genoa station was twelve, thirteen kilometers away. Outside the window, the Italian Riviera jiggled by, its beauty mutilated, Coca-Cola signs and BP stations; all the world was turning into Newark.

Twenty after eight. No hurry, Alessandro told them. The Milan train didn't leave till nine or thereabouts and—Alessandro was a talker—they'd been lucky he was up so early. It was Filomena, six months old, she had the croup, poor angel. Sleepless night for him and Carla, Carla was his wife, she came from Tuscany and on and on.

She let the words flow past her. They were going to Milan by train. They had to. Nothing flew from Genoa directly to the States. They'd found that out from Alessandro who produced an airline schedule that proved it.

Milan it had to be. Way out of town, up in the mountains: Malpenza Airport. When they got there? Well, God knew. The search for them might still be going on in Corsica. Then, too, a lot depended on how big an item they were in Italy. It shouldn't be like France or England, not unless the Papacy had lost its mind. They might, they just might be able to breeze through. As for New York, they'd face that when they got there.

Genoa looked fairly grim. They came in on the coast road from Savona, past the docks, the *porto nuovo,* into town. Down the Via A. Cantore, whoever he was, then the old port, on their right, and then the station.

The deal they'd made with Alessandro was for fifty dollars. Alessandro didn't mind the dollars, got them all the time from people off the yachts, no problem. West gave him a hundred and they took the change in lire, which they needed.

She asked Melvil for a bill or two and he went off to buy their tickets while she beelined for a newsstand, bought a copy of *Il Messaggero* and a *Herald-Trib.* She headed for the gates. The train was leaving soon and there were lots of people milling, getting on. She saw him coming through the crowd. He looked terrific in his uniform.

They headed for the dining car. Good smells and everything looked fresh and clean. She felt like ordering the menu, top to bottom. Newspapers first.

She didn't have to look beyond the headlines. They had caught the public fancy like the last assassination. News from everywhere. She handed him the Roman paper but his Italian was medieval so she translated; voice low, politely conversational. From Corsica: the shooting in the mountains and the chase, the search still going on. From Paris: confidence that West and Gardener would be apprehended and a photo of a minister of something taking off for Washington. From London: Hunter-Donne at Downing Street. From Washington: big pressure on the Met to give up all claims to the chalice. Quotes from VanStraaten, holding firm: the Met had bought the chalice in good faith, the provenance was solid, that was that. And finally, from Rome: some Senator was claiming that the chalice was the Grail and half of Italy believed him and a fund was being formed to buy it for the Vatican.

So much for breezing through at Malpenza. The airport would be covered like a blanket. Out the window, towns went by: Tortona, Castelnuovo. There were heavy clouds; it looked like rain. They ordered tons of pasta and some wine. Maybe they should call VanStraaten from Milan and tell him what they knew and lay low while he handled things. But it was so complex, their story was so convoluted, so many questions might arise. No, they would have to sit down in the same room with VanStraaten, tell the whole thing to him face to face.

The train was due in at 10:46. Another half an hour, if they were on time. Then what? The line of pitfalls stretched, like Macduff's children, on to doom. Airport police, for openers. Then the tickets and they always asked to see your passport. Dead before they had their tickets. Then came Immigration; passports again. And Immigration in New York, with all of New York's Finest looking for them. Hopeless? Way past hopeless.

"Hey," he said, "come on, it's not that bad. They haven't got us yet."

Was "Go down fighting" what he wanted? O.K., it was what he'd get. She squared her shoulders. "Right."

"And anyway . . ." He reached across the table, took her hand. "Whatever happens, I've got you to show for it."

Cheap sentiment. She bit her lip.

Milan. The station was an iron palace. They went striding down the platform. Carrie scanned the signs. Out: out was that way. Rain was falling and the day was dark. She stood on the sidewalk looking at the traffic: motorcycles, buses, everything but taxicabs. She saw an empty, started for it but an old man beat her to it. West was calling to her, pointing diagonally across the street.

An airport bus was pulled up at a bus stop. She took off for it. She heard honking, shouts. No squealing brakes, they didn't brake for you in Italy. A motor cycle whipped around her, little bastard, and a

Fiat, driven like a weapon, see Milan and die. West was there ahead of her.

The bus was fairly full. Some businessmen, some tourists and some airlines personnel. A steward and a stewardess sat side by side, up near the front. The driver smiled and waved them through, not asking for a fare. Nice man. They started down the aisle and, ahead of them, the steward did the damnedest thing.

He smiled at them in a smeavy way, saluted, spoke. He had what sounded like a Texas accent. What he said was, "*Ciao, Capitano.*"

Funny thing to say. They sat. Two rows behind the steward and the hostess. Close enough to hear the steward say, "Dumb wop bastards, fly like morons, stupid wops." The motor revved, the bus lurched forward.

"Carrie?" West was frowning. "If we found ourselves some uniforms, do you think we could get away with it?"

She nodded. Yes, she did. They'd fly back to the States as crew. She heard more swearing from the steward. She leaned forward. It was hard to hear now but enough came through. They had been shacking up, a two-day leave, their first time in Milan, the leave got canceled, Malpenza all fogged in, no crew, the goddam crew that should have taken their flight couldn't goddam land and you could take the goddam country and the goddam wops and fuck 'em all.

The steward was a big man, close to forty, and the stewardess was fairly tall. The idea came so naturally she didn't feel it happen. She was looking at their uniforms, the uniforms they needed, there they were, two rows in front. She turned, looked out the window at the bleakness; low heavy clouds. The bus was rising, up into the mountains and the mist. The only way to get those uniforms was by taking them. By force. Some risk involved, it bothered her a little. But what bothered her a lot was afterwards, what happened afterwards? The flight to New York took eight hours. How to keep them from reporting what had happened? Short of killing Woppo and his girl friend, how did you put them on ice for eight long hours?

When the answer came, they talked about it. West kept pointing out the risks involved but there was nothing they could do but risk it.

Malpenza looked like every other modern airport in the world: straight lines, all rectangles and glass. The parking lot was jammed. No people, just a mass of cars; with nothing flying in and out, she'd thought it would be. Good. The terminal would be a madhouse. Even better.

They were pulling up. She looked at West. His face was set and pale, lips tight. He jumped a little when she touched him.

"Ready?"

"As I'll ever be."

The bus slowed down. It stopped. She nodded. He stood up. Moved forward. Just two rows. He tapped the steward on the shoulder. Then he spoke.

"*Signore?*" West said.

"What?" The steward turned, looked up. The smeavy smile again. "*Paisano, Capitano, come va?*"

"You picked yourself the wrong wop bastard and I'm going to kick your faggot ass around."

The steward blinked. "Did you say faggot?"

Yes, indeed; she'd told him to, she had a hunch about the steward. He was on his feet, fists clenched. West moved straight down the aisle, out, not one look back, and strode across the pavement, straight into the parking lot. The steward followed on his heels, the hostess just a step or two behind.

The lot was huge. Deserted, not a soul. They needed something big, a screen to work behind. There; West had seen it, big Bianca truck, bright yellow.

They got there ahead of her, the hostess well to one side and the two men face to face.

"You calling me a faggot?"

"Bet your faggot ass."

"If anyone's a faggot, you're a faggot."

The hostess watched, eyes bright, mouth slightly open; riveted. Carrie moved in quickly, right hand rigid, flat. She'd done it in Iran and once or twice since then. The neck—if she remembered right—just there. She brought her hand down and the girl went slack. Then arms out quickly, and she caught her as she fell.

"For Christ's sake, Carrie." It was West. "Don't hurt her."

Not unnaturally, the steward turned to look, and it was then West let him have it. Dreadful blow, the stomach, just above the belt. The air whooshed out of him, his eyes turned up, he crumpled. West stood over him as if he weren't sure what he'd done or where the man had gone to.

"West!" He heard her. "Strip him."

"Yeah."

He nodded slowly, knelt beside the steward, started fiddling with his shoes. It isn't easy, taking clothes off someone who's unconscious, but she had experience with drunks, she'd put a lot of them to bed. And, careful not to hurt the girl, she slipped the jacket off and then the blouse.

"Shit." West was having trouble with the steward's trousers, couldn't get them off, man's legs kept rubbering away. Like something out of Chaplin, really funny, only not now. Lots of laughs tomorrow. How much time? Three minutes, four? They'd start to come around, she didn't want to hit again.

She left the girl, gave West a hand; the trousers came, the shirt. She went back to the hostess while West changed. Redressing them was hard. They had to look right, proper button in the proper buttonhole, the steward's necktie was a bitch and Nancy's dress zipped up the back.

"Let's look at you." He turned around. It didn't fit, not really, but he'd get away with it. She turned around for him. He nodded and she reached down for the flight bag by the hostess, pulled it open. Passport, papers; right. She opened up her Vuitton bag—a shame to see it go—took out the chalice and her passport, mustn't leave her passport, had her picture in it, just the charge cards, driver's license, stuff with Carrie Gardener printed on. She slipped the chalice in the flight bag, straightened up.

"Ready?"

"Just a sec." He kept his passport, slipped his keys in one back pocket, was about to stuff the steward's wallet in the other, and stopped and opened it. "I'm Jerry Fuller."

Hadn't thought. She scrabbled for her passport, flipped it open. "Jacqueline Moran."

"Hi, Jackie." He was grinning.

"Let's get out of here."

She turned and started running. Through the drizzle, feeling damp and clammy; chilled, like Dublin in December, to the bone. She dodged around one puddle, didn't see the next one, kept on going, straight ahead, between the cars, across the road and like a bullet to the *carabiniere* lolling by the lobby door.

"*Sergente.*" Breathless, in a state.

"*Sì, signorina?*"

This was it. She let it fly. They'd come out on the bus. With two other Americans. She should have known, the way they acted, strange and furtive, whispering. The bus arrived and the Americans, they said they had a gun. They forced them to the parking lot. Behind that yellow truck. Asked for their passports, they were desperate, didn't have a gun, there was a fight and Jerry, this was Jerry, Jerry was a hero and the two Americans had fallen and—

That's all it took. The cop tore off, across the road, between the cars. She took a deep breath, let it out. It might work, it was possible. The cop would find two wallets filled with cards and papers: Melvil West's and Carrie Gardener's. Big arrest, excitement, take the prisoners into town; an hour, maybe more. Their photos hadn't been in that day's *Messaggero* and she didn't think the local cops would have the London papers. Eventually, they would think of calling Interpol and Interpol would call Inspector Drum. Because he was the only one who'd met them, could identify them positively. Another hour? Easily. And Drum, if only Drum were still out in the *maquis* searching for them, more time. Then what? Drum would have to find an airport, catch a plane and land, if they were landing, at Malpenza, drive to town. Eight hours? More like nine or ten. Of course, a lot of things could screw up, things like—

"Here we go," said West and in they went. The airport lobby was a jungle. People milling everywhere, not going anyplace but moving. Children crying, benches mobbed, long lines for everything. She let him shoulder through, stuck close behind.

He stopped, looked up. Departure board. She hadn't checked her papers. If she had them.

"What's our flight?"

He grinned. "I don't even know what line we're working for." He took his cap off: TWA *Flight 843. Departs 11:45. Postponed.* A good thing; it was 12:15.

"Now what?" He looked at her.

She tried to think. She'd known a girl or two who'd flown but it was years ago. Nice girls, not very bright but—

"Personnel." It came to her. "We go check in at Personnel."

It was as big a mess behind the scenes as out in front. Small quarters, people pressing, metal lockers, office desks, a counter, bulletin board. No one seemed to notice them. Stale air. They saw some people sign in so they did it, someone gave them papers. When was takeoff? A bald man at a desk said the clouds were lifting; maybe half an hour, maybe more. Someone said "Hi" and waved. At her? She couldn't tell, waved back. Cigarette smoke, smell of coffee, perfume, powder; it felt good to leave.

The plane was empty when they boarded, just the crew around, a lot of girls all named Doreen or something, friendly smiles, and "Hiya." West was working First Class, hugged her, quick kiss on the lips, and went away. O.K.—and all she had to do was watch the other girls and do what they did: she'd be fine.

She was fine till the passengers began to board and all the girls got busy, people everyplace and everybody with a problem. Seating mix-ups, hang up coats and where for God's sake were the closets, could they visit First Class, see the bar, would she refrigerate this package. Yes, but where and how, she couldn't ask, what kind of hostess was she?

She was standing in the aisle, in everybody's way, piled high with coats and packages when one of the Doreens said, "Come on, Jackie, don't just stand there." Always play it near the truth. She poured it out. Her leave was canceled and her boyfriend furious. She'd never worked a 747, lots of 727's sure, but everything was different. Everybody had so many questions and her arms were aching. It worked. Doreen would show her all the ropes.

Eventually, the coats got put away and everyone sat down. Including hostesses. She leaned back, closed her eyes, deep roaring, bouncing, going faster—airborne. Out of Italy. God had been good. She thanked Him—knew He wasn't there and didn't watch the sparrows if He was but she was in the mood and thanked Him anyway. The plane rose through the clouds, gray-black and swirling, clutching at the windows. Let it rain, they'd made it.

The seat-belt sign went off. The other hostesses got up, so she got up. The flight had left an hour and a half late, it would land an hour and a half late: 3:50 in New York and she had had enough of hostessing, yes thank you very much. She slipped up front to look for West.

He was drinking a martini when she found him. Upstairs in the little bar, all by himself. He made her one. She took it in one gulp, she needed it. He made them both another and she took it slower, sipping, feeling the delicious cool and bite of it. She sighed, sat back, and closed her eyes. Someone said "Jackie?"

"Jeezus, Jackie." On the stairs; Doreen again. "You must be crazy, they could fire you."

She drained the glass. "I'm thinking of quitting anyway."

"Well, you can't quit on us so you come right downstairs 'cause we've got work to do."

Work? It was past work. It was galley slavery. Up and down the aisle with Wash-n'-Drys, then up and down collecting them. Then up and down with mints and gum and someone wanted magazines and could they have a blanket and the toilet door was stuck and up and down with drinks and running out of ginger ale and going back for ice and making change and picking up the empty glasses and then lunch. Good God and it was up and down again with napkins, spreading them on trays, some kid with toys, then up and down with trolleys, trays were hot and someone wanted kosher, was this kosher, no she didn't think so and the woman got so angry, up and down with coffee, trying not to spill, and cream and sugar, say it with a smile, and up and down to pick the trays up, fingers in the slops and leavings, always smiling, please and thank you and it was the captain speaking, turbulence ahead and fasten seat belts and the barfing started, little kids first and she promised, cross her heart and hope to die, that she would never ever be impatient with a stewardess again and barfing sounds from everywhere, she didn't feel so good herself and she was in the galley when her spirit broke.

She stood there, all those trays with garbage and she couldn't bear it. Tears.

"Jeez, Jackie, what's the matter?"

"Oh, Doreen," she sobbed and threw her arms around the girl.

# XXV

To open: *(1) Move Lever A to Position B.*

He nodded. He could do that. If he didn't, someone else would.

*(2) Take Handle C and Rotate Counterclockwise to Position D.*

The plane was inching, barely moving. One last tremor. Stopped. The motors whined, then cut. The time in New York: ten to four. He reached for Lever A.

He'd had a quiet flight. Nobody wanted him for much of anything. He'd poured some wine and served some pâté, listened to some stories. It was easy. Lots of time to think. Of Dido, for example. All these days, how little he had thought of her. It was as if he'd penciled out a section from an article he'd written: a vital section, central to the argument, and when he scratched it out it left no trace. Not missed, not needed, all unnecessary. Would he see her? Yes, he thought so. They had wasted precious time together and he owed it to her. He had used her badly and he wanted her to know he knew it. He was sorry, truly, and he wished her well, a good life with a good man, someone just as right for her as he'd been wrong.

And Pieter, he had thought of Pieter, too. The rough time, all the pressure he'd been under. What would Pieter think and feel and would he understand? The truth did matter, even if it meant he lost the chalice to Sir Winston.

*Take Handle C.* Eight hours—more like nine—since dress-up in the parking lot. A long time. People standing, stirring in the aisles. Just how smart was What's-his-name, the steward, Jerry Fuller? Had he blown their story open, found a way, or was it holding? Handle C was turning.

Were there cops outside or not? And if there were, would they come charging in like gangbusters or would they wait until the plane cleared out? Position D. If it was gangbusters, what could he do? His hands were on the handle and his body pulled the door.

No cops. Just one man, in mechanic's uniform: stood by a little board of buttons, pushing them, maneuvering the mobile corridor. It came up, touched the plane, connected.

Stewardesses, beside him now, all smiles as the passengers went past. Bye-bye now, see you soon, fly us again. First Class all emptied out. They started in from Tourist.

"Carrie-I-mean-Jackie." Stupid but it just popped out of him, she looked so terrible. Like one of Cranach's women, faintly green. "What happened?"

"I was okay until the barfing started." She moved close. He put his arm around her. People filed by, a steady flow; some sleeping kids, some jumping ones, a lot of pallid faces.

The plane was nearly empty. It was coming soon if it was coming. His impulse was to take off, break and run, but their best chance of slipping through was with the others, staying close and clearing Immigration in a clump. And so they stood there, chatting, listening to the jokes, relaxed and natural, trying not to sweat: just Jerry and his Jackie to the end.

Doreen came up along with Kim, Melissa, Debbie, Sandy, B.J.—Carrie introduced them all and off they went together down the corridor, about a dozen of them. Carrie's hand was tight in his. He listened to the babble. Debbie had a date with someone groovy who was taking her to the Icecapades. Sandy's guy was in Miami with his mother but Melissa had a friend who had a friend and they were through the corridor and out the other end. Ahead were signs for Customs, Immigration; lights and arrows. Then Doreen, or was it Kim, was saying "Hiya, Bobby" to the Immigration officer and down his stamp came. Down and down, it was that easy.

The taxi was a joy ride. Twenty after four and they were heading for the Met. VanStraaten liked to work late; any luck at all, they'd find him there and little old New York looked good enough to eat and so did Carrie. Everything was funny now. She told about the spilling and the barfing and the tears. They'd done it, they had brought it off, the two of them against the world. They would bound out at the Met, bounce up the stairs, past Bindle, hello Bindle, and they'd give the chalice back and tell their story and the world would fall down dead.

Light traffic. They were past LaGuardia, the bridge ahead. He felt like having her; right there, why not, she wouldn't mind, she'd laugh and love it. Throw her arms out, kick her heels, roll over. Alessandro would have understood and if they'd been in Italy, who knows?

They came down from the bridge and took the Drive, turned off at 96th Street, up the hill and straight across to Fifth and down. Old friends went by: the Jewish Museum, the Guggenheim—and sixty seconds later, there she stood. The Metrofuckingpolitan.

He couldn't ask the man to change a hundred so he took two tens from Carrie, paid, got out and stopped. He stood there for the longest time, not moving. Looking up, that's all; just looking up.

"West?"

He heard her but he didn't answer right away. It

felt like going back to school. He'd done it once, gone back to see Wisconsin after years and years. A handsome campus, handsomer than he remembered: beautiful. But he had never been there. Someone seventeen had done it all.

"Come on." He took her hand and started up. He used to know how many steps there were but he had lost the number. It was after hours, after five: doors closed. Bindle stood there, let them in. He looked old.

"Hello, Bindle."

"Evening, Dr. West. The conference just started—"

He had never really seen a double take before. Amazing; just like in the movies. "Sorry, Bindle. Didn't mean to startle you. What kind of conference?"

"In the Patio."

"Is Pieter there?" Blank look. "VanStraaten. Is he there?"

"I always liked you, Dr. West."

"I'm fine."

He reached out, lightly touched the old man's arm, then started out alone across the lobby. Two steps, three before he stopped. Old habits: he had always been alone here. She caught up, took his hand. Her smile wobbled at the corners. Nerves? So many things might go wrong: he hadn't thought. His stomach tightened and his lips were dry. They started off across the marble wastes with little steps, like naughty children late for school.

There, straight ahead, the great grand staircase, gateway to Western European Art. No: Arts, Arts with an *s*. Dead silence, echoes, of all kinds. They veered left at the stairs, a few steps more, and then the Patio.

He stopped cold in the doorway. It was like a jump in time. Exactly as it looked—when was it, not two weeks ago? The room was crowded, everyone was there. Kropotkin of the *Post* and Sitwell: was he thinner? Nothing all that odd about his butt and the abominable Racine-Brissac: a little man, that's all he was, with puffy chins and frightened eyes. And Potter Grant: no chin at all. Around the room, just like before, stood blowups of the chalice. Dais, lights, the empty pedestal and Pieter speaking.

His ears rang just a little. What was Pieter saying? It came in like shortwave, like his Philco when he was a kid and it was late at night and Canada kept slipping in and out. "... this opportunity to make a statement ... our position stands. The chalice is undoubtedly authentic and its provenance beyond dispute . . . Believing in the justice of our cause, we must respectfully decline to place the chalice and its disposition in the hands, no matter how well-meaning they may be, of Washington ..."

Murmurs, scribbling, turning heads. How tired Pieter looked, what dreadful pressures. Carrie squeezed his hand. It would be nice to be alone and stationary, all the running over with.

"... new hope this sad affair may soon be ended." Pieter's voice again. "I spoke to the Attorney General late this afternoon and he informed me there is reason to believe that Dr. West and the unfortunate Miss Gardener have been apprehended in Milan . . ." Ho-ho; he felt a giggle rising, pushed it down. "... and while they do not seem to have the chalice with them, as had been supposed, they surely know its whereabouts and we shall press our case with vigor for its prompt return." A lot of buzzing this time. Boy, if they thought this was news, they had a shocker coming.

"... hope that Dr. West will not be prosecuted. He was a distinguished member of this staff, a gifted scholar and a friend. The matter rests with the authorities, of course, but our hope is consideration will be given to the possibility that he was mentally unbalanced at the time he took the chalice. That ends my formal statement. Are there any questions?"

Were there? Up his hand shot. "Here."

"Gentleman back in the doorway." Pieter squinted through the lights. "Yes, sir?"

"My question is . . ." He reached for Carrie's flight bag, took the chalice out. There were a lot of questions but he had them narrowed down to one, the only one that mattered. He took Carrie's hand in one hand, and the chalice in the other and moved forward past the people to the pedestal. He put the chalice gently on the velvet.

Everything was very quiet. It was hard to see, the lights were in his eyes. Someone said "Melvil." It was Pieter.

"Hello, Pieter." His voice sounded strange to him, recorded, but he knew what he was doing and he asked the question.

"Pieter, were you in Geneva in December?"

"Was I where?"

"Geneva. In December. Were you there?"

"No. No I wasn't. Why?"

The Why? was muffled by the rising hubbub in the room. People were shouting questions at him, shoving, pressing to get near him. Someone called out "This way!" It was Pieter, heading toward the door. He reached for Carrie, kept her close behind him, pushed and shoved. They made it, out into the corridor. Pieter was there. He gestured to the guards. They moved in, blocking off the door.

"Christ." Pieter shook his head. "We've got to talk." They started for his office, moving fast, through the deserted entrance hall and into Greek and Roman. Just the way he'd left it: boring. What a dull exhibit. Academic, stifling and he'd liked it all those years, no life in it at all. Then down the sculpture hall; nice statues but they stood there all lined up, like dummies in a shop that dealt in pyramids.

They turned left at the Sardis column, up the stairs and through the private door. Miss Burton sat there at her desk. She had a pretty face, he thought; but pale, washed out. She had been nice to him, though, so he smiled. They went on, into Pieter's office.

"Jesus Christ, West." Pieter stood there, all keyed up, excited. Was he angry? "What the fuck have you been doing?"

"Take it easy. I can—"

"Take it easy? Do you know what it's been like here?"

"Look, I can explain—"

"It's been sweet bloody hell."

"I'm sorry but I had to do it, Pieter, and I found the truth."

"What truth?"

"I found out where the chalice came from, whose it was."

"It's Kalman's, part of his collection."

"No, it's not."

"It has to be, I've got the papers, Mannheim swore to me—"

"Look, do you want to hear what we found out or don't you?"

"Sorry, yes, of course. It's just that . . ." Pieter shook his head and went to the decanter, poured them stiff ones. "Okay, Melvil, what's the story?"

"Well . . ." Melvil looked at Carrie and made a formal introduction, calling her Miss Gardener, but she said to call her Carrie. Pieter said he would and she said, "Well, it started at the airport . . ."

They sat down at the big oak table and they poured it out together, talking fast, excited, breathless, interrupting one another. All about their meeting with Sir Winston and their day with Kalman, how their stories could be true or false, you couldn't prove them either way. But Mannheim's story, Mannheim's was the false one and they told how Mannheim made his slip, his big mistake, the thing that gave it all away: that he'd seen Pieter in December.

Melvil summed it up. "So that's what happened, Pieter. Mannheim got the chalice from whoever stole it from Sir Winston. But he couldn't sell it, not without a provenance, and Kalman had the perfect one. He went to Kalman, set it up, then wrote to you. It was a damn good story, you believed it, so did I. And you know what? If Mannheim hadn't gotten greedy, if he'd given Kalman what he promised, he'd have gotten clean away."

"I see, I see." VanStraaten nodded, frowning. "But what I don't see is, I can't see any proof. How can you prove it?"

"What?"

"I mean, put Mannheim on the witness stand, he'll say he never said it."

"But he did. We heard it, we were there."

"I know and God knows I believe you, but . . ." VanStraaten slowly shook his head.

He looked at Carrie. Was it true? Was there no proof at all? Just theories? No: he felt it in his guts, but absolutely. Mannehim was a liar, he had lied.

"Look, Pieter, I don't care what Mannheim says, his story won't hold up. Not when they start investigating. Scotland Yard, the CIA, they're not fools, they'll go into everything, they'll dig up every move that Mannheim made, who saw him, where and when. They'll find it all."

"Yes . . ." Pieter nodded slowly. "Yes, they will; you're right. And what you want from me—" He stood up, brisk, eyes bright, convinced; they had convinced him. "What you want from me are Mannheim's letters, right, and proof I wasn't in Geneva in December."

The intercom went off and Pieter picked it up. "For Christ's sake, no. Get rid of them. Not now. No interviews. The Patio—in half an hour. West'll be there."

Pieter slammed the phone down, "Damned reporters," started toward the files in the corner.

Melvil reached for Carrie. This was it. They'd brought it off. His eyes were full, all blurry. Pieter had the file open, stuffed something in his pocket, took some papers out—the Mannheim letters—came and put them on the table. February: there they were, all dated February.

Melvil smiled. "Pieter . . ."

"Wait; there's more." He held his passport in his hand.

This clinched it: proof he wasn't in Geneva in December. Pieter gave the passport to him. He opened it. A handsome picture. Pieter did a lot of traveling, pages filled with stamps. More pages. Then the end and there it was: GENEVA, 20 FEBRUARY. Smudged but clear enough. And just above, not smudged at all: GENEVA, 21 DECEMBER. Christmas week.

It made no sense. Was Pieter in Geneva in December? How? How was it possible if Mannheim lied? It must be Mannheim told the truth; he hadn't meant to but it slipped. And that meant Pieter lied; just now, in front of all those people. Why? Why two trips to Geneva? Why was one of them a secret? And the chalice—who did it belong to? Not Sir Winston, not if Pieter saw it in December, weeks before Sir Winston dug it up. Did Pieter see it? Ask him.

"Pieter, did you see the chalice in December?"

Pieter's lips moved. "Yes."

"You're certain? Mannheim had it in December?"

"I should know, I brought it to him." He was smiling in a funny way.

"You brought it? Where'd you get it from?"

"I found it."

"Where?"

He frowned as if he couldn't quite remember, smiled again. "Think on it. It will come to you."

It came. Like nothing new, as if he'd known it all

along. "The Lowenthal Bequest. You found it in the tunnel in the Lowenthal Bequest." It meant the Met had had the chalice in a crate downstairs since 1899.

"It's all your fault, you know." Pieter said it wryly. "All your talk about the tunnel and the jolly times you had. The thing was all caked over when I found it. Had good lines, though, and I fiddled with it and the muck along the bottom fell away." He shrugged. "It wasn't hard to read PASITELES. I'd found a fortune, do you see. It was all mine because nobody knew the thing existed. I could sell it to myself, three million dollars, but it wasn't worth a dime without a provenance. I had to have a middleman, someone to give the piece a provenance and then approach me, offer it for sale." He wiped his forehead, frowned, as if he'd lost the thread.

Melvil felt shaken, couldn't seem to take it in. "That's why two trips?" He went on. "Mannheim had to have the chalice first, before he came to us. He took it, went to Kalman, set the story up—"

"Yes, you were right about that much of it. And it's a damned good story, do you know? Still is. Just three things wrong with it: one passport and the two of you."

It couldn't be, his Pieter couldn't be a thief, his good friend Pieter, standing there so pale and reaching with his right hand to his jacket pocket, taking out a pistol. Pieter wouldn't use it, not on him.

"For God's sake, Pieter—"

"Everybody thinks you had a breakdown. All I've got to do is say you went berserk, I had to shoot."

He meant it. He was going to do it. Carrie, too; he'd shoot her, too, he'd have to.

Melvil stood up. "Pieter, don't."

"I'm sorry, Melvil." And he looked it, really sorry. Silence, just a second's worth. Then sirens. Dozens of them, howling up outside the window. Pieter spun across the room, looked out. The cops. Who called them? Bindle. Bindle called the cops. The cops were there for them, not Pieter. Did he know it? Was he cool enough?

"They're coming for you, Pieter!"

"No . . . !"

His gun was pointed at them but his eyes were blind. He pivoted. He almost fell as he went lurching past them toward the door. He had it open. One look back, then he was gone.

"West?" She was standing, pale as chalk.

"It's okay, the police'll get him."

"No, they won't. It's us they want. He'll get away."

He started for the door. "Stay here."

"Not on your life."

She grabbed his hand. They raced out, past Serena, ashen at her desk. The stairs. Which way? Down. There was noise from down. They raced. The halls were dark. Economy: the lights went after hours. Toward the entrance hall, feet pounding. Lights ahead—and people. Cops. A hundred of them? Swarming, fanning out. They skidded to a stop.

"You! There! Don't move!"

The cops had seen them. "Back," he said. They spun around, took off, back past the statues, pulled up at the stairs. Which way had Pieter gone? Not up, not when he wanted out. The entrance that he always used. Downstairs.

The ground floor. Hard to see. Streetlight through window bars. No sound. Sharp right, three steps, sharp right again. The door. He pressed. It opened. Cops and cop cars everywhere. No Pieter.

"Other door." He whirled around. The entrance to the parking lot. That way. He caromed off a wall, kept going, straight across, there, threw himself against it. Chains, it hurt, all chained up for the night. Another door? The kid's museum? They'd have it chained up, too. Which way? He stood there gasping. There was thudding on the stairs. Cops coming.

They were cornered.

"Shit."

He turned, kicked at an office door. Keys, keys, his keys. Back pocket. Had he kept them? They were there. The first one jammed. The thudding closer. Carrie breathing. Steady, for the love of God, stop shaking. Third one did it. Through they went.

He softly closed the door. Receiving room. Huge place. New acquisitions came here. Shipping crates, as tall as he was, taller. Statues, stones, half-opened boxes; he could barely see them.

"West?"

He touched her lips. It was important to be quiet now. Because he knew where Pieter was.

He took her hand.

"This way," he whispered. Didn't see the carton, stumbled, stood and listened. Silence. Moving slow, the door was that way. Hard to see the wall. He felt his way along it and found the tunnel door. It stood half-open.

Stone steps going down. Faint glow of red: the exit light. He took his shoes off, set them down. She put hers next to his. Soft. Cat's feet, like the fog, down through the red glow. It was cold, the air was cave air, dead and cold.

They heard it when they reached the bottom. Pieter weeping.

Heartbreak sounds. High, soft, choked off, ashamed to cry but home is somewhere far away and it's so dark out. Carrie shivered, pressed against him.

Down the tunnel. Halfway down it, in the Greek and Roman cage. He sat there huddled on the floor, as small as possible, legs pulled up, shoulders rounded, choking, pistol lying at his feet. He didn't seem to see them.

"Pieter?" Softly said and gentle. "Pieter?"

"Go away." He shook his head.

"It's all right, Pieter."

"No, it's not. I'm so ashamed, oh God . . . " He looked up then; and saw them. "Hello, Melvil."

"Hi." He stepped into the cage, knelt down. The pistol lay there, inches from his hand. He tried to smile. "Everybody's looking for you."

"Can't have that." A grin from Pieter as he snatched the pistol up. "That's mine."

"It's over, Pieter."

"No it's not." He wiped his nose. "You know what?" And then he smiled. "I didn't need the money."

Carrie screamed and Melvil lunged but Pieter was the quickest. What he had to do was easy, after all. Just open up his mouth and pull the trigger.

* * *

## CHALICE CASE GOES INTO THIRD DAY

By WALDO SITWELL

Special to The New York Times

GENEVA, August 14—The trial of noted film producer Adolf Mannheim for conspiracy and fraud entered its third day today with testimony from Dr. Melvil West and Miss Caroline Gardener.

Dr. West, formerly Curator of Greek and Roman Art at the Metropolitan Museum, is currently residing in Madrid where he is at work on a critical reevaluation of the so-called "Black" Goyas, in the collection at the Prado. Miss Gardener, also in Madrid, is near completion of her book recounting their experiences with the Pasiteles chalice, to be published in the spring both in America and abroad.

Their testimony today disclosed nothing new to American readers familiar with the case.

Scheduled to testify tomorrow is Stefan Kalman, key witness for the prosecution. Dr. Kalman, who resides in Florence with his daughter, is a new but active figure in the International Art scene and has figured prominently in the sale of several highly valuable (Continued on Page 21)

## ABOUT THE AUTHOR

JAMES GOLDMAN has won accolades as a playwright, screenwriter, novelist and lyricist. His plays include *They Might Be Giants, The Lion in Winter* and *Blood, Sweat and Stanley Poole* (with William Goldman). For the musical stage, he has written *A Family Affair* (with John Kander and William Goldman) and the award-winning *Follies* (with Stephen Sondheim). His adaptation of *The Lion in Winter* for the screen won an Academy Award in 1968 as well as Best Screenplay Awards from the Writers Guild of America and Great Britain. His other films include *They Might Be Giants* and *Nicholas and Alexandra.* Two other screenplays, *The Death of Robin Hood* and *The Man from Greek and Roman,* are soon to be produced. For the ABC television network, he wrote *Evening Primrose* (with Stephen Sondheim). Mr. Goldman has also written one other novel, *Waldorf.* He lives in New York City.